FUTURE

F-BOMB: SEALS LOVE CURVES, BOOK 8

MARY E THOMPSON

F-BOMB: SEALS LOVE CURVES

Welcome to the world of F-BOMB where a group of former SEALs have come together to protect the curvy women they love and the country they call home from the dangers of the world. They have the training and the knowledge, and they have the ability to kick some ass when needed. And it'll be needed.

F-BOMB: SEALs LOVE CURVES

Freedom (free everywhere)

Fiancée (subscriber exclusive)

Forgotten

First

Failure

Friends

Family

Forbidden

Future

Finally

SUBSCRIBE NOW AT MARYETHOMPSON.COM

1

———

TAYLOR WRIGHT CARESSED THE MULTICOLORED BOW ON THE box with a satisfied smile. She'd been getting gifts from supporters and investors for weeks, each more lavish and thoughtful than the last.

After years of killing herself to make it to the top, she'd finally arrived. She was doing exactly what she wanted to do, and she was doing it exactly how she wanted to do it.

She had her enemies, but they were people she'd left behind her. People she wasn't interested in involving in her success. She'd built her company from the ground up and she was going to open up to customers in two weeks. Initial reviews were overwhelmingly positive, proving she was doing things right.

Taylor lifted the lid with a curious smile on her face. She peered inside and screamed, "Gah!" She dropped the lid and backed away from it. Cement filled her gut and ice flooded her veins.

"Are you okay? What happened?" her assistant Jessica's near-permanent grin faded to confusion when she saw the panicked look in Taylor's eyes.

The only thing Taylor could do was point to the box. Jessica turned to it, then back to Taylor with narrowed eyes and a tilt of her head that assumed Taylor was being dramatic and crazy.

Jessica had worked for Taylor for almost a year. She was the closest thing Taylor had to a friend, even though they really weren't friends, but Taylor thought her assistant had a little more trust in her than to think she was nuts.

"What—? Oh, my God. Is that what I think it is?"

"If you think it's a dead bird nestled in decaying roses with a note that reads *you're next*, then yes, it's what you think it is."

"Who the hell would send you something like that?"

"Someone who wants us to fail."

"Okay, but who?"

Taylor shook her head. "I have no idea."

"I'll send you the list, officer," Taylor said for the third time in thirty minutes. "I want to be thorough."

"Does the bird have any significance?" the young cop asked.

Taylor fought the urge to roll her eyes. She was exhausted. It had been a long day before she walked into her office and found a dead bird in a box. She glanced around at the walls, covered in birds. "Yeah, the bird is significant."

Taylor called her company Birds of a Feather because she wanted the women she targeted to know they weren't alone. It was important to her since Taylor herself never felt like she connected with the women she knew, but she hoped to create a world where other women didn't feel the same.

Birds of a Feather was more than a company to her. It was her baby. Her dream when she was in grad school and imagining her future, a future she thought she would share with her boyfriend. Mark was ambitious and studious, just like Taylor, but what she couldn't see at the time was that he was also jealous of her creativity and lacked his own.

It didn't bother Taylor, but it was a sore spot for Mark. So sore that he stole an idea he and Taylor came up with together and pitched it as his own to get himself a job at the company where they both first interviewed. When Taylor pitched the same idea, as a joint venture, they all but accused her of stealing it and said the only reason they weren't reporting her to the school was because they knew the truth.

That was when Taylor learned not to trust other people. Especially men.

"Do any men work here?" the officer asked, dragging Taylor's focus back to the issue in front of her.

Again, she had to resist an eye roll. "Birds of a Feather is an inclusive work environment. We hire the person who is best for the job, but when developing a company of size inclusive exercise clothes for women, it attracts more women than men."

The officer stared at the rear end of one of the interns as she rushed past Taylor's office. Sure, she was cute and perky and perfect, but the man was on the damn job.

"Ahem," Taylor said loudly.

The cop almost dropped his notepad as he yanked his eyes from the woman's ass. Minor victories.

He pressed his lips together in what she assumed was supposed to be a smile and gave Taylor and her ample curves a dismissive once-over before announcing, "I think I have all I need. If we find anything, we'll be in touch, Ms...."

"Wright," Taylor provided.

"Yes, of course." He picked up the evidence bag containing the box and nodded, then left her office.

Taylor's sigh was more of a groan as she scolded herself that flipping off a cop was not in her best interest, just in case he turned around and caught her.

She watched until he made it to the bank of elevators, then sank into her chair. She was drained. Dealing with threats and cops could do that to a woman.

"What did he say?" Jessica was another one the cop admired on his way to see Taylor. She had jet black hair, a curvy hourglass figure, and a smile that would make any man drop to his knees and beg for her to flash it at him, but Taylor hired her because she was also crazy smart and could think quickly on her feet. She'd saved Taylor's ass more than once in the last year.

"He said they'll be in touch."

"Which means we'll never see him again."

"Yep. Whatever."

"Why don't you call Braden?" Jessica suggested.

Taylor took note of the way Jessica's voice lifted at the end, as though there was more than one reason she might want Taylor's brother aware of what was going on. Taylor resisted the urge to call either of her brothers about anything, but Braden was the worst. He was the worrier. The one who was always telling her she needed to be more careful. Being a firefighter, he saw some of the worst the world had to offer, but he was paranoid. And Taylor wasn't going to be afraid to live her life.

"I don't think I need to tell Braden about this."

"Tell me about what?" Braden asked from Taylor's doorway.

Taylor sighed and gave Jessica a look that asked if she set

Taylor up. Jessica flushed fifty shades of pink and tucked her hair behind her ear before she hurried out of the office, sneaking past an oblivious Braden on her way back to her desk. Braden's gaze followed her for half a second, then snapped back to his sister. "What happened?"

"It was nothing."

"Then why did I pass Officer Shaw on my way up here?"

"Dammit," Taylor hissed.

"What happened?"

"Just someone being an ass."

"Which means?"

"I got a dead bird in the mail. Wrapped up in a pretty box and nestled in a bed of decaying roses." Taylor delivered the words with a pissed-off smile that hid the threat of showing her brother what she had for lunch.

"What?" Braden stalked across the room to her side. His fists clenched, and he twisted his neck to release the tension that immediately locked it up.

Taylor shrugged like the whole thing was a minor inconvenience instead of a not-so-thinly veiled threat to everything she'd worked her ass off to build. That was exactly why she didn't want to tell him. And why she didn't mention the note.

"You need protection, Tay. Someone with you to make sure you're safe."

"No," Taylor said. Now that was why she didn't want to tell him. The last thing she wanted was to feel like a prisoner in her own life.

"Taylor—"

"Would you be telling Aaron this? Or Wray or one of your other firefighter buddies? Is it because I'm a woman?"

"It's because you're my sister, Tay-tay. I don't want anything to happen to you."

Taylor's frozen heart melted whenever he called her by her childhood nickname. Especially when he tilted his head to the side and gave her the same lost little boy look he'd worn on a daily basis growing up. As the oldest of four, Taylor took a mother role with her younger siblings. She started babysitting them when she was able to use the microwave for dinner, and she was changing Braden's diapers, the youngest, the day he came home from the hospital. Taylor's greatest accomplishments were her siblings.

Until Birds of a Feather.

"I'll be fine," she assured Braden. "Whoever sent it is just trying to scare me."

"Which is exactly my point. I know a guy—"

"Don't go there, Braden." Taylor's sharp look and sharper tone would have made most people shut up quickly, but he was her brother and knew she was like a chihuahua pretending to be a Great Dane.

His matching glare had the punch of a pissed off hornet, but she wouldn't tell him that. "Taylor."

"Braden."

"I'm worried about you."

Taylor shook her head to dislodge the equally powerful sting of his soft words. "I have the best security system money can buy, both here and at home. There are cameras all over this building. I have no reason to think this is anything more than some sick joke, but if it's not, I have a baseball bat under my bed and you know I can swing it."

Braden's entire face softened at the mention of their shared memories. One of the many roles Taylor took on was coaching his baseball team when he was seven. She'd just turned eighteen and knew little about the game, but she learned fast. Just like she did with everything else in her life.

"At least meet the guy. Talk to him."

"Braden."

"Taylor, please. It'll make me feel better if you have a conversation with him."

"Let me think about it."

Braden's sigh was his annoyed sigh, the one that Taylor had grown accustomed to him using on her since he realized he was finally bigger and stronger than his big sister, and that she still wouldn't let him take care of her. "I guess that's all I can hope for."

Taylor's grin bordered on a smirk. "Yep."

RYKER HAMILTON SAT in the briefing room and listened to his boss talk about their latest job. Ryker, known as Dex to the rest of the team, had taken his turn as lead on a few cases, but he was happy when Dunn filled the role. It was natural for him, but Dex... he liked to be behind the scenes most of the time. He was comfortable being in second place.

"Dex, are you with us?" Dunn asked.

Dex nodded, meeting the gaze of the other man. It didn't matter what the task was, Dex was up to it. F-BOMB was as much his baby as the others'. They'd built the company from the ground up over the last few years, working to protect the borders of their country and keep people safe. That included stopping all sorts of bad guys, and brought them to their current asshole.

Dennis Parker.

Parker was the kind of scum that gave scum a bad name. He was involved in anything and everything bad. But he was smart enough to stay a step or two away from it and never get his hands dirty.

Dex hated men like him because everyone knew they were the ones pulling the strings, but their puppets always protected them. It wasn't because of loyalty, though. He had something on everyone who'd ever worked for him. And he wasn't afraid to use it to ruin their lives if they ever thought about ruining his.

"How are we going to handle this?" Archer asked.

Archer was their smash and grab guy. He could tear someone apart with his bare hands if he needed to. He was a good man to have on your side, and he was smarter than he gave himself credit for.

"The sheriff is out for blood. We have to bring the entire organization down," Dunn said. He met the gazes of the rest of the team with his own dark one.

"And we're sure it was one of Parker's men who took the sheriff's daughter and did that to her?" Rocky winced at the picture of the bruised woman on their board. He was the rational one of the group. Rocky thought through their actions and made a decision long before he acted.

"We're sure," Dunn said. "The guy bragged to her about other cases they've been tied to. He knew too much to be spouting rumors. He was a part of it."

"What's the play here?" Dex asked. "Normally, the powers that be would bring in someone like this guy and cut him a deal in order to get his boss. I can't imagine that's the plan with this one."

"No, it's not. We want to take down the entire organization. To do that, we need to know what he has on his people," Dunn said. "We need his files."

"Where do we think they are?" Jack asked.

"They're not digital," English said. As the team's computer expert, if something existed online, English would find it. A self-professed nerd, English was the kind of guy who could shoot you with one hand and ruin you with the other. He was as badass as they came, but he stayed in the shadows more often than not.

"That means everything is on paper. Files somewhere. Probably more than one copy if he's smart, and we know he is. I'd be willing to bet he has a copy at his home, one in the office, and another somewhere that we don't know about," Dunn said.

The frustration in Dunn's voice matched that of the rest of the group. It wasn't that they were simply frustrated that they couldn't bring the guy down, they were frustrated that he impressed them. Not in a way that made them want to be like him, but in a way that made them wonder how he pulled it all off without being caught. After everything they'd seen, not much got past them, but Parker did. More than once.

Dex's phone rang, prompting a pause to the meeting. He looked up at Dunn for permission to answer during the meeting. Dunn nodded.

"Hamilton."

"Ryker, this is Braden Wright. I wondered if I could call in that favor."

Dex waved off Dunn's look to let him know it wasn't anything relevant to the current case, then left the conference room to talk to Braden. After Braden went undercover with Dex and saved his life at an illegal poker game a few months earlier, Dex vowed to return the favor anytime Braden needed something.

"Everything okay?"

"That's why I'm calling. My sister is about to launch her newest company and she's getting threats. Most have been stupid online things, but the latest was a dead bird. Do you have time to act as private security for her? A few weeks, maybe?"

"For you, Braden, anything."

"Thanks. I owe my sister everything, and she doesn't like to admit when she needs help."

"I've met a few people like that."

Braden chuckled. "Yeah, well, she did raise me. I'll send you her company's address. You're on her calendar for tomorrow afternoon. Thanks, Ryker."

"Any time. We'll talk soon."

Braden hung up, and Dex went back into the conference room. Dunn raised a brow at him, pausing his sentence just long enough for Dex to nod in response to the unasked question. *Everything is fine.*

"So," Dunn said, "how are we going to bring this asshole down?"

EVERYONE HAD LEFT for the day, but Taylor still sat at her desk. She refused to leave anything to chance this close to her launch. Years of working jobs that made ends meet had led her to where she was. On top of the damn world.

She checked and double checked her notes and confirmed everything with her suppliers and manufacturer. She'd thought of everything, except sabotage.

Taylor tried to come up with a list of people who might be out to get her, but she was having trouble. The top of the list was relatively easy with former bosses and coworkers and a few people who didn't get the jobs they applied for, but after a handful of names, she was drawing a blank.

She groaned and pushed her chair back. She stretched her neck from side to side, loosening the tight muscles.

Maybe she could book a massage before the launch. God knew she needed it. She laughed to herself. Like she had free time.

A massage was a luxury, sort of like a date was. She couldn't remember the last time she went on a date. As she got closer to her dream coming true, men were less and less important to her. And less and less willing to see her as a potential partner. Nope, she was a mark, someone to use for what they wanted. She was done being used.

Taylor considered going home, but she was too tired to drive. She kept a small closet of clothes in her office for the too many nights she stayed there. Her executive bathroom was almost as lavish as the one in her home, so she gave up the fight and moved from her desk chair to the couch that was even more comfortable than the one she had at home.

She sank back and closed her eyes. Deep breath in, and out. Again in, and out. She forced her mind to clear and let go of the day. Nothing was going to stop her from moving forward with her plans. Nothing.

Her phone rang, startling her out of her relaxed state. She wasn't asleep yet, but she was on her way. The price of running an online business.

Taylor answered without bothering to think about the blocked caller ID knowing many of her investors had blocked numbers. "Taylor Wright."

"Did you get my gift?" a man's voice asked.

"Who is this?" Taylor asked. Her voice trembled, and so did her hands. She looked around the silent office, feeling exposed.

"I wanted you to know I was thinking of you."

"What do you want?"

"I want you to appreciate me, Taylor. You wouldn't be

where you are if it weren't for me. I want you to acknowledge that."

"Why don't you tell me who you are so I can?"

He chuckled. "That would be too easy. I understand, though. All the people you stepped on as you were climbing the ladder... It's easy to forget us all. But we never forgot about you."

"I didn't step on people."

His laugh sent ice to her heart. She shivered from the chill and grabbed her blanket.

"Taylor, Taylor, Taylor. You're so forgetful when it doesn't serve you. But I know exactly who you are. You're still that white trash who grew up on the wrong side of town. A cheap whore who tried to pretend she was someone she's not. But I know the real you, Tay-tay. I know everything about you. And I'm not going to let you destroy more lives."

"What are you talking about?" Taylor asked. Her mind raced to come up with a name. The list of people who knew her childhood nickname was short, but the voice... She couldn't place it.

He chuckled again, a breathy sound through the phone. "Don't play dumb with me. You're far too smart for it."

"I don't know what you're talking about."

"Yes, you do, Taylor. But I need to go now. We'll talk again very soon."

She tried to say something else, but he was gone. Taylor stared at her phone, shaking in her hand. The fear overtook her and the phone slid from her hand to the floor. She couldn't stop shaking.

The phone buzzed on the floor, making her jump. She looked at it as if it were a snake ready to strike. The screen lit up with an email. An update from a supplier.

Taylor drew a long breath, letting the air fill her lungs

until they ached. She held it to the count of four, then slowly released the air. After a few more deep breaths, her hands stopped shaking and her heart slowed to normal. She picked up her phone and opened the email.

She didn't have time for threats. She had a job to do.

2

———

TAYLOR REFUSED TO LET THE MAN ON THE PHONE SCARE HER into backing down. She was going to do what she set out to do, and she was going to do it the way she'd planned.

That didn't mean his words didn't play in her mind the entire next morning. She was an ambitious woman, but she never set out to step on others on her way to the top. She worked hard and pushed herself, but she didn't intend for her own drive to stop others from moving up with her, or moving up in their own way.

The first job Taylor had was working at an ice cream shop the first summer she was old enough to work. It was near the touristy areas of Niagara Falls and she made most of her money in tips. She learned quickly if she softened them with a friendly smile, then asked people about their days and shared suggestions about the city, people would give her bigger tips. The money she earned helped her to buy Christmas presents for her three younger siblings that year.

Every year after that, Taylor learned what it took to be successful at whatever job she was doing. It didn't matter to her if she was bagging groceries, making sandwiches, or running her own company, there was always a secret to the job that helped her to get ahead.

Stepping on others was never her plan, though. Which was what kept her mind on the man on the phone. He made it sound like he knew her from her childhood, and he made it sound like she used him to get ahead.

Taylor's first boyfriend was someone she met the year she worked at the grocery store. He stocked shelves, and she bagged groceries. They joked about being invisible to the people they were serving. They dated for about six weeks, but her job changed and they saw each other less and eventually fizzled out.

Could it be Jesse?

Her phone rang in her hand, startling her. She fumbled with it and dropped the offending item onto her desk where it rattled across the surface until she snatched it back up.

She paused and looked at the screen, then shoved away her fears. She had to answer her phone.

"Taylor Wright."

"Ms. Wright, this is Steven Anthony." The head of her security for the building.

"Hi, Steven. What do you need?"

"We have a package here for you. I was told to call you before delivering anything. Would you like me to open it?"

Taylor hated that she wanted to hide behind a man for any reason, but especially for this reason. Whoever sent her the bird got to her. He got into her head and made her doubt her abilities and her strength.

"Yes, please," Taylor said after a long moment.

"Hold on, Ms. Wright."

Taylor strained to hear something as Steven unwrapped whatever was delivered to the building. She was grateful for the barrier between herself and the outside world, but she resented it more than anything.

The building didn't just belong to Taylor and Birds of a Feather. She leased the third floor, but there were five in total. The ground floor was security and retail spaces that were open to the public. One of those retail spaces was going to be the Birds of a Feather flagship store in a few months. Other companies leased the other three floors. A visitor had to check in with security to get a pass to access any of the companies through the shared elevator. All the stairs were only accessible from inside one of the upper floors or with a keycard. The building was secure. As secure as possible.

"It's clean, Ms. Wright. I'll send it up."

"Thank you, Steven. I really appreciate it."

"Any time, Ms. Wright."

Taylor set the phone down. Her hands quivered. She squeezed them and flexed them, but the fear running through her was making it harder for her to simply be. She drew a shaky breath and blew it out slowly. She needed to walk.

She left her office and turned toward the marketing department. They were spread out at the conference room table, shouting ideas and scribbling them on the board. Taylor stood in the doorway and listened for a few minutes, letting their excitement fuel her.

She didn't step on any of them.

Next was accounting. They were a more subdued group, but they were no less important to the success of her company. Taylor felt her confidence returning as she continued past the quiet collection of people way smarter than her.

The art department was another active group with one

team that focused on the design of each piece and another that focused on the fabrics and patterns. Taylor wanted her clothing to be bright and colorful. Sure, they had some solid colors, but she insisted on adding pops of color to those, too. She'd been told to hide her shape her entire life, but she was done hiding. She wanted to celebrate her size, and she wanted to encourage other plus-size women to do the same.

Birds of a Feather.

Taylor was finally feeling like herself when she made it all the way around to her office. Jessica was at her desk with a large box covering most of the surface.

"What is that?" Taylor asked.

"This is the package that came for you. It's gorgeous." Jessica pointed to the large painting.

Taylor recognized it right away. She'd bought it weeks ago at a showing the artist had. It was the perfect piece for her office. In the center was a brightly colored bird on a full color branch. The birds and branch next to it were outlined in black and white, but the colors of the bird in the middle were flowing outward and painting the other birds, giving them all the same beautiful colors.

The artist titled it *Birds of a Feather*, and Taylor couldn't resist the purchase.

"I want to put it up right away. I love it."

"You have an appointment first. He's already in your office."

"Who is he?"

Jessica avoided Taylor's gaze and focused a little too intently on her computer screen. "He's on your calendar."

Taylor gave Jessica a not-too-happy look. Jessica was the one responsible for Taylor's calendar, which meant she was the one who added the meeting. A meeting Taylor didn't remember setting up, or asking to have set up.

Taylor walked into her office and froze. His back was to her, and she had to stare for just a moment and appreciate the beauty of him. She had no idea who he was, but she was going to enjoy the view inside instead of the one outside her windows that showed the Niagara Gorge.

He shifted his weight and the black jacket he wore stretched tight across his shoulders. He blew out a breath and glanced at his watch, then turned to look at the door.

Taylor flinched slightly at being caught staring at him. His dark eyes pierced into her, scanning and cataloguing her in an instant. Dismissing her, no doubt. She was used to it. Men were interested in her because she was a powerful woman but immediately lost interest when they saw her and realized she wasn't a stiletto and pants-suit wearing woman who could have been a pin-up model but started a company instead.

"Ms. Wright?" he asked, his voice rough, like he wasn't accustomed to using it.

Taylor nodded and stepped toward him. "Yes. And you are?"

His dark brow lifted just enough to say he was surprised by the question. The corner of his lips turned up in a tentative, amused way. He tilted his head and said, "I'm Ryker Hamilton," like that explained his presence. "Your brother asked me to come by. He said you would be expecting me."

Taylor groaned internally and gave him a you-weren't-invited smile. "Thank you for coming by, Mr. Hamilton, but my brother is mistaken."

Her quick dismissal left him with his hand halfway between them. He closed his fist and tucked both hands behind his back, standing at full attention. He definitely had all of hers, but the glint in his eyes that said he thought she was foolish had her standing firm in her refusal of his help.

"I see. Would you mind giving me a few minutes? We can sit and talk. That way, if you change your mind at some point, you know who I am."

Taylor breathed a laugh and moved behind her desk. She wheeled her chair out of the way and sat down. "My brother is being ridiculous. I appreciate you coming down here, but I assure you, I don't need whatever kind of help he led you to believe I needed."

"And you're not willing to speak to me. Or let me make an assessment of your situation."

"I don't have a situation. I receive threats all the time. I'm a powerful woman, and men don't like that. Men have a tendency to think they're the only ones who know how to do things. I'm shaking things up. I'm making waves in their pool. They don't like it. But that doesn't mean I'm in any real danger. My brother wants to protect me, but he's forgotten who raised him. Who protected him when we were younger. I'm very capable of taking care of myself."

Mr. Hamilton studied her closely for a long moment. Taylor refused to squirm under his steady gaze. She knew he was waiting for it, but she learned a long time ago not to show weakness. Men thrived on it. She herself used it in negotiations. She was not going to show him how he was affecting her.

"If you change your mind, here's my card." He set it on the corner of the desk. "My company is willing to help you. My personal number is on there. You can call me day or night and I will make myself available for you."

Taylor choked out a breath, her hand catching it on her lips. "You're an escort? I thought you were here for security."

His lips curled up before he had a chance to wrangle them back into submission. "I am, Ms. Wright. But my company is not your typical security company. Plus, I owe your brother a favor."

"And I'm your favor?" Taylor asked, incredulous that she was a bargaining chip.

Mr. Hamilton shook his head. "Keeping an eye on a beautiful woman is certainly not a hardship."

"I..." Taylor fumbled over her tongue. She needed to call her brother. What the hell was he thinking sending this guy to her. Taylor could get her own damn dates. Just because she hadn't had any in longer than she could remember did not mean she needed her brother to set her up.

Mr. Hamilton stood still, waiting for her to say something. Taylor glanced at the card on her desk and drew a breath.

"Thank you for coming in today, Mr. Hamilton. I am sorry I can't help you pay back the favor you owe my brother."

He shrugged and moved toward the door. "I'll find another way. It was a pleasure to meet you, Ms. Wright."

He nodded and walked out her door, turning toward the elevator and walking away like he was the one who owned the place instead of her.

Taylor sank into her chair and sighed heavily.

"Who was that?" Jessica asked, pausing at the doorway to watch the man walk away. Jessica knew everything about Taylor, including how long it had been since she had gone on a date. Taylor couldn't help but wonder what Braden said to her to get Jessica to add Mr. Hamilton to her calendar.

"That was a gift from my brother."

Jessica snorted. "I wish I had a brother who sent me gifts like that. Are you going to go out with him?"

Taylor grabbed the business card from the edge of the desk and stuffed it into her bag. She'd get rid of it later. After giving herself a private moment to fantasize about letting go and giving in to a date with a man like Ryker Hamilton. Private security or not, the man was nice to look at.

"No," Taylor finally said, answering Jessica's question. "We have work to do. I don't have time for dating. What's next on the agenda?"

DEX WALKED into the office with his jacket over his arm and the ghost of a damn-she's-hot smile on his face. Taylor Wright was not what he expected. He wasn't sure what he expected, but when Braden called and asked him to meet with his sister, Dex assumed she'd be a lot less... intoxicating.

He smothered the look before he ran into his teammates. They would notice in about three seconds and destroy him for it. He had become a loner since their days in the service. Not that he wasn't interested in women. He'd been focused on himself for the last few years. If he didn't, he would have ended up another footnote in history of a warrior who returned home and lost his damn mind. A traumatic brain injury could do that to even the strongest of men.

Dex knew he was lucky that his TBI wasn't worse, but he also knew it meant he had to be careful, which meant putting himself first.

Taylor Wright was the first woman he'd looked at twice since he returned. And damn if she wasn't worth that second look.

"How was the meeting?" Dunn asked, sticking his head in Dex's office.

"Nothing came of it."

"Are you free?"

"Yeah. What's up?"

"Need to bounce some ideas off of you. Parker is out there and we need to find him."

"Conference room?"

Dunn nodded, and the men walked down the hall to where they had a board set up with Parker front and center. They had pictures of the man, but they were from years earlier. The sheriff was the one pushing the case forward after his daughter was assaulted, but Homeland had a file on Parker. All their leads had dried up, though, and they were eager for the assistance. Dunn agreed, but digging up new dirt on a ghost was proving to be more of a challenge than any of them expected.

"His old shell companies have gone under, but we're struggling to find the new ones. The assumption is he's set them up under the names of his closest advisors, but we don't know who they are. He's obviously not afraid to drop a body, so anyone he's willing to trust must be someone very close to him."

"Does he have any family?"

"Not that we know of."

"What do we have on him?"

"Obviously not enough. Most of the data is old, which is a big part of the problem."

"And aside from the latest victim of one of his associates, whose name we don't know and who we also don't have an actual photo of, we believe he's still operating out of this area?"

"We're fairly sure of that."

"Why?"

"It seems obvious with this case. Darcy Harris, the sheriff's daughter... All the cases he told her about were older, but they're still local cases. She knew about them because of her dad, but he obviously didn't know who she was. If they were gone, if Parker was gone, I doubt someone who's been a part of his world like that would still be here. Plus..."

Dunn shuffled papers on the table and handed over a grainy photo and a report from the local medical examiner's office.

"The photo is Parker. It was taken only a few months ago. It's not good enough to use for facial rec, so English is still aging up old photos. And the report is classic for this guy. He's not a quick and dirty killer. He relishes it. He enjoys making them pay for turning on him."

Dex's stomach flipped as he read the report. He'd read others, but the detailed way the report was written was almost like a love letter to the trauma Parker inflicted on the deceased.

"Who's the ME?"

"What do you mean?"

"This report is a bit much. Almost like the medical examiner was impressed by what was done."

Dunn reached for the report and scanned it quickly. "Dammit. We need to talk to him."

"I'll go with you. I need some fresh air."

"We're going to the morgue. I think that's the polar opposite of fresh air." Dunn raised a mocking brow at Dex.

Dex pretended not to notice the look. "Just want to get out of the office."

Dunn let it go and took the file with them to see the ME. With any luck, they'd get some answers.

"WHAT DO you mean he no longer works here?" Dex asked Jerry, the man behind the desk.

"He only worked here for a few weeks. I think that was the only case he worked on alone, but I can't remember. I can pull up his files, but we let him go right after this," Jerry said. He tapped the keys on his computer and stared at the screen. He pushed his glasses up his nose, but they kept sliding down, making him look much older than he likely was.

Dex catalogued him, focusing on Jerry instead of the overwhelming smell of death in the basement. Unruly dark hair that looked like he ran his hands through it constantly. Wide rimmed glasses, a brown cardigan and stained white button down. He could have been the crazy college professor everyone laughed at, or he could have been the crazy head of the ME's office.

"Here he is. He worked here for two weeks and three days. Everyone spends the first two weeks shadowing another employee. After that, they're on their own unless there's a reason they can't be. He had a good recommendation, but he broke all the rules. Really seemed like his documentation was faked."

"Faked?" Dunn asked.

Jerry shrugged. "Who knows? When I fired him, I had a list of things he'd done wrong, right down to eating in the exam room. It was a lot of basic stuff he messed up."

"Do you have any contact info for him?"

"Of course. But, uh, who did you say you work for?"

"We're contractors through Homeland," Dunn said. He handed over a business card. "You can call Agent Andrews if you need to verify anything."

Jerry looked at the card and clicked another button on

the computer. The printer behind him came to life and spit out a single sheet of paper. "This is what I have."

Dunn took the sheet and looked it over before handing it to Dex. "Thanks for your help," Dunn said.

The two of them left the morgue and the darkness. Dex gulped the fresh air, willing it to clear his head and take away the beginning of the migraine barreling toward him.

"You doing okay?" Dunn asked.

Dex nodded, trying to pretend he could see straight and nothing out of the ordinary was going on. He hadn't been completely open with his team about his condition, preferring to keep it quiet as much as possible. Dunn knew he got headaches, but Dex never elaborated on how bad they were.

"Notice anything about that name?" Dunn asked.

Dex shook his head and looked at the paper again. He groaned. "Dammit."

"Yep."

"Do you recognize the address?"

"No. I'm not even sure it's valid. What I do know is we need to get this information to English to find out if Damien Parker is related to Dennis Parker or if it's just a coincidence that they share the same last name."

"What are the chances of that?"

Dunn snorted. "Doubtful, but I'm not counting on that easy of a coincidence yet."

3

"WHAT THE HELL WERE YOU THINKING?" DENNIS BARKED.

Jonah shrugged, trying not to piss his pants. He'd seen his boss's wrath directed at many others over the years, but he'd always stayed on his good side. To remain unscathed.

"She's the sheriff's fucking daughter! What is wrong with you?"

"I didn't know that."

"Yeah, well, now everyone in the county knows that. He's gunning for you, and since you work for me, he's gunning for me. What the hell did you tell her?"

Jonah squirmed. He could still see her face in his mind. Her beautiful brown hair and her stunning eyes. She wasn't a perfect match for the woman he really wanted, but she was close enough. And she'd been easy to talk to. Too easy.

"I... I don't remember."

Dennis raised an eyebrow. A single lift that said more than any words could say. He was calling bullshit, and they both knew it. They also both knew if Jonah didn't tell the truth, he wouldn't get a second chance. Any of the men waiting outside the immaculate office would happily clean up his dismembered body and dispose of it in a way that made it clear that Jonah had betrayed their boss. He would be a lesson to others.

Just like the man who had Jonah's job before him was.

"I mentioned a few things. But nothing recent. Nothing that we're tied to."

"Apparently, you were wrong about that, too. Shaw said my name was on all those cases as a person of interest. She sang like a bird to her daddy and now they're looking for me. They even brought in an outside team to help with this one. We're fucked because you couldn't keep your damn mouth shut."

"I'm sorry, boss. I didn't realize. I didn't mean to cause any trouble. I'll do anything. Anything. Let me fix this."

He shook his head and said, "This is why I'm thinking of bringing in my oldest to take over instead of you. Fucking worthless."

Jonah swallowed his rage at the man and clenched his fists. He was not going to let him know how much he got to him.

Dennis leaned back in his black leather chair. With his elbows on the armrests, he steepled his fingers in front of his jaw and glared down his long nose at Jonah. His dark hair was all gray around his temples with sprinkles of gray over his entire head, but instead of making him look weak, he was seasoned and even more deadly. He'd survived longer than many men who'd taken up the mantle of an organization like theirs. And he knew how dangerous that meant he was.

Dennis cleared his throat and leaned forward again. "Fine. I'll give you time to clean up your mess. Don't fuck up again or you'll be the mess that needs cleaning up."

Jonah nodded rapidly. He scrambled to stand and leave the office before Dennis changed his mind.

Jonah hurried down the long marble hallway to his own office, only pausing once he was inside. He wasn't safe in there, since Dennis owned his entire world, but he was safer than sitting across from the man he'd known most of his life.

Jonah's hands rattled, and his bladder and lunch threatened a revolt. Jonah took a deep breath and stilled them all. He was not going to lose it. Not after all the work he'd done. He was close to getting everything he wanted. Victory was within his sights. He couldn't stop now. Even better, his two goals were coming together.

Taylor was scared on the phone, and she had no fucking clue who he was. That stung, but Jonah didn't expect her to recognize his voice. He knew he was invisible on her quest for success. But he wouldn't be invisible forever. Soon she'd see him. She'd have no choice.

TAYLOR WALKED into her bathroom and stripped. It had been another long day, and she needed to relax. Steam from the shower blocked out her reflection. She drew a breath and let the warm air fill her lungs and heat her up from the inside. She'd been cold since the bird arrived in her office. Cold and scared.

She walked under the stream and tipped her head back. The water ran through her hair and down her back, washing away the last two days.

After a minute, Taylor grabbed the shampoo and started to wash herself. She let her mind go gloriously blank as she went through the motions of her shower. She didn't want to think about her company or the mystery man or her brother's friend. She just wanted quiet in her mind.

She stepped out of her shower, and every hair on her body stood up. She froze, trying to place the uneasy feeling that wrapped around her throat and tried to choke her. The cool air settled on her wet skin and pushed goosebumps to the surface, making her hyperaware of everything. Taylor reached for her towel, trying to pretend she was fine. If there was a problem, her alarm would have gone off. It was just her mind playing tricks on her.

She still couldn't shake the feeling as she dried off and dressed. Something was off. Something wasn't right. Someone was watching her.

Taylor grabbed the baseball bat she kept next to her bed and crept out of her room. All her windows were covered, so whoever was watching her had to be inside her home. Her sanctuary.

Her alarm never went off, but she could feel it. She could feel the air, the change. Something was wrong.

She made it downstairs before she heard a sound. The soft intake of breath, a moment of panic. She was definitely not alone.

"What are you doing in my house?" she asked the silence.

"I just wanted to say hi, Tay-tay," someone answered. A man. The man from the phone.

Taylor spun toward his voice, but he was in shadows. All she could see was that he was bigger than her. His clothes were dark, but the light flashed against the knife he held in his hand.

"Get out of my house," Taylor said, her voice shaky and unreliable, just like her knees.

"Is that any way to talk to an old friend?"

"If we were friends, you would have rung the doorbell and waited for me to invite you in. Get out now and maybe you won't get arrested when the police arrive. I have a silent alarm, and someone is on the way as we speak."

His laugh sent a chill up her spine. It reminded her of something, someone. Her mind tried to find the memory deep in the recesses, but it came up blank.

"We both know no one is coming, Tay-tay. Why don't you put that bat down and we can chat? Or you can get down on your knees for me right now."

"I'll bite it off, you sick fuck."

That pissed him off. He lunged for her, swinging the knife. She tried to block it, but he caught her forearm. The bat was still in her hands, but he was stronger than her. His breath reeked, even from a few feet away. His body smelled like he needed a shower and had for days. The pungent odor made her eyes water and made it harder for her to fight back.

He punched her in the ribs, knocking the wind out of her, but knocking some sense back into her. He wasn't there for a chat. He was there to hurt her. Maybe kill her. If she wanted to see daylight again, she needed to fight back.

Taylor swung the bat, albeit weakly, and connected with his shoulder. He growled in frustration and swung at her with his knife again. A sting on her side said he got her, but she didn't care. Adrenaline pumped through her body and swung the bat for her. She got his hip that time, a blow that had him stumbling backward and howling in pain.

"You bitch. You were always a bitch. And one day, you're going to be my bitch." He held his hip with his hand and hurried for the sliding glass door that was wide open. Taylor's hands shuddered as he vanished into the night, blending into the darkness as soon as he was outside.

She followed him to the door and pushed it closed, locking it and yanking the curtains over it. Sweat beaded on her body as her fear pumped through her bloodstream and fueled her actions.

Without thinking, she dumped out her purse and found what she was looking for. She fumbled with her phone and punched in the unfamiliar numbers, keeping her gaze locked on the traitorous back door.

"Hamilton," he barked in answer.

"Mr. Hamilton?" she asked, even though he already said his name.

"Yes. Who is this?"

"Taylor Wright. We, um, we met earlier today in my office."

"Yes, of course." His voice softened with recognition. "Is there something I can do for you, Ms. Wright?"

"Someone was just in my house. I, um..."

"What's your address, Ms. Wright?"

Taylor drew a shaky breath and held it. She blew it out slowly, forcing the panic from her body for the second time in less than thirty minutes. Had it really been less than that since she stepped out of her shower and felt like everything was going to be okay? "I'm sorry. I shouldn't have called you."

"What is your address? At least let me check out your property and make sure no one is still there."

Her eyes flipped to the other doors, doors she'd loved when she moved in. They meant she could open her home and let the outside in. Doors that allowed her siblings to flow through her home and enjoy the riches she'd earned with her blood, sweat, and tears. Doors that now felt like a burden instead of a blessing.

"I, um..."

"Ms. Wright, I will call your brother and get your address from him if you don't tell me. Someone was inside your home. I'm assuming from the frantic call, this was someone you don't know and someone you didn't invite into your home. You're scared, and you have every right to be scared. Let me come over. Let me make sure you're safe for the night. Please, Ms. Wright."

Taylor sighed and pulled in another shaky breath. He was right. And she knew he would definitely call Braden if she didn't tell him where she lived. She recited her address and whispered, "Thank you."

"You're welcome, Ms. Wright. I'll be there in five minutes. Keep the doors locked. I'll send you a text when I arrive and come into the house first. I will not be walking around outside until after I've come in to see you. I'm on my way."

"Thank you."

"I'm not going to let anything happen to you."

"Can you... um, I mean, do you mind..."

"Do you want me to stay on the phone with you?"

"Yes," she said quietly, the word painful to admit.

"Of course. Why don't you tell me about your company? Birds of a Feather. Where did you come up with it?"

Taylor took a breath and started talking. She could talk about her company all night if she had to.

DEX LISTENED to Taylor's voice as it went from panicked and wild to calm and happy the longer she spoke. He liked listening to her, almost as much as he liked that she called him when she needed something.

He kicked himself for not having gone there. She told

him she didn't need or want his help, but he should have known if Braden was calling, there was a reason to be concerned. Instead, Dex had left a beautiful woman unguarded and in danger.

He pulled into her driveway and told her he was there. Her voice changed back to the panicked one, and he wished he could have kept her talking about her company.

"Should I unlock the door?" she asked.

"Hang on. I'll knock twice when I get to your door. I'm getting out of my car right now. I'm walking up. Okay, this is me, Ms. Wright." He knocked twice.

The door opened before he'd pulled his hand back. Her wet locks hung down her back and teased their way over her shoulders. She wore a pair of loose pants that fluttered with her jerky movements. Her tank top was tight and bright and hugged her curves in a way that made his mouth water.

But Dex wasn't there for that. She was Braden's sister, not some woman he was going to sleep with.

"Mr. Hamilton," she breathed, her voice doing things to his cock that a woman hadn't done in far too long. Dex used to think of himself as a little bit of a ladies' man, but it had been far too long since he let himself enjoy all the treasures of a woman's body.

"Ms. Wright. Are you hurt?" His gaze scanned her body, landing on the bloodstain on the side of her shirt. "You are. Let me see it."

She lifted her arm as he backed her inside and closed the door. He locked it, making a mental note that the lock didn't appear to have been tampered with.

Dex held her arm up and walked with her toward the kitchen. Her home could have been in a magazine or on one of those shows Lily, Ashleigh, and the other women liked. Everything was white and bright, with pops of color throughout the space. Her kitchen had white cabinets and white countertops with mismatched, colorful pulls. Pendant lights hung over the island and cast bright blues and reds around the room. It reminded him of her office with the blank, bright canvas and the brilliant colors that brought the place to life.

"Do you have a paper towel or something I can use to clean the blood away?" Dex asked.

She pointed, then reached under one of the upper cabinets. She pulled a roll of paper towels off a hidden holder and handed it to him.

"Thanks." Dex ran a few sheets under warm water and got to work cleaning up her arm. The cut wasn't deep, but it was long. When he finished cleaning it, he asked if she had other cuts.

"I'm not sure. Um, but, maybe on my side? And he punched me."

She was starting to crash. Dex could hear it in her voice. "Why don't you sit and I can look?" He held her arm and guided her to the stools on the other side of the island. The dining room chairs were fabric and would stain, same as the couch, but the stools were shiny and could be wiped clean.

Taylor didn't fight him as he helped her sit. She leaned against the counter and winced. "Ow, yeah, it hurts. I didn't realize..."

"It's fine. Can I lift your shirt?"

She nodded and turned away.

Dex lifted the edge of her shirt and let his gaze flip between her face and her wounded skin. She pulled her lower lip between her teeth as her cheeks darkened. He wondered if it was pain or something else that had her pulling back from him.

The gash on her side was similar to the one on her arm.

The blood he noticed on her shirt definitely came from this cut, which told him before he got a good look at it that it was likely deeper. He cleaned it carefully, watching her face for signs of pain as he worked quickly.

"I don't think either will need stitches, but I'm not a doctor. I can take you to the hospital."

"No," she blurted. "No hospitals and no cops."

"No cops? What do you mean?"

"I can't have anyone else find out about this. If I report it, it becomes public record. That means people will find out. I'm so close to launching my company, and if this gets out, it'll take all the focus off *Birds*. I can't have that. No one can know what happened."

"Ms. Wright—"

"No, Mr. Hamilton, no. I'm sorry. I shouldn't have called you and put you in the middle of this." She made a move to stand, but Dex blocked her escape.

"Ms. Wright, please at least let me bandage your cuts."

She looked up at him. Their faces were close since she moved to get away. Close enough that Dex could feel the warmth of her breath on his face. They stared at each other, neither of them moving. She swayed toward him, just slightly, then pulled back and settled in her chair again. "Okay," she whispered.

Dex wasn't sure he would ever breathe normally again. His body pumped with desire. But she was off-limits. She was a client and a friend's sister and a favor, not... available for him.

Dex focused once more on the task at hand. Taylor had a well stocked first aid kit. He closed the wound on her side with butterfly strips and covered it with a gauze pad. The one on her arm got the same treatment. Dex tried not to memorize how soft her skin was or how good she smelled as he worked, but it was pointless. He knew the first chance he got, he'd fantasize about all the things he couldn't do with Ms. Taylor Wright.

Once her wounds were bandaged, Dex cleaned up and asked if she was feeling better.

"I think so. I just…" She sucked in a breath and stared at her back door.

"Is that where he came in?" She nodded. "Do you have a security system?" She nodded again. "And it was set but didn't go off?"

"Yep."

"I'll check everything out. Are you okay in here for a little while?"

"Yeah. I can—" She made a move to get off the stool and winced. He reached for her, but she waved him off and walked across the room and settled on her purple couch. "Is it okay if I sit here?"

"Of course. I'll check around the house and see if I can find out how he gained access. Do you have a hidden key or anything?"

"No, nothing."

"Okay. Where are your keys?"

"My keys?"

"I will lock the door on my way out and let myself back in so you don't need to get up. You're injured, Ms. Wright. I want you to rest."

"Oh, okay. In my purse."

Dex found them and looked at her once more, then walked outside into the darkness.

He slipped effortlessly into warrior mode once he was outside. Protecting Taylor was all that mattered. He walked around the entire house, checking windows and doors and looking for anything that seemed off. He didn't know what normal looked like for her, but he didn't see anything that alarmed him.

Which alarmed him.

He let himself back into her home. Taylor hadn't moved from the couch, but she was staring at the door when he walked in. Her teeth left an imprint on her lower lip. "Anything?"

"No, unfortunately."

"I thought that was good. You sound like that's a bad thing. Why is that not good?"

Dex moved across the room toward her. "It means I don't know how he got into your home. Which means he could do it again."

She pulled her knees up onto the couch and hugged them. "I... He knows me. I don't know who he is, but he knows me. He keeps calling me by my childhood nickname."

"Keeps calling you? This wasn't the first time he's been in your home?"

"It was, but it wasn't the first time I'd spoken to him. He called me last night. He's the one who sent me the bird."

Dex tried not to let his anger show, but he was pissed. She had a stalker, a dangerous one, and she was only now telling him. After she refused his protection.

He felt even more guilty for not being there. It didn't matter that he didn't have all the facts, he was a soldier. He was supposed to have a sixth sense about these kinds of things. Instead, he was fantasizing about the client and worrying about another case.

"Tell me everything, Ms. Wright. Now."

4

TAYLOR DIDN'T HOLD BACK. NOW THAT HE KNEW ABOUT THE phone call, Mr. Hamilton wasn't letting her hide any of the details. He asked questions and pried it all out of her until she felt like laundry on a clothesline. Exposed and wrung out.

By the time she'd answered all of his questions and he was satisfied with the details she'd shared, Taylor was drained. She needed some pain meds for her cuts and sleep.

"Ms. Wright, I'd like to stay here tonight," Mr. Hamilton said.

"You don't have to do that."

"I know, but I'd like to. I'm assuming your bedroom is upstairs. I'd like to stay on your couch, if that's okay. It doesn't appear as though someone could access your room from the outside, so you should be safe up there. I'm happy to look around upstairs if you would like me to. But I am either spending the night on your couch or in my vehicle in your driveway. Your choice, Ms. Wright."

Taylor sighed and admitted to herself it made her feel

better to know he would be there. "Okay, but you should probably start calling me Taylor."

He gave her a rusty smile that hit her right in the center of her chest. "Ryker. Or Dex. Whichever you prefer."

She tilted her head to the side before voicing her thought. "Is Dex your middle name?"

"Uh, no. It's my nickname from my SEAL brothers."

"What does it mean?"

"It's short for Poindexter."

"Uh, interesting. Does that mean you're really smart or is it ironic and you're... not?"

He chuckled at her blunt question and said, "The first one."

"Lucky me. Hopefully that means you're smart enough to keep me from getting killed before I can launch my company."

He sucked in a breath at her words, his smile melting into a scowl. "That's definitely my goal, Taylor."

She liked the way he said her name, like it was something important. Like she was important. She watched his mouth form the word, his tantalizing tongue barely peeking out between his open lips.

It felt like days instead of hours since she stepped into her shower to wash away the day and relax for the night. She hadn't let herself relax in far too long, and a man like Dex was... she didn't want to relax with him, but she could think of something they could do that would definitely leave her feeling boneless.

She dragged her focus from her self-appointed bodyguard and led the way upstairs. She felt exposed letting him into her bedroom, but she'd prefer him to the man who kept letting himself into her world.

When Dex declared the upstairs safe, he headed back down while Taylor sequestered herself in her bedroom. She took a deep breath, then another, and one more, and struggled to find her peace. It wasn't like that was the first time she faced down an intruder, but the last time she had a lot more at stake than stuff. Last time, she was protecting her siblings.

Taylor shook her head and tried to clear away childhood memories. She opened her eyes and focused on her room. She needed to get ready for bed. The routine would calm her mind. A routine always did.

By the time she was sliding between her luxurious sheets, Taylor was feeling slightly better. Her hands had stopped shaking, and her mind was focused on each task as she did it. *Pull back the covers, climb in, then tug the covers up to your chin and hide from the world.* Her mother's words played in her head, another memory she wanted to forget.

Taylor closed her eyes and slowed her breathing. She counted as she inhaled and again on her exhale. She went through everything she'd learned to relax. She flipped onto her side, winced, and repeated the process. The other side. To her back again.

She threw the covers off in a huff. The digital clock on her nightstand told her it'd been almost two hours since she closed her bedroom door.

The fan above her bed whirred and pushed cool air toward her. Maybe she was hot. Maybe that was the problem. She climbed out of bed and took off her pants, laying them on the edge of the bed for the morning. And because there was a strange man in her house.

Dex. The name suited him. She could see the calculating glances he made whenever they were close. She also trusted him, something she hadn't found in a man in far too long.

Too many men from her past saw her as an easy mark and did everything they could to push her out of the way and take what they wanted. It was the main reason Taylor was baffled by the mystery man. He claimed Taylor stepped on him. But she didn't. She knew she didn't.

She was still warm without her pants on, but now she was wide awake again. She replayed the phone call in her mind, then repeated the words the man said downstairs. She tried to place his voice and his anger, but both eluded her. He knew her, but she didn't know him. How? And why?

Taylor went to her bathroom and got a glass of water. She sipped it and used the bathroom, then washed her hands and went back to bed. She tossed and turned again, wincing with each move as the cut on her side protested. She sat up and looked at it, remembering the fear coursing through her.

"I need to stop," she whispered to herself. She tugged her shirt down over the white bandage and laid down again. She pulled the covers up and closed her eyes.

Going to sleep scared was a regular occurrence when she was a child, especially shortly after her dad left the last time. When he lived with them, he was the barrier, but once he moved out, Taylor had to be the one who stood up to people wanting to hurt them. She learned how to talk tough and which knife in the drawer would send unexpected visitors running. Most of them, at least.

Taylor drew another deep breath and focused on her counting. If she could push away all other thoughts, the counting would put her to sleep. It was a big if, but she had to try.

One, two, three, four. Hold, two, three, four. Out, two, three, four.

Again, two, three, four. Hold, two, three, four. Out, two, three, four.

Once more, two, three, four. Hold, two, three, four. Out, two, three, four.

She felt her body relax slowly. Her hands loosened their fists. Her thighs let her legs melt into the bed. Her butt lowered her body. Her chest eased. She was able to draw a deep breath that didn't make her lungs hurt. And another.

She drifted, grateful for the bliss that came after so much fear.

DEX STRETCHED out on the couch and studied the room he was in. It was lavish and expensive and almost exactly what he expected when he met Taylor. Her brother? Not even close. But Taylor? Yeah, she was fancy.

It was good, though, because it meant he wouldn't get any ideas about her interest in him. She was grateful for his help, but she wasn't his type. He caught her staring at his lips and every part of his body begged to drag her closer and let her do more than look, but he was not there to touch her or taste her or do anything other than protect her. No matter how tempting she was.

Dex listened to Taylor toss and turn in her big bed upstairs and had to close his eyes and repeat the steps to disassemble and reassemble his handgun to get his erection to go away. She was not the woman for him.

Taylor finally settled, and Dex was able to relax just a bit. He wasn't going to sleep, not when there was someone threatening the woman who slept upstairs, but he operated better if he was relaxed. If his body was in a constant state of tension, his brain didn't respond well. He needed his brain ready for anything with this assignment.

Every twenty minutes, Dex got up from his seat and walked around the downstairs. He checked windows and doors and listened for movement upstairs. He changed where he settled with each check, moving around the large first floor in a way that he hoped wasn't predictable.

He was fairly certain whoever was there was long gone, but Dex never counted on bad guys to do what they were supposed to do.

When the sun finally made an appearance through the filmy curtains of the sitting room under the master, Dex got his first good look outside. The house was lavish, but the outside was like an oasis. A line of trees circled the yard, giving it more privacy than Dex expected. A large seating area complete with a grill and full outdoor kitchen were on the patio just outside the sliding door. A swing set was off to one side, the swings swaying gently in the morning breeze. A fire pit was surrounded by more chairs and far enough from the swing set to allow everything to be enjoyed at once.

Taylor Wright was a woman of surprises.

Dex didn't want to leave the house before she was awake, so he made his rounds inside and watched the property from the windows as the sun continued its climb. When Dex heard her moving upstairs, he started the coffeepot and sent a text to Dunn with his whereabouts and that he'd check in soon.

Taylor breezed downstairs like it was perfectly normal for a man she'd only met once before to be in her home. She avoided his gaze with a fake smile at the coffee and even faker cheeriness in her voice. "Good morning."

Dex saw right through her before she opened her mouth. She didn't sleep for shit. Her gaze never settled anywhere for longer than a second or two, her body wound tight with tension. She was exhausted and stressed and eager to get the hell out of her own home.

"Morning. I started the coffee. I figured you would need some."

She finally met his gaze and her guard slipped just enough for him to see the sincerity behind her grateful smile. Her makeup was perfectly applied to hide her exhaustion, but Dex had spent too many years surrounded by people who didn't sleep. Makeup didn't cover everything.

"I checked the house all night and didn't see anything. I still think you should notify the police."

"No," Taylor argued before he even finished speaking. "I can't. It's bad enough with the bird. This would... I can't."

"Okay, but I think you need protection, Ms. Wright."

"Taylor. I told you to call me Taylor."

Dex hated her name. He didn't want to use it. Calling her Taylor was personal, intimate. It was what he should say when he was buried deep inside her, not what he should say to the woman he was tasked with protecting. Tasked by her brother, for fuck's sake. "Whatever I call you, you need protection. Until we can figure out who this is and why he's after you. He hurt you last night, and he could have killed you."

She sucked in a sharp breath and closed her eyes. She blindly reached for the edge of the counter.

"Taylor, I'm sorry. I don't want to scare you, but I don't want you dead either."

She released her breath. "Thank you. And you're probably right. Obviously, my security system is not what it should be. I need to call someone about that—"

"I can take care of that for you. Our team can install a

new system today. We can have it up and running by noon. If you're okay with that."

"I can't ask you—"

"Taylor, I know you don't know me, but my team is good at what we do. Your brother knows it, which is why he called me. I'm sorry I wasn't here last night when you were attacked, and for that I'll never forgive myself, but—"

"I told you I didn't need protection. Why would you have been here?"

"Because your brother said you did need it. I should have listened to him and been here for you, anyway. I'm sorry I wasn't."

Taylor shook her head, her chestnut hair catching the light and glowing. She really was stunning. Beyond beautiful.

"I didn't think this would happen. I... Thank you for coming when you did. I'm not... Full time protection feels like overkill."

"I understand. It is your decision, however, I feel the need to tell you that I will be sitting in your driveway every night until we catch this man, so..."

Taylor laughed, and the rich, husky tone was the most beautiful sound in the world. Her eyes sparkled with unexpected joy and he found himself replying with the same.

"I'm sorry," she said after a minute. "I'm picturing you sitting in your car in my driveway, peeing into a cup and forgetting which one is pee and which is your drink. I shouldn't be laughing, but—"

"But that would be funny," Dex provided for her with a smile.

She nodded and laughed again. "It would be so funny. And I clearly did not get enough sleep last night." She sobered quickly. "Fuck. I hate this. And I'm sorry my brother got you involved in it."

"This is what I do. Don't be sorry, just let me do my job."

She drew a slow breath and held it, then released it and nodded. "Okay. I'm in. Whatever you think, I'll follow your lead."

"Good. First, I need permission for my team to enter your home and set up a full system."

"Done."

"Okay, second, you're with me. We're leaving your car here and you're not going anywhere unless it's with me."

"But I have meetings and customers and work. I can't wait around for you—"

"I never said this would be easy. I will take you to your office this morning, then go to mine. I'll get some things that I need so I can work from your office. Is there a desk somewhere I can occupy for the next few weeks?"

"Yes, we have open desks."

"Okay. I won't sit in on your meetings, but when you are in the office, I'll work. If you need to leave, you ride with me. At the end of the day, I'll bring you home and stay here with you."

"You're offering to sleep on my couch?"

Dex chuckled. "I've slept in much worse places."

"I have a guest room upstairs. I should have offered it to you last night. I was just too—"

"Taylor, it's fine. I didn't sleep last night, anyway. Once our system is in place, I'll sleep. But last night, I needed to be awake."

She nodded but was visibly shaken. Her hands squeezed into fists, and her body tensed. For a minute, they were almost like friends having a chat, but Dex reminded her of why he was there and brought her fear right back to the forefront of her mind.

"Taylor…"

"I'm fine," she said. "It's not the first time I've had to deal with… I'm fine. Is there anything you need to do before we go to the office?"

"No, I'm ready when you are."

"I'm ready. Let's go." She grabbed her coffee and her oversized bag and headed for the door. She locked up and handed over her keys so Dex could pass them off to whoever was setting up the alarm system, then followed Dex to his SUV.

Their drive to her office was quiet. The radio played softly in the background, but Taylor stared out the window and didn't speak. Dex didn't push, letting her have her quiet.

He followed her directions to park in her designated spot and trailed behind her as she made her way to the front door. She stopped at the security desk and introduced him to the guard, Steven.

"I need a pass for Mr. Hamilton, please. He's going to be working for me for a few weeks and will need to be able to come and go."

"Of course, Ms. Wright," Steven said. He hit a few keys and asked for Dex's license. Within minutes, a pass was printed and clipped to Dex's belt loop. "Keep it on you at all times when you're in the building. It's your key card to access the employee elevators, but obviously it only gives you access to Ms. Wright's floor. You'll need to scan it when you're going past security also."

Dex nodded his understanding. "Thank you."

Steven nodded back sharply, then turned his focus to Taylor. He offered her an overly familiar smile that had Dex wondering if he was more than security, or if he just wanted to be. "Have a nice day, Ms. Wright."

"You, too, Steven."

Dex hated that his job made him suspicious of everyone he encountered, but he had no choice. He saw danger everywhere. And after what his team had been through, he knew sometimes danger was closer than anyone suspected.

"How well do you know him?" Dex asked once they were in the elevator.

"Who? Steven?"

"Yeah."

"I don't know. Not well. Why?"

"Does he fit the profile of the man who attacked you?"

Taylor glanced at the other people in the elevator with them and glared at Dex. "No."

Dex linked his hands together and leaned back. She was right. He shouldn't have asked with others around. He was silent until they made it to her floor and got off the elevator and were alone again.

"He doesn't fit the profile?"

Taylor huffed a sigh and spun on him. "No, Steven doesn't fit. Plus, I speak to him every day. I'd recognize his voice."

"Not if he was disguising it."

"The man... he wasn't disguising his voice. And he's smaller than Steven. Shorter and thinner. Steven is paid security for the building and you think he's breaking into my home and sending me dead birds?" She rolled her eyes at the ridiculous implication.

"Have you ever slept with him?"

"Excuse me?"

"If he's a pissed off ex, he could have hired someone—"

"I've never slept with him. Or anyone else who works in this building."

Dex cleared his throat as Taylor stomped away from him. He trusted her, but there was something about the other man he didn't like. He was extremely familiar with Taylor, and that rubbed Dex the wrong way. Why, he wasn't sure, but he was going to do some digging on the other man to make sure there wasn't something he was missing.

5

TAYLOR SETTLED INTO HER CHAIR, PAINFULLY AWARE OF THE large man sitting outside her office and watching her every move. He shuttled her into her office when they arrived and searched the entire floor to make sure no one else was there, then instructed her to stay in her office and not leave.

He didn't know her well if he thought he could order her around.

Taylor went through her emails from overnight and read the updates from all her vendors. She reviewed her schedule for the day and added a few meetings she wanted to have with marketing and accounting.

Everything was on track with the launch, which meant she was getting her dream, but the threats tainted all of it and kept Taylor thinking she wasn't the hero she imagined herself to be.

Dex shifted in the chair near her door and drew Taylor's attention. She got up and went over to him. "You can leave, you know. You don't have to stay here. You've got to be exhausted."

"I'm not leaving until other people are here."

"Steven and the other guards are here. I'll be fine."

He looked up at her with a glare.

Taylor rolled her eyes at his attitude. "Fine. I'm going to get a bottle of water. Do you need anything?"

He jumped to his feet. "I'll get it. You stay here."

"Why? You said the entire floor is empty."

"It is, but—"

"What difference does it make if I'm in my office or I'm in the break room if there's no one else here?"

"I'm here to make sure nothing happens to you."

"And you think I'm going to injure myself getting a drink?"

"Taylor."

"Dex."

He sighed heavily. "Just stay here. I'll get whatever you need. Or if you insist on going, I'll go with you."

She stared at him for a long moment, irritated by his insistence. There was a small part of her that appreciated his presence, but there was a much larger part that resented the fact that she couldn't even walk around her own office without feeling like she was doing something wrong.

"Fine, but you need to find out who this asshole is so I can go back to my life."

Dex nodded. "I'll do my best."

Taylor huffed and walked away, leaving Dex to follow her. She walked into the break room and straight to the fridge. She pulled out two bottles of water and handed one to him, then went to the breakfast bar. She knew some of her employees weren't able to get something to eat before they came to work, so she offered options that suited every-one. Taylor debated between the sugary cereal she loved as a kid and the smarter option of fruit and yogurt. Thinking she had a choice almost made her laugh as she reached for the fruit and yogurt. With the way her stomach felt after almost no sleep and getting attacked, sugar was a bad idea.

"Do you want something to eat?" Taylor asked Dex as she found a bowl to mix her food together.

"I don't want to take things from your employees."

"There's always plenty. Please, help yourself."

Dex grunted and moved next to her. He did opt for the sugary cereal, pouring a large bowl of it and filling it with milk. She stared longingly at the cereal as he took his first bite.

"Are you okay?"

"What? Oh, yeah. Sorry." She pulled her focus back to her own breakfast and tried not to wonder where the man put that big of a bowl of cereal. There wasn't an ounce of fat on him. She could only imagine how he worked it off.

She licked her lips slowly, her gaze lingering on his chest. He was there to keep her safe, not to be her morning, noon, and evening entertainment. No matter how badly she wished he was.

"Taylor?" he said, his voice low and husky.

She looked up at him. He'd set his bowl on the counter. Was he closer than a minute ago? She wasn't used to a man focusing so intently on her, giving her his undivided attention. Her body flushed with heat and desire. She could skip breakfast and just have him instead.

She took a step toward him, and he didn't retreat. Their gazes collided and held, the air between them sparking. Tension and anticipation flooded Taylor. She couldn't remember the last time she'd felt so turned on by a man before he even laid a hand on her. Usually, she needed more than a little warm up to feel half as ready as she was in that moment.

The ding of the elevator sounded loud in the empty

office space. Dex went from sex-god to warrior-god in a heartbeat. He turned toward the doorway and blocked Taylor with his body.

It took her a little longer for the fog to clear, but once she heard the humming that was indicative of the head of her marketing department, Taylor told Dex it was fine.

"Do you know who that is?"

"It's Sharon. She's the head of marketing. She'll put her stuff in her office, then come in here for breakfast. She has a son in high school and drops him off on her way in to work. She's always the first one here after me."

Almost as soon as she finished speaking, Sharon rounded the corner into the break room. She pulled up quickly when she saw Dex, then relaxed when she noticed Taylor behind him.

"Good morning?" Sharon said, her words tilting up at the end and making the greeting a question.

"Hi, Sharon. This is Ryker Hamilton. He's going to be hanging around for a while. A little extra security after the bird," Taylor said.

"Good idea." Sharon extended her hand and gave Dex an almost imperceptible one-over. "I'm the head of marketing. My office is right next door. I haven't personally received any threats, but I appreciate you being here. Taylor is an amazing boss and what she's doing for women is so important. It's why I came to work here. I believe in her and her vision."

"Thank you, Sharon," Taylor said, her heart swelling with gratitude. Sharon was her first big hire, stealing her away from another clothing company that focused on providing fitness wear for fitness buffs. Taylor never thought she'd be able to convince Sharon to make the move, but she was the only person Taylor wanted for the job.

Sharon fanned herself and pretended to faint when Dex wasn't looking. Yes, Taylor had to agree. He was a hell of a man to look at. She gave a barely there shake of her head to silently tell Sharon he wasn't anything more than security, but Sharon was clearly not interested in that part of the truth.

"I'm going to get some breakfast and start my morning. I'll leave you two to... whatever you were doing." There was no mistaking what Sharon thought was happening.

Taylor tried to argue, but Dex grabbed both of their bowls and jerked his head toward the door for Taylor to proceed him out of the break room. Sharon gave her a thumb's up and mouthed *he's hot*. Taylor shook her head, admitting defeat.

Back in her office, Taylor finished her breakfast with Dex sitting at the edge of her desk eating his. He kept his eyes on the door, waiting and watching for anyone who dared get close.

By the time they finished eating, Taylor needed a break from him. A few minutes of air that wasn't shared by the sexy man who was working his way under her skin.

"I'll be back," she told him, getting up from her chair and taking their bowls.

"Where are you going?"

"Okay, listen, you can't follow me everywhere. There are people here now, and there is security downstairs. I know you're here to protect me, but I need to be able to go to the bathroom without you peeking over the edge of the stall."

"Is that where you're going?" Dex asked, ignoring the rest of what she said.

"I... I just need a minute without you up my ass, okay?"

Dex stilled long enough to tell Taylor he didn't appreciate her words, then nodded. She took his nod as acceptance and hurried out of her own office before he could tell her to wait for him.

The break room was empty, giving her a moment to catch her breath while she put their bowls into the dishwasher. The cleaning crew had emptied the dishwasher overnight, leaving it ready for the employees to fill it so it could be run again when everyone left for the day.

After the break room, Taylor took a walk around the floor before heading back to her office. When she finally arrived, Jessica was sitting at her desk, pretending to not stare at Dex.

"I didn't agree to him being here. I'm so sorry. I don't know why he's here," she whispered. "I can get rid of him."

Taylor put her hands on Jessica's to get her attention. "I called him." She glanced around the floor at Jessica's confused look. "The man who sent the bird broke into my house last night."

"Oh, my God. Are you okay?" Jessica blurted.

Taylor's head bobbed around in a noncommittal way. "Yes, but really no. I'm scared. But I didn't want to call the police because I don't want this guy to dominate the news of our launch. So, I asked Dex to come over last night and he's going to be around until we find whoever is doing this."

"At least he's nice to look at," Jessica said. "He could probably break a person in half."

Taylor allowed herself a full appreciative look at the man who'd been volunteered to keep her safe. She owed her brother, but she wouldn't tell him that. Braden would lose it if he found out about the break-in.

"I didn't tell Braden about anything other than the bird. Please don't tell him."

Jessica's cheeks flamed, and she avoided Taylor's gaze. She shuffled papers on her desk and shook her head in a twitchy way. "I won't. I mean, I wouldn't. I don't talk to Braden except when he comes here. We're not... friends or anything."

Taylor knew her assistant had a not-so-secret crush on her brother, but she was fairly sure Braden was too dense to notice. Maybe once the launch was over, she could invite them both to her house and... she had no idea what. Taylor was not a matchmaker, and she was clueless when it came to what people liked to do on dates or how to connect them. Maybe her sister, Melissa, could help. If she wasn't busy with her own family.

Taylor pushed the thoughts away. She needed to live long enough for all of that. And at the moment, staying alive and launching Birds of a Feather had to be her priorities.

"Okay, but just, if he shows up, don't say anything."

Jessica did an impressive impression of a bobble-head and sat down at her desk.

"We have a meeting in ten. Let me know if you need more time than that to get through your morning stuff."

"Nope, I'll be ready," Jessica said, sounding like herself again.

"Sounds good. Thanks." Taylor went into her office and circled around her desk on the side that didn't have a muscled badass.

"Feel better?" Dex asked.

Taylor glared up at him.

He chuckled.

"I have a meeting in a few minutes, and, as you can see, this place is getting busy. I know you have other things to do. If you want to head out..."

Dex looked at the bustling office outside her door. He stood to his full height, then focused on her again. "Don't leave. Please. Promise me you'll stay in the office, on this floor, and you won't go anywhere else."

"What if I have a meeting somewhere else?"

"What time? I can be back whenever you need me to be."

"I usually go out to lunch. What about that?"

"Have something delivered. What time is your meeting?"

"What if I need some fresh air?"

"Dammit, Taylor, someone was in your house last night. They sent you a dead bird in the mail a few days ago. He called you. He knows you. He knows your number and where you live and how to rattle you. This might be a joke to you, but I promise you, it's not a joke to me. If something happens to you, your brother will kill me, and I'm not looking forward to letting you get hurt again. I'm not leaving if I don't have your assurance that you're not leaving."

"I'm not leaving," she mumbled.

"Are you just saying that so I'll go?"

She looked up at him and sighed before admitting the truth. "I don't have any reason to leave today."

He raised one dark eyebrow and glared at her with his near-black eyes.

"I don't like being told I can't do something. It pisses me off."

"So, you just want to torture me and make me think as soon as I turn my back you're going to run?"

Her satisfied smirk was the perfected product of the oldest of four. "Pretty much."

Her admission pushed a laugh from him and transformed the angry ogre into a sinfully sexy specimen with a smile that could launch a thousand ships. If women were as reckless as men and started wars over dicks.

He leaned over her desk and invaded her personal

space, ratcheting her pulse up in the process. Maybe she would launch a thousand ships for him.

"I'm going to go to my office and get a few things and hand over your keys so my team can install your new security system. Then I'm going to run home and shower and pack a bag so I can stay with you for two weeks. I should be back in a few hours, but if you need to leave before I'm back, call me and I will come back and get you."

Taylor nodded, unable to do anything beyond what he asked when he focused on her. He really was a stunning man. And she was as sex starved as a eunuch. Once all this was over, she needed to get laid.

"I'll see you soon, Taylor. Don't leave the building."

Taylor rolled her eyes as Dex walked out of her office, even though she had no plans to disobey. She watched him until she couldn't see him anymore. Jessica walked in and asked, "Are you ready for our meeting with Sharon?"

"Yep. We need to make sure this company is a success."

"It will be. Nothing is going to stop that," Jessica said with a confidence Taylor really needed to believe in.

DEX MADE it to the F-BOMB offices in a fog. Exhaustion was setting in. The only thing keeping him awake was the blinding migraine that pulsed behind his eyes as he made his way down the hallway.

He'd barely sat behind his desk when there was a knock on his door. "Yeah?"

"Hey. I thought I saw you walk by. Everything okay?"

He nodded and put his head in his hands. "Yeah, it's fine. Braden Wright's sister is getting threats and someone broke into her house last night."

"And she called you? I didn't realize you knew each other aside from your visit yesterday."

"We don't. I gave her my card when I was there. She doesn't want to tell the police or her brother. Her business is launching in a couple of weeks and she wants the press to be talking about that, not about this guy that's harassing her."

Dunn drew a breath loaded with disagreement.

"I know. I already told her she needs to report it, but she refused. Her security alarm clearly sucks because the guy was in her fucking house, Dunn. He had a knife and cut her twice. She nailed him with a bat, but he got away. I checked the house when I got there and stayed on her couch, but I can't walk away from this one."

Dunn sighed heavily. "Fine. I can't tell you not to do this because she obviously needs the help. Our job is to protect people. Are you out then? For the Parker case?"

"No. I was going to grab some stuff from here and take it with me to her office. She said she'd have a desk available for me to work at. I'm not leaving her alone, so I'm going to stay in her guest room and work from her office. Any word on Damien Parker and a connection to Dennis Parker?"

"Damien Parker appears to be a ghost. We can't find records of anyone with that name attending med school or doing a residency anywhere. It was definitely all fake."

"Shit. I wonder why that worked to their advantage."

Dunn tilted his head and raised his brows. He knew.

"What?"

"Probably to cover up the true cause of death in the case. We would have to get permission to exhume the body, but I'm guessing there was more to it than is in the report."

"Yeah, that makes sense. There's a lot more to this case than we realized."

"Yep. We're going to see if we can find the guy on security cameras, but you need to stay focused on Braden's sister. Do you want to use a safe house?"

Dex snorted, knowing exactly how Taylor would respond to that one. "She won't stop going into the office. She has a lot going on. If someone is watching her, they'd find us at a safe house or my place or wherever we end up. There's no reason to hide, which goes against every fiber of my being."

Dunn chuckled. "Yeah." He paused long enough that Dex looked up at him. "You doing okay?"

"Monster headache. I didn't sleep at all."

"Do you need help on this one? Someone to switch off with you?"

"Nah, I should be fine once we have our system in. Whoever this guy is won't be able to work around it. She'll be safe, and if she's not, the alarm will wake me up. She was in the damn shower when the guy broke in. He was in her living room when she made her way downstairs. Just standing there like he had a right to be in her fucking house."

"Shit. She's tough if she fought back and scared him off."

Dex agreed. Taylor had impressed him more than once in the few hours he'd spent with her. "She's very tough. And smart and strong and caring. She really takes care of her employees."

"Is she pretty?"

The question earned Dunn a glare. One he met with an expression that said he was willing to wait for an answer.

"Yes, but that's irrelevant."

"Because you're just there to protect her?"

"Yes."

Dunn snorted. "I said the same about my wife. The one who's home with our son right now."

Dex flipped off his boss and friend as Dunn walked out laughing.

Fucking hell.

6

———————

"I WANT EVERYTHING PUT INTO THAT HOUSE. THERE IS A credible threat to her life, and we're not going to let her down," Dex said to English and Jack. They'd been assigned the task of installing Taylor's security system, and Dex wasn't taking any chances.

"We'll load it up. I think I have everything here that we would need for a house that size. I'll use what's in place and reroute the feeds, but we'll add more, too," English told him.

"Good. If you can do a perimeter alarm, that would be good, too. Better to know if he's getting close before he tries to break into the house. Her cuts weren't deep, but they wouldn't have happened at all if her original system had worked."

"Any idea how he bypassed it?" Jack asked.

"No. I tried to look last night, but it was too dark to see much of anything. This morning I didn't go outside except to leave. It was still armed, as far as I could tell, but he came in the slider so he did something to it."

"Damn," Jack said. "Glad you were there to help her out."

"Yeah. I'm not sure how much sleep she got, but knowing her alarm wouldn't go off, I couldn't leave her." Dex scrubbed a hand over his face to wipe away the exhaustion.

"Are you going to stay with her again? I can trade off with you if you need me to," English offered. "Or you can bring her back to our house so we're both there."

Dex shook his head. "Nah, I got it."

The snicker from Jack was his first indication that his friends were messing with him. Dex looked up at them with a glare. "What?"

Jack crossed his arms and assessed Dex. "Just curious that you're so invested in this case."

"I owe Braden. He saved my ass. His sister is important to him. I'm not going to let anything happen to her."

Jack jerked his head toward English. "And you think he's going to?"

"I didn't say that," Dex growled.

Jack and English exchanged an all-knowing, shit-eating smirk. "Didn't have to," Jack said. "We'll take care of your woman's house. You watch out for your woman."

"She's not mine," Dex said as the other two left his office, laughing.

Dex let them walk away. It didn't matter what they thought. He was doing Braden a favor. Sure, they would have taken Taylor's case if she'd asked them to, but they weren't above doing favors for family and friends either. Dex wanted to figure out who was after Taylor, and he would, but his primary concern was keeping her safe.

He finished up what he needed to do at the office and packed up his computer to take with him to Birds of a Feather. He had his assignment for a few days and would focus on what he could without being on site. With any luck, he'd also get some sleep.

Dex went home and took a quick shower. His headache pounded behind his eyes, threatening to take over if he didn't find some way to alleviate the pain. He laid down on his bed, naked and damp from the shower, and let the cool air of his ceiling fan dry his body and soothe his mind.

The alarm on his phone snapped him awake thirty minutes later. Not nearly enough of a nap, but it was all he could give himself. He considered taking his muscle relaxants with him, but they knocked him out and he couldn't afford that when he was on a job. Ibuprofen would have to work well enough.

Dex dressed and packed a bag. He added a few extra weapons, just in case, and drove back to Birds of a Feather. He parked in the spot assigned to Taylor, then walked through the front door. Steven was still there, watching as Dex scanned himself through. The elevator whisked him up to the third floor and opened out into a busy space.

On his first visit there, Dex didn't pay attention to the noise or the brightness. He was there for a job and didn't care about the rest of it. When he arrived that morning with Taylor, the place was silent and grew louder slowly enough that he didn't notice it. But now? The noise and the lights and the entire place made his head pulse with tension and his body hum with anxiety.

So much for that ibuprofen he took.

Dex worked his way past employees to the large office in the corner that Taylor occupied. He could see her inside on her phone, not looking happy. When her eyes widened and she drew back, he picked up his pace to get to her and make sure she was okay.

"Mr. Hamilton!" he heard before he could open Taylor's office door.

With his hand on the handle, he spun to meet the gaze of Taylor's assistant. "Jessica. What's going on? Is she okay?"

Jessica looked past him to Taylor, her shoulders tight to her ears. "There's a minor issue, but she's handling it. She asked not to be disturbed."

Jessica's pointed look had Dex pulling back. He looked at Taylor once more, her glare telling him not to enter. She was a strong, successful businesswoman. He wasn't there to fix all her problems. His job was to keep her safe so she could do her job and fix her own problems.

"Taylor said there was someplace I could work?"

Jessica rose from her seat and crooked her finger for him to follow. "She assumed you'd want a spot where you could see pretty much everything." Jessica walked around the edge of her partition and back toward the elevator. She stopped at a corner cubicle with a desk facing the center of the room. From that position, Dex could see the whole floor from the elevator to Taylor's office in one quick glance. "Will this work?"

Dex set his computer bag on the desk. "Yep, it's great. Thanks."

Jessica pulled open the top drawer. "Here's our Wi-Fi password. And that's the number for the IT person, just in case there's something you need from her. If you need anything at all, this is my extension and direct line. I can get you her schedule or contacts or anything you need." She looked up at Dex, and her smile faltered. "I love working here. For Taylor. She's a great boss and I believe in what we're doing. It might not seem like much, but it's important. She told me what happened. Thank you for helping her."

Dex nodded, believing even more in Taylor. "What

you're doing here is very important. It's huge for a lot of women. Don't diminish that."

Jessica beamed at him, then skipped back to her desk.

Dex settled into his space and pulled out his computer. He connected to the internet without any issues and started to dig. There were two dangerous men out there, and he needed to find them both.

TAYLOR FELT like all she had was meetings all day. She was tired and hungry and cranky. And it was barely noon.

When Jessica walked in with a bag of food, she nearly fell at the woman's feet and worshipped her. "Thank you so much."

Jessica didn't falter at Taylor's overly excited appreciation. "Of course. I ordered in so we wouldn't have to leave the office. Dex said that was okay."

"Oh, crap. I forgot about him. Is he back?"

Jessica opened the bag and handed over Taylor's food. "He is. I set him up at his desk and he's working, I guess. I ordered him a sandwich, too." Jessica unwrapped her sub and took a bite. After a minute, she met Taylor's gaze with a smile that said she knew the answer before she asked the question. "Are you okay? Really?"

Taylor shrugged. It was the best she could do. The truth was, she was far from okay. Her home had been violated. Her company. Herself. She was under attack from someone who thought she caused them harm, and she had no idea who he was. But she couldn't tell Jessica that. She didn't want her to worry, and Taylor knew she would. "I will be. Or at least, I hope I will be. Right now, I'm trying to push it all out of my head and focus on work. I'm not willing to let this guy ruin what we've been building. We've worked way too hard on this."

"I agree. But I don't want you to feel like you're alone. If you need someone to vent to, I'm here."

Taylor appreciated the gesture, but they both knew she wouldn't take Jessica up on the offer to talk. Jessica was kind and excellent at her job and someone Taylor would call a friend, if she had friends, but Taylor was her boss, and that made it impossible for them to be friends. Taylor needed those lines and descriptors between her and the people around her. She needed to know where she stood with everyone. It made her feel safe to put people in boxes.

"Thanks," Taylor said, not offering anything else. She wasn't ready to vent, and she wasn't willing to vent to Jessica. She wasn't sure who she could vent to. Maybe a bottle of wine would listen. It definitely wouldn't interrupt her.

"Do you have any idea who the guy could be?" Jessica asked.

"No. I've been trying to think. I made that list for the police, but it was tough to come up with that many people. I don't think of myself as having enemies."

"And I can't imagine you stepping on anyone else to get ahead. You've always been willing to bring people up the ladder with you. Even from when we first met. You didn't have to make me your assistant, let alone keep me on when you started Birds." Jessica's gratitude was apparent in her smile, but it was the sincerity in her words that warmed Taylor.

"You're excellent at your job, and I couldn't have done all of this without you. For me, that also means knowing that I'm going to have to find a new assistant one day because you might want to move on. And I will support you doing that, whether it's here or somewhere else." Taylor meant every word, even though she hated the idea of not having Jessica working side-by-side with her.

"I... I don't want another job," Jessica said.

"Good, but if you do one day, I hope you'll talk to me about it so I can help you."

Jessica smiled absently as though filing the thought away for later. "Thank you. I... This is why I don't understand someone thinking you pushed him out of the way for your own advancement. It's insane."

Taylor had been trying to figure out the same thing. "We're all the heroes of our own life. I guess he feels I wronged him."

"Men."

Taylor laughed. She couldn't argue with that.

When they finished lunch, Taylor had more meetings all afternoon with the launch team. Everything was in place. They'd sent out pieces to influencers and were already receiving positive feedback from a few of them. It was the one piece of the puzzle Taylor was unsure of, but her team had pushed for it.

She was happy to be wrong, as long as she was actually wrong.

"Do we have any negative reviews?" Taylor asked.

"So far, not one," Sharon said. She flashed her proud mama smile at Taylor. She'd done amazing work getting the word out about Birds of a Feather. Sharon was the kind of person who could talk to anyone and make them feel comfortable. She wouldn't take shit, but she was subtle and smooth about it, slapping you with her words in a way that made you grateful for it.

The team Taylor created worked like a team who'd been together for years. They bounced ideas around and played off each other's. There was no competition among them, only cooperation, something that made Taylor very proud. She had confidence the company would succeed because of the team she had around her.

Taylor asked a few more questions and issued a few directives, then turned the conversation to other things happening in the office she needed to share.

"I want you all aware of what's been going on with me lately," she began.

No one spoke, but they all shifted in their seats and gave Taylor their full attention.

"I think everyone knows about the bird." She met the gazes of her team as they each nodded. "The man who sent the bird also called me, and last night he was in my home."

A collective gasp went around the room, followed by questions of her safety.

"I'm okay. Mostly shaken up. He had a knife and got a few slashes in. It was terrifying, to put it bluntly. The man sitting in the corner is a friend of my brother's, and he's going to be here until we find out who is behind this and take care of him. His name is Ryker Hamilton, or you can call him Dex. Jessica and Sharon have already met him. If he asks you anything, please help him out. His organization helps people. I think. I'm not really sure, but he's here to help all of us, so if you need him to walk you to your car or you notice anything strange or whatever, he's here to keep us all safe." Taylor again met the gazes of her team and tried to reassure them with a full-of-shit-but-pretending-to-be-confident smile. The worried looks that met hers said she might have missed the mark.

"I don't want anyone to worry. I just want you all aware."

"Are we in danger?" Emily, the head of design, asked.

Taylor knew she had to reassure her employees without making them think it was business as usual. "I have no reason to believe that. He seems to be targeting me. And he's made it sound personal, although I don't know who he is."

"Are you okay?" Sharon asked.

Taylor forced a smile for her team. "I'm as good as I can be."

"Well, I'm all for the eye candy around the office, so I'm not complaining," Megan, the social media manager, said with a not-so-subtle peek at Dex.

The others in the room murmured their agreement, and Taylor laughed. Dex was better than eye candy, but she wasn't going to talk to them about how sexy he looked when he was protecting her, or the way his rough morning voice skittered up her spine and made every inch of her tingle. Nope. She was keeping those things to herself.

"Okay, I think we can adjourn our meeting. Thank you, everyone."

Taylor cleaned up the conference room as they filtered out, stealing glances at Dex on their way to their desks and offices. She definitely didn't blame them.

Over the next two hours, her entire staff headed home. Dex sat quietly at his desk, watching the floor and working. Taylor wondered if he was as exhausted as she was and assumed he had to be since he got even less sleep than she did the night before.

She finished up a few things on her computer and packed up to head home. Her stomach growled at her, reminding her she needed to eat something before she went to bed. Maybe Dex would be willing to stop for takeout on their way back to her house.

"Are you ready to go?" he asked from her doorway. His messenger bag was thrown over his shoulder like he knew she was leaving soon.

Taylor glanced around her office once more, accepting

that she was done for the day. She slid her phone into her purse and slung it over her shoulder. "I am. I have a tendency to work long hours. I'm sorry if I kept you."

Dex shook his head. "You are my priority, Taylor."

She liked the way that sounded. It would be even better if he meant it in a way that said she was more than a job to her, but she knew that wasn't the case. He was a sexy badass who kicked ass for a living. She was an overweight business owner who made clothes. They didn't match in any way possible.

But when she looked up and met his gaze, she wondered if she was wrong. His stare was intense and made every nerve in her body notice. If she hadn't been looking at him, she still would have known he was looking at her. Assessing her.

"Thank you," Taylor finally replied.

He held her gaze as if he was unable to look away. "Should we pick up dinner on the way to your place?"

"I was thinking that, too. Is there anything you don't like?"

Did she imagine his gaze sliding down her body? He rubbed his jaw and shook his head, breaking the connection that left Taylor dizzy. "No."

"There's a great Vietnamese place not far from here. Is that okay with you?"

Dex nodded. No words, just a nod.

They ordered food and went by to pick it up. Back at her house, they sat at the breakfast bar to eat.

"Do you need a drink? Or any sauces?" Taylor asked, feeling uncomfortable with him in her home. Her home had never belonged to anyone but her. She worked hard for it, and when she bought it, she moved in with the belief she would always live alone.

"I'm good. Sit and eat," Dex ordered.

Having a man like Dex in her space was unnerving. He acted like he belonged there, like he was meant to be there. It was temporary, only until she felt safe in her space again. But he was there. He was filling up her small home with his bigness and his warmth. He was making her feel like he should be there. Like she needed him for more than just protection.

Taylor finally sat and finished her dinner. With her stomach full, she felt better. There hadn't been any threats, no surprise visits or packages. It was almost like a normal day.

Except for the beautiful, dangerous man in her home.

Taylor could feel her anxiety ramping up with each passing second. Darkness had settled outside her house, and with Dex in her living room, she had a physical reminder of what happened the night before. He was there to protect her, but she knew the man who was after her was smart. He could take out Dex and leave Taylor exposed.

Her heart pounded, and her palms dampened. She wanted to run and hide. To leave behind whatever pain she caused and forget about it all. She wasn't strong enough to fight the man who was after her. She needed a break. A release. A way to forget.

"Are you okay?" Dex asked. He stopped in front of her, studying her face with narrowed eyes.

Taylor had stopped in the middle of the room. She felt frozen. She looked up at the man in her home, the man who'd rushed to her side with one phone call. The man her brother trusted to make sure she was safe.

She shook her head. Braden was the last person she wanted on her mind at that moment.

"You're not okay?" Dex asked, misinterpreting her head shake.

"No, but I know how I can be," Taylor said. She drew a breath and held all her courage inside and threw herself at the strong, sexy, stoic man who'd been by her side for twenty-four hours.

And she knew he would catch her.

7

———————

Catching a beautiful woman when she threw herself at him was the easiest thing Dex ever had to do. Resisting that same woman... not so easy.

The first press of her lips to his was sloppy and uncoordinated and dick-hardening. He indulged in her for a moment, admitting only in that brief pause of sanity that he never wanted to let go.

But he had to. She was scared, overwhelmed, emotionally spent, and he was there to protect her. She didn't really want him, he knew that. He was convenient, and temporary.

Reasoning with himself was almost impossible. He wanted her, so much he could taste it around the edges of her perfectly plump lips and tantalizing tongue, but he was working. He was on the job. And the job required keeping her safe, not sated.

Dex allowed himself one more mind-numbing minute of his lips against hers, then he gently pushed their bodies apart like he was bench pressing a weight far greater than he was able. His arms trembled with the effort, and his entire body resisted rejecting her, but she deserved better than a battered man who'd never be whole.

He drank her in for the moment they were apart, his eyes memorizing every detail of her heart-shaped face. Her eyes were still closed, giving her an ethereal quality she didn't have with her piercing gaze locked on him. Her lips were wet and red from their kiss, inviting, making him want to dive back in and forget all about what was right and what was wrong because everything about her had to be right.

In the next moment, she realized he'd separated them, and all the things he soaked in vanished. Her eyes snapped open and instead of a regretful look, she gave him one of indifference. One that said he was the one who kissed her, not the other way around.

Was he?

The look was so convincing he scratched his head to stimulate the memory and mumbled, "Sorry."

"It's fine," Taylor said, her voice like a twig snapping on a fall morning. "I'm going to go upstairs." The only betrayal of her words was the faint blush staining her cheeks.

She walked away as though she had all the time in the world. Her head held high and her oversized purse slung over her forearm, Taylor Wright was not the kind of woman a man said no to. Not if he had two brain cells and a functioning cock.

Dex's lungs failed to work, trying to force air out to call her back. His lungs had no more control than his cock did, which left him standing in the middle of her living room, staring at the balcony walkway above his head and listening to the door he couldn't see close.

And lock.

"Fuck." He finally breathed the word, the only word he

could materialize. The only thing he wanted, needed, couldn't have.

With the pulsing of his erection, Dex stumbled to the couch. He collapsed onto the cushions, needing one part of his body to have a break. It definitely wasn't going to be his dick anytime soon.

He leaned forward and rested his elbows on his knees. The woman was a force. He knew that after watching her work all day, but to have her throw herself into his arms and abandon all pretense... He had no idea how he resisted her. Only that it was the right thing to do.

If only it didn't feel so fucking wrong.

Dex leaned back against the couch and exhaled all the breath in his lungs until he felt deflated. He looked upstairs again, but no sound came from Taylor's room.

He had a job to do. A job that required him to protect her, not whimper about having to resist the stunning woman who kissed him. He needed to pull his head out of his ass and focus.

Dex walked around the house and checked that everything was secure. He had the app for their security system on his phone already so he logged in and pulled up the report on Taylor's house to see what English and Jack had installed.

The system was as complex as what they installed at their own homes with window and door alarms all linked but operating independently of each other. It guaranteed the alarms couldn't be bypassed or disabled unless you had access to the system.

There were also alarms around the property that would alert them if someone approached the house from any direction.

Since the alarm had been installed that morning, nothing tripped any of the sensors.

Dex sent a thank you to English and Jack then settled on the couch again. It was still quiet upstairs, with no sign that Taylor was going to leave the sanctuary of her bedroom. She'd mentioned him sleeping in the guest room, but without confirming that with her, he didn't want to creep upstairs and let himself into a room.

The couch would do for another night.

Dex scrolled through his phone and read emails he'd missed during the day. The blue light strained his eyes and before long, his headache was returning.

He set the phone down and decided to get some sleep. Even if Taylor was awake, the alarm was on and the company they contracted with to monitor the F-BOMB properties was watching Taylor's home. Dex could close his eyes and rest for a little while.

TAYLOR HAD another restless night of sleep. Her cheeks still flamed when she thought of the way she launched herself at a completely unaware and uninterested Dex. She didn't know how she would face him, but Taylor had never been one to back down from awkward situations. She was the one who answered for her siblings when they didn't get their homework done, and the one who called out her old boss for his mistreatment of the female employees. It earned her the trust and respect of her coworkers, and a pink slip, but Taylor was fine with the consequences when she knew her actions were in the right column.

She still struggled to go downstairs and face Dex. She wasn't willing to avoid him, but she wasn't right on that one.

She never should have thrown herself at him. He wasn't there for that, and he never gave her the impression he might be open to it, so the situation was all on her. Which meant fixing it was all on her, too.

With her game face on, Taylor tossed her freshly washed and dried hair behind her, licked her glossed lips, and straightened her perfectly dressed spine. She opened the door to her bedroom and stepped out.

She expected to hear... something. When she got up the morning before, Dex was in her kitchen making coffee. Her guest room was comfortable, but she didn't like the idea of having to wake up the man who rejected her. Especially having to walk into the bedroom and find him sleeping.

One image after another, each more pulse-skittering than the last, flickered through her mind, demanding Taylor's attention. Did he sleep naked? Or maybe in boxer briefs? Would he be facedown on the pillows, making love to the bed? Or would he be on his back with a tent in the middle?

Heat raced to her cheeks as she fantasized about the man she couldn't have. She pressed her hands to her warm face and drew a shaky breath. She indulged for the briefest of moments, grabbing the railing for support before she ruthlessly pushed away the images her imagination conjured of Dex.

She exhaled fully, letting go of all the fantasies, and walked downstairs. Her heels clacked across the tile floor into her kitchen and she set down her purse. Dex's computer was slung over the back of the stool, like it had been the night before. His jacket was there, too.

Taylor spun when she heard a soft breath behind her. Her heart thumped with fear before her gaze settled on the couch, and then her heart thumped for a very different reason.

Dex was asleep on her couch. His feet were on the ground, like he'd been sitting there and just passed out. His phone was beside him on another cushion. His chin rested on his chest as he slumped to the side, his shoulders wedged between two cushions to keep him in place. His hands were linked together on his lap, cupping himself.

Taylor couldn't move. She couldn't even breathe. She just stared at him, taking him in. When he was awake, he was a badass alpha who left women panting and men wishing they were half as tough. But asleep... he looked calm. Peaceful. Like nothing could shake him or upset him or worry him.

Taylor longed for that feeling, even in sleep. She hadn't been able to stop worrying since the day her parents brought her brother home from the hospital. She was only two when Aaron was born, but she knew from the moment she saw him that her life had changed forever. Her earliest memories included him. By the time Melissa was born five years later, their dad was gone more than he was home, and Taylor and Aaron had become the best of friends and each other's only playmates. She loved her siblings, but she worried about them every minute of every day.

Taylor dragged her gaze from Dex before tears ruined her carefully applied makeup. She couldn't wish for her life to be different. She'd grown up with a mother who did that so much Taylor blamed herself for her mother's failures. She was in charge of her own life, and worrying about her siblings was her job as the one who raised them. It didn't matter that she was their sister and not their mother, she was the one who made them who they were.

While Dex slept, Taylor busied herself with making

coffee as quietly as she could. With the grounds in and the water added, she started the pot and looked out the back window to her backyard.

She used to go out there with her cup of coffee. Enjoy the morning as the world started to wake up. Taylor had grown accustomed to only a few hours of sleep as a teenager, and had never adjusted to more than that, even as an adult. It was her secret weapon. But it was lonely. Everything about her life was lonely.

The coffee sputtered and spat its last drops of the brew. Taylor winced at the sound as Dex jerked awake. He looked around the living room in two seconds, taking in Taylor's life, before his gaze snapped to hers.

She expected fuzziness and confusion in his eyes. A question, even temporarily, of where he was and why he was there. Instead, his eyes darkened and widened as his lips parted. His chest rose with his quick inhale. The pink tip of his tongue wet his lips, readying them for...

Taylor broke their connection. Her cheeks flamed at the unanticipated reaction from Dex. She moved to the coffeepot and poured herself a cup. "I'm sorry I woke you. I didn't realize you were down here until after I'd started the coffee."

She tucked her hair behind her ear and hoped he didn't hear the lie in her voice.

"It's fine." His voice was rough and strong, like she'd fantasized about his fingertips being when she'd taken her shower the night before. Her own secret she wouldn't share with anyone, ever.

"Do you want—"

"About last... night," he started at the same time.

Taylor exhaled a laugh, and her shoulders sagged when he did the same. She turned to face him once more and pulled up her best I'm-sorry smile, one she hoped assured him she'd never touch him again. She wasn't the kind of woman who repeated her mistakes.

"I'm sorry," Dex rushed to say. "For... If you want to have someone else stay with you until this is over, I can make a call and have one of my teammates meet us at your office."

"Is that what you want?" Taylor blurted, unable to keep the sharp question from landing between them.

Dex held her gaze and slowly shook his head.

"That's not what I want either. I apologize for kissing you last night. I shouldn't have done it. I know you aren't interested in me, and you're not my type at all, but the emotions and the fear and the gratitude..." *Dear God, stop talking.* "Ahem, anyway. I'm sorry for putting you in an awkward situation and making you feel like..." Taylor rolled her lips in and pressed her fingers to them before it got worse. She tried to unravel the twisted apology she weaved with a simple, "I'm sorry."

The tension between them felt like gelatin, until he took a step toward her. She fought the urge to back up and run away. The look in his eyes said he saw her. The Taylor she didn't show to anyone. The Taylor she hid from the world because the world was a cruel and evil place. The Taylor who wanted to run and hide and not have to care about anyone. He saw her.

"I am impressed by you. You are a strong, smart, beautiful woman who is far too good for me. I'm here for muscle, not brains. I'm smart, but I'm not educated, Taylor. I never should have made you feel like your safety was less important than my desire for you. For that, I apologize."

If Taylor could have handpicked a man for herself, made him in a lab or created him out of thin air, he would not be as perfect as the man standing in front of her apologizing for her shitty behavior the night before. She'd spent her life accepting the blame for things other people did, especially her parents, but this man, this man she'd known for less than two days, he was accepting blame and apologizing to her for her own actions.

"Dex, it's not your fault," she said with a laugh. "I was the one who threw myself at you. I was the one who wanted to get lost in the moment and forget about all the shit surrounding me. Your only fault was that you are friends with my brother and got roped into this and assaulted by a crazy woman you barely know."

"Best assignment ever."

The crooked smile he flashed her set her panties on fire and scorched her last bit of resistance to him. She pressed her thighs together and bit the inside of her lip to stop the moan that wanted to escape.

Dex cleared his throat and scrubbed a hand over his face. "Um, anyway. You're ready to go. I, uh, we can head out if you want."

"If you need to take a shower or get some coffee or something, that's fine, too. I can check emails on my phone before we go."

"I don't want to hold you up."

"No, it's fine. I... stormed off last night and never showed you to the guest room. I'm just doing all this wrong."

"Taylor." His tone drew her gaze to his lips. She wanted to feel them again, on her lips and her breasts and her clit.

She cleared her throat and focused on a spot behind him so she didn't get lost in him again. "Yes?"

"You're not doing anything wrong. If you're okay with it, I'll take a quick shower and we can go. Assuming there's plenty of breakfast at your office again?"

She allowed herself the chuckle she knew he was hoping

for. "Yes, there's always breakfast. I'll show you your room so you can shower and then we can go."

Dex grabbed his things and carried them up the stairs behind Taylor. She opened the door to the guest room and stepped to the side for him to go in ahead of her.

"It's a suite, so the bathroom is through that door over there. There's a closet if you want to put anything in there. And the desk... it's girly, but it works. I hope."

Dex nodded and took in the room with the fluffy white rug, the pink gauzy curtains, and the teal bedspread. Taylor wondered what he thought of it, but she didn't ask. She just waited for him to say something.

"It's all fine. It's your home, Taylor. Nothing needs to change for me."

The pang Taylor felt at his words was misplaced and irrational but there nonetheless. She wanted him to want to be there, to want to stay there, to want to want her in his life. A man she'd known less than forty-eight hours. She'd never been so drawn to a man in her life, and if there was ever a good time to let one in, it was not now.

"Good," she said a little too loudly. "Um, so, I'll be downstairs. Take your time. We can, um, go when you're ready." She backed up toward the door, slamming her elbow against the door frame. She winced and shook her head at his step toward her, then backed into the hallway and closed the door between them.

Taylor hissed, "Ow," and rubbed her elbow as she walked away from the door and retreated to the kitchen so she could drown her embarrassment in her coffee.

Too bad she couldn't drown her shame in something a little, or a lot, stronger.

8

<hr>

DEX HURRIED THROUGH HIS SHOWER AND THREW ON CLEAN clothes. He'd never thought much about the way he looked, but working for a woman who designed clothes for a living had him feeling like he should step up his game. Except he didn't have anything nicer than khakis and polos. That was fancy in his book.

When he walked down the stairs and caught Taylor staring at him with her mouth slightly open and a big, bad wolf look in her eyes, he figured his version of fancy was good enough.

She snapped her mouth shut and her eyes away, and he missed that tiny glimpse of Taylor like she'd actually walked out the door and left him behind. When she pressed her lips together in what was supposed to be a smile, then asked if he was ready to go, he was sure he'd never see the real her again.

The drive to her building was nearly silent. A question about her day from him, a comment about the weather from her, and they were awkward companions thrown together in an even more awkward situation.

Dex had been tasked with protecting people before, but none of them were like Taylor. None of them had captivated him the way she did from the first look. And none of them threw themselves at him and forced him to use every ounce of his strength to resist fulfilling her every wish and desire.

Taylor Wright was in a category all her own.

He gave a terse nod to Steven when they walked into the building. His nod was met with a look that said the other man did not like that Dex was showing up at Taylor's office with the woman herself. Dex may or may not have rested his hand on her lower back in a show of possessiveness he had no right to make.

Thankfully, Taylor didn't call him on it.

But she did retreat to her office as soon as they were on her floor.

Dex went through the floor and verified everything was as it should be. His stomach reminded him he hadn't eaten breakfast. He glanced at Taylor's office and allowed himself a moment to watch her through the glass walls, impressed once more by her focus and obvious determination.

After his breakfast, Dex positioned himself at his desk and tried to make some headway on both of his cases. The local PD had nothing new on Taylor's dead bird. They tried to find out where it was sent from, but that was a dead end. There was no return address on the package, but the code at least told them what post office it went through. The tiny location had nothing in the way of security or cameras and couldn't remember a thing about the box.

Dex tried searching around Taylor's house for any indication of the man who broke in, but he was smart. He stayed away from the street, avoiding all cameras in the area. There had to be a way he got onto her property, but Dex couldn't find his trail. The wooded area behind Taylor's house provided cover for an army if it was needed, which gave one man a lot of room to work.

The other case was just as frustrating for Dex. They hadn't found anything about the ME who wrote up the one report, then vanished. The sheriff's daughter didn't know much more than she already shared the night she was attacked. The rest of the team looked into the bar where she met the man, but it was another hole in the wall without cameras or any form of security. Unless you counted the shit-kicker at the door, who was great in a bar fight but not so great at remembering one man who kept to himself and walked out with a dark-haired woman.

Dex stood and stretched, then went to the break room for a cup of coffee. He needed to clear his head. Sleeping on Taylor's couch was fine, but his neck was sore and his headache still lingered from the day before. He needed answers to all the questions he had so he could spend a night in his own bed with a muscle relaxant. God, his life was pathetic.

Dex had just sat down at his desk when his phone rang. The office around him was waking up with more than half the desks full and quiet conversations taking place. He wasn't sure if he should answer his phone in front of all the people, but he couldn't walk away from Taylor.

"Yeah?"

"How's the fashion mogul?" Slade's voice rang through the phone.

"She's safe. That's all that matters."

"Keep it that way. Kyra loves her clothes. She's waiting for the drop. Not very patiently."

"The what?"

"Drop," Slade repeated. "It's the release. When new products are available. How have you been there two days and don't know all this? I should be in charge of monitoring her. She can stay with Kyra and me."

Dex growled, his intention loud and clear through the phone.

Slade's answering laugh was just as loud and clear. The conversation was a fucking trap.

"Fuck you. I'm hanging up now," Dex snarled.

"No, don't. I actually did call to see how you're doing."

"I'm fucking fabulous."

"That kind of answer makes me think you might be lying. How's your head?" Slade's tone was muffled and understanding. He didn't know Dex's official diagnosis, but he knew enough to get that it wasn't easy. Dex still kept a lot to himself, but Slade covered for him when he needed the help. If he admitted it, and sometimes when he didn't.

"My head is okay. I'll be better once I get some sleep."

"Why aren't you sleeping? The mogul keeping you up?" And Slade was back to teasing.

"Do I need to repeat my earlier statement?"

Slade chuckled. "Nope. Hey, so everyone's getting together at my place tonight. Bring the mogul."

"I'm not sure that's a good idea."

"Why not? We all promise to be on our best behavior."

"Your best behavior makes a monkey throwing shit at his enemy sound reasonable."

Slade laughed again, a loud sound that made Dex's lips lift.

"You know me too well. But seriously, you guys need a night off. Come have a drink. Maybe she'll relax with all of us together. If nothing else, it means you can have a few minutes of not being the only one on duty."

The hard thing about working with the people who kept your secrets was that they knew everything about you. How you operated and what you needed. Dex found himself agreeing to Slade's request with the understanding he had to check with Taylor. If she didn't have plans, he told Slade they'd be there.

"Fabulous. And hey, if you happen to see something Kyra might like, I wouldn't mind if you swiped it from that place."

"I'm hanging up now."

"She's a size—"

Dex ended the call with a shake of his head. He adored Slade's wife, who was also their office manager, but he was not going to steal from Taylor for her. He would warn Taylor in advance though, just in case she had something extra lying around.

Dex kept himself busy the rest of the morning, alternating between the work he was doing on his computer and monitoring the office. Both bordered on boring, but boring was good for his headache. And for the task he'd taken on that morning.

When it was almost time for lunch, Jessica approached him once more with a wanting-to-help smile. "How are things going today?"

Dex shrugged. He wasn't about to tell her anything about his work, but he also didn't get the feeling she was fishing. She was being friendly, a trait he'd gotten too used to not being present in his day-to-day life. "Not bad, but not great either. Is everything set for the drop?"

She tilted her head with an impressed look on her face. "It's getting there. For now, I'm ordering lunch. Taylor usually forgets to eat if I don't force her to. Some days we go out, but I'm guessing that's not such a great idea right now."

Dex winced internally when her hopeful smile faded at

his head shake. "I know this isn't easy. Why don't you order lunch for everyone. On me."

Jessica took a step back with her hands up in protest as Dex dug into his pocket for his credit card. "No, you don't have to do that."

Dex peeled his card from the too small wallet and held it out to her. "I insist. I'm charging it back to my company as a business expense because that's why I'm here. And if it keeps everyone here and minimizes the risk, it's a good thing. Unless you think it's too late to take care of something like that?"

Jessica looked at the rest of the staff with their heads down, hard at work, the clock and food clearly long forgotten. "I don't think anyone has eaten yet."

"Please, Jessica. Don't worry about the cost, just order food. You guys are busy."

She nibbled her fingertip for a long second before she stepped forward and grabbed the card from him. She tapped it against her other palm and nodded. "Thank you. This is really nice of you."

Dex pressed his lips together in what he hoped looked like a genuine smile. The truth was, he'd started digging into all Taylor's employees and didn't want any of them to leave in case he found something on them. So far, he hadn't, but he was only about halfway through the list.

As Jessica walked away, Dex turned back to his computer. Jessica, Sharon, and all the other department heads were clear. He couldn't explain why he was disappointed to see, at first glance, so was Steven from security. Dex kept looking through the employees as he waited for lunch to arrive and wondered what Jessica was going to order.

When the elevator dinged with the arrival of lunch,

Jessica rushed past and waved for Dex to meet the delivery people. They carried four large bags of food. Jessica led them to the conference room while Dex followed behind, watching for any trouble.

Dex's mouth watered once the taco and fajita bar was set up on the conference room table. The hint of spiciness and sizzle of hot food drew the staff over, ready to enjoy lunch. Dex walked the delivery people back to the elevator and hurried back to the conference room.

Taylor was ahead of him in line and turned back with a shy, grateful smile that made him want to go into debt to buy lunch every day. "Thank you for this. It wasn't necessary, but it's very much appreciated."

"Jessica said you only eat when she forces you to. I figured this way you have no choice."

Taylor focused on the chicken in front of her. "I could stand to skip a few meals."

Dex growled, drawing her attention back to him. "Your company is built on women being perfect exactly as they are. You need to listen to your own lessons because you're perfect, too."

The pink stain sinking from her cheeks under the collar of her shirt had him wishing he hadn't turned her away the night before. He'd love to know where that flush ended, and how else he could make it appear.

"Thank you."

"It's the truth, and every person who works with you agrees. These people believe in what you're doing. Our office manager is one of your fans, apparently. She's anxiously awaiting your drop. I just learned that word today."

Taylor's eyes lit up with her sarcastic smile. "Really?"

She moved from the conference room toward her office.

Dex followed her, happy for a minute alone with her. "I'm clearly not the fashion mogul you are. But Kyra always dresses very nice."

"Yeah?" That smile was a trying-to-be-nice-but-dying-inside kind of smile.

"Yep. Her husband is one of my teammates. Everyone is getting together at their house tonight. We've been invited."

Damn if the mention of Kyra's husband didn't put the light back in Taylor's eyes. Until Dex said they were invited to go out.

She sat behind her desk and avoided his gaze. "Oh, um, I'm sure I have a lot of work to do. But you can go. I don't want to mess up your social life."

"First of all, I have no social life. My teammates get together most weekends because we don't have other friends. Second, if you're not going, I'm not going. I'm here to protect you, Taylor, and that means not leaving you alone."

"I... I don't do well with people."

Dex paused with his taco halfway to his mouth. He'd been watching her for two days. She had the respect of her employees, but also the admiration of them. They genuinely liked her. It wasn't fake. She listened to them and talked to them, and she was a great boss. If she thought she didn't do well with people, it was because she wasn't paying attention.

Dex put his taco down and wiped his hands, ensuring he had her full attention before he spoke. "Taylor, you're amazing. You're kind and thoughtful. You provide for your employees and you care for them. Every single person here is doing this job because of you. Because you sold them on your vision and you convinced them to bring it to life with you. They love you. And my friends and teammates will also. If you don't want to go or you have something else you need to do, we don't have to go, but don't say no because you think you're anything less than amazing."

Taylor looked at him, their gazes locked in a game of chicken. Dex leaned forward, inexplicably drawn to her in a way he couldn't resist. She licked her lips and pulled the lower one between her teeth, and he happily lost their game to enjoy the fantasy of replacing her teeth with his.

Taylor cleared her throat and straightened in her chair. "We can go to your friend's house."

Her words were soft and loaded with doubt. He saw what it took from her to agree to something so far outside her obvious comfort zone. He wanted to make everything better for her, to take away her panic.

"You know, Kyra loves your stuff. I'm not sure if you have anything lying around, but..."

Taylor grinned proudly, the business woman back in charge. "I'm sure I can find something. She might be too small for my products, though."

Dex shook his head. "Nope. I would guess you two wear the same size, but I have no experience guessing that kind of thing. I can ask Lily."

"Who's Lily? Your sister?"

"Lily is married to another teammate. Almost all of them are married or heading that way."

"You're the holdout?" Taylor asked with a teasing smile.

"Me and one other. Seven have gone to the dark side."

Taylor shivered. "I'm with you. Life is better alone."

Dex thought back to their one and only kiss. "I don't know if that's always true."

She sucked in a quick breath, stealing all the air from the room. Her eyes widened, and that lip went back between her teeth.

Definitely not always better alone.

"Um, well, I need to finish some work," Taylor stammered. "I shouldn't be too late tonight. Is there something we should bring?"

"Bring?"

"To your friends' house?"

Right. Dammit. Dex was already plotting being alone with Taylor, not spending the evening with his team. "Yeah, um, no. They'll take care of it. I'll let you get back to work."

He backed toward the door as he spoke. She winced half a second before he ran into the glass panel. The vibration echoed through the office and his head.

Taylor covered her grin with her hand and asked, "Are you okay?"

"Yep. All good."

Her laughter carried him back to his desk, where he looked back and saw her still watching him.

He could not sleep with her. He couldn't.

He was going to really try not to.

TAYLOR WAS NOT LOOKING FORWARD to going to a party, but she was looking forward to spending time with Dex. If they went back to her place, the night would drag on and it would get awkward. The last time they had unlimited time, she made a complete fool of herself and tried to sleep with him.

She was not going to repeat that mistake.

Although, she wasn't willing to take all the blame for that error after the way he looked at her all day. When he backed into the glass, she couldn't help but laugh and wonder if that was how she looked when she ran into the doorframe in her guest room.

Then he looked back at her when he got to his desk, and she thought she was going to burst into flames.

She finished up her work earlier than usual for a Friday, but Taylor rationalized it with the promise she'd work through the weekend since sitting around with Dex would only lead to naked times. Hot, dirty, sexy naked times that would have her feeling like she'd forced herself on him. Again.

Taylor convinced herself going to his friends' house would be fine until they were on the way, and he started telling her about all of them. Nine men, seven women, and a few kids thrown in. All under one roof. And she was going to walk in there and act like she belonged.

Fat fucking chance.

Why did she agree to go?

Oh, yeah. Because there was a psycho sending her dead birds and breaking into her house, and she didn't want to tell her brother. So, she was going to a party and wishing she'd gone to more in college so she didn't feel like such an outsider for once.

It was definitely too late for that. They were there.

9

TAYLOR SQUARED HER SHOULDERS AND DREW A DEEP BREATH. She held it, letting it soak into her lungs and give her strength. She needed it. She was walking into a lion's den with a man she barely knew and had to pretend she was happy about it.

She was not.

Dex walked up to the door and knocked once, then opened it. He stepped inside as the noise knocked Taylor back a step. She paused, wishing she had time for another deep breath before she had to walk into a stranger's home. Why did she agree to this?

No one noticed them as they moved inside and closed the door behind them. A group of men sat at the table arguing about something. A few women were in the kitchen. More men were on the couch with another mixed group on the back patio.

Taylor couldn't remember the last time she'd been around such a large group of people she didn't know. As sweat trickled down her spine and an uncomfortable heat settled in her gut, she wished she could say the same thing tomorrow, but she would remember the night with a clarity that only came with panic.

A hand settled on her lower back, stirring an entirely different sensation inside her. Taylor resisted the urge to lean into him when he drew closer. He was responsible for her, not interested in her. That was why he reached out. That was the only reason.

"Let me introduce you to everyone. Kyra is in the kitchen with Lily. We'll start there. Watch out for Howler, though. His hind legs don't work real well and he has a tendency to topple over. He doesn't let it stop him, so he can be like a bowling ball at times. Once he figures out someone new is here, he's going to come running."

"Who's Howler?" Taylor asked as a wolf let loose an ear pitching howl. She winced and looked toward the back door, wondering why no one was rushing inside and locking out the animal.

"You had to ask," Dex said with a chuckle.

A beast of a dog came around the edge of the couch. He headed straight for them, his tongue lapping to the side and his eyes wide. His teeth had Taylor pulling back, torn between ready to swing her purse at the offending creature and climb the man behind her like a tree and have him fight the dog off.

"Hey, buddy," her would-be protector crooned. He was crouched down, reaching out for the demon dog.

"He's going to bite you," Taylor hissed.

Dex looked up at her for half a second, then a crash drew their attention. The dog was on his side against the cabinets that lined the kitchen. He scrambled to get up and continue his race toward Taylor's face. She took a step backward, ready to let herself out if no one was going to protect her.

"He doesn't bite," Dex said quietly, calmly. "Are you afraid of dogs?"

"That's not a dog. That's a monster."

Dex chuckled as the dog finally made his way to him. The dog licked him and flopped on his back again, his tongue hanging down to the floor as he panted for every breath. There was a part of Taylor that thought he was kind of cute, but he was still a dog.

"Howler is the biggest wimp on the planet. He's all bark and no bite, and he couldn't attack a person if he wanted to. He's too gentle. Look at this face. Is this the face of a monster?" Dex's childish tone said he thought Taylor was being silly, but she most definitely was not. She knew the wounds a dog could create. She lived with one of the scars on her ankle and another on her heart because she couldn't protect her sister from a dog when they were kids. Dogs were not cute. They were animals.

"I'm not a dog person," Taylor said. It was her standard response. Her family could barely afford to feed four kids let alone a dog, so they never had any pets. She knew dog people couldn't understand not loving dogs and if she told him about her experience, he would laugh it off and say the dog he was giving a full body rub to wasn't like that, but Taylor wasn't interested in toxic positivity and fake encouragement. Nothing anyone could say would make her into a dog person.

"I'm really not either, but I like Howler." Dex rose to his full height, leaving the dog to lie in a puddle of appreciation. Dex stepped over him like he wasn't an animal that could kill him, but Taylor gave the dog a wide berth as she made her way around his beady, watchful eyes and long, sharp teeth.

"Okay, so, now that you've met Howler, this is Kyra and Lily," Dex said, hugging two women in the kitchen.

They stopped their conversation and met Taylor's gaze with bright, welcoming smiles.

"Hi," the first woman said. She had dark wavy hair and a confidence in her that felt natural and easy. "I'm Kyra. We're so happy you came tonight. We've heard a ton about you."

Dex flashed her a panicked look that had Kyra's friendly smile faltering. She plastered it back in place, but the damage was done. "I mean, um, shit. This is why I'm the office manager and not on the team. Sorry. Are you okay?"

Taylor's entire face felt tight. The smile she forced her lips into felt like it might splinter. After the week she'd had, the last thing she wanted was to pretend she was fine and enjoying her evening with a bunch of strangers who knew everything about her.

"I'm good. Thanks." She lifted the small bag she'd brought for Kyra and handed it over. "Dex said you're waiting for the drop. I brought you a few pieces. He wasn't entirely sure of your size, but I think most of these will fit."

"I'm so jealous," the other woman said. "I'm Lily. My husband is Archer."

Taylor nodded like she knew who Archer was and realized it was going to be a very long night. She had a lot more people to meet in the crowded house and a lot more smiling to do before she could go home, curl up on her bed, and finally relax.

"You did not have to do this," Kyra said, clutching the bag to her chest after a peek inside.

Taylor flashed her camera ready smile and realized Dex had left her alone with the two strangers. "I'm your guest. I didn't think it was right to come empty-handed."

Kyra gave her a smile that was filled with pity and

sympathy. A smile that said she saw right through Taylor's insistence that it was only a thank you gift. Not even close. It was a please-like-me gift, an I'm-awkward gift, an I-shouldn't-be-here-but-thank-you-for-letting-me-invade-your-home gift.

"Do you drink? Wine or beer or anything? Lily and I were going to sit on the patio and have a drink with the others if you're interested in joining us."

"Of course, you don't have to drink," Lily said. "I'm nursing so I'm not drinking. That little one is sucking me dry and I can't risk it." She pointed to a tiny baby wrapped up in the bulky arms of a stunningly sexy man.

Taylor's ovaries whimpered at the sight. A gorgeous man cuddling a tiny baby, surrounded by other men who looked at him with admiration and a touch of jealousy. Had she fallen into an alternate universe? What the hell was going on?

"It's intoxicating, isn't it?" Kyra asked, her voice conspiratorially low. "Seeing the men crowd around the baby and looking at her like that? My husband is Slade, the one in the red tee. We've only been married a few months, but every single time we all get together, he spends the next few days trying to talk me into having a baby."

"You don't want kids?" Taylor asked, turning back to her.

Kyra gave her a smile tinged with sadness, regret, and maybe a little hope. "I do, but I can't, so we're talking about adoption. But we haven't been married for that long and I want it to just be us for a little while longer. We're still in the newlywed bubble. I like it in there."

"The newlywed bubble is fun," Lily agreed. "This is a different kind of fun. When I met Archer, I never would have thought he'd be the kind of man who would look at a baby like that. I don't think he ever thought he'd be a father. But he's amazing with her."

Taylor watched as Archer handed the baby over to Dex. Her protector kissed the baby's forehead and nuzzled his jaw next to her face before tucking her into the crook of his arm and bouncing her just enough to make her settle again. She smacked her lips and jammed her fist in her mouth, her eyes still closed, content and peaceful in his arms.

Dex's wanton smile had Taylor wishing she could give him that. It was insane to have the thought, but it floated in and sank inside her. Dex wasn't hers. He wasn't interested in being hers. But she was watching him cuddle someone else's baby and fantasizing about having one with him. It was official. She'd lost her damn mind.

The baby started to fuss, her tiny cries barely audible over the rest of the noise in the room. Dex looked at Archer, who jerked his thumb toward the kitchen. Dex swung his gaze, likely looking for Lily, but his eyes connected with Taylor's.

In that instant, all the promises she made to herself shattered like a glasshouse in a rock slide. The promises to keep her hands to herself, to stop thinking about a future that wouldn't happen, to be okay with her choices to put her career above all else and that she didn't need a family or friends or anything other than her brothers and sister and for them to be happy.

Her entire world shifted. Tipped upside down and shaken like a snow globe in the hands of an over-excited child, then righted so everything could settle again. But nothing returned to the same place. The things Taylor thought were important that morning had been moved around to make space for other things.

Like her sudden, intense desire to have a family of her own.

"Is your bathroom…?" Taylor asked Kyra, pointing to the hallway as Dex started toward them with the baby growing louder.

"Yep, first door on the right," Kyra said with an oblivious smile.

Taylor moved the opposite way around the large dining room table from Dex, his eyes following her every move. She avoided looking at him, knowing he would see everything in her eyes if she met his gaze. She had to lock it all back up, throw away the key, and never dig it out again.

At least until he was done protecting her and she could indulge in those mental fantasies without an external audience to judge how ridiculous they were.

Taylor made it to the bathroom and closed and locked the door behind herself. She closed her eyes and tried to suck in a deep breath, but her chest was too tight. A pain, something frighteningly close to loss, made her whole body ache. She tried again for a deep breath, but the pain pushed out a sob instead of letting in a breath.

Taylor slapped her hands over her mouth and stared at the door. Beyond it, she could hear the noise of the large group. She had to pull herself together, before someone heard her, and keep it that way until she got home. Then she could fall apart. A little bit. Not enough that she couldn't recover quickly, but enough that her fragile emotions weren't so close to the surface.

Taylor closed her eyes and focused on her breaths until they weren't shaky or painful. The emotions lingered, but she was fairly sure she could handle them. She hoped she could handle them.

Taylor used the bathroom and washed her hands, giving

herself another moment alone, then plastered her best all-good smile on her face and opened the door. The hallway was blissfully empty, allowing her to walk out without anyone paying attention.

Kyra was in the living room showing off the clothes Taylor brought to three of the women Taylor hadn't met yet. When Kyra saw her, she waved her over.

"Ladies, this is Taylor. She's the wonderful mind behind these items," Kyra said with an honest and grateful smile.

"I have a great team working with me," Taylor said, always praising others for their hard work. Her team busted their butts, and they deserved the credit.

"That makes a huge difference," one of the other women said. "I'm Pilar. It's nice to meet you. Kyra has been talking about Birds of a Feather for weeks."

Taylor liked her instantly. She was warm and welcoming, just like Kyra and Lily, but there was something about Pilar that Taylor felt a kinship to. She'd known pain in a way not everyone did. She was fragile, but strong.

"Nice to meet you," Taylor said.

"I'm Megan," another woman said. "Slade is my brother, and Mason is my boyfriend. Although I hate that word." She rested her hand on her clearly pregnant belly. "Do you make maternity clothes?"

Taylor shook her head. "Not yet, but that's a good idea."

Megan rubbed her belly absently. "I don't get a lot of exercise anyway, but everything is different when you're pregnant. It feels that way."

"Does Mason still rub your feet every night?" the third woman asked.

Megan nodded, a dreamy look in her eyes. "He does. He's amazing. I don't know how I would have handled all this without him."

"He's always been such a good guy." She turned to Taylor. "I'm Kelsea. I know how overwhelming this is, and I'm sorry."

"It's fine," Taylor said with fake dismissal. It was fucking torture.

"No, it's not, but that's okay," Kelsea said.

"Stop analyzing her," Kyra warned.

Kelsea's cheeks pinked, and she ducked her head. Taylor narrowed her brows at the other women and tilted her head to the side with her unasked question.

"Kelsea teaches psychology. She's a psychologist herself and is always telling everyone how they feel. We still love her, but when she does it the day you meet, it's very awkward," Pilar explained.

"I'm sorry," Kelsea said. "It's hard to turn it off."

Taylor waved her hand. "It's fine. I'm a treasure trove of psycho-analysis waiting to happen. Being here is the least of my worries."

"This is stressful, though. Meeting all these people. Trying to remember names and connections. It's not easy," Kelsea said.

Taylor considered herself good with names, but so many at once was a challenge. "It's not, but it's fine." Something hit her leg, and she looked down and jumped away. The dog was leaning against her and looking up at her with his teeth exposed. Taylor did her best not to scream. Her palms dampened, and her throat tightened. All of a sudden, it was hot. Very hot.

"Um, I'm going to go outside," Taylor said, her voice too high.

"Are you afraid of dogs?" Pilar asked, a hand on Taylor's arm keeping her from moving away from the offending animal.

"Um, no, not all dogs. I had a bad experience," Taylor explained, making another move to go.

"Howler is so sweet, though. He's trying to be friends with you," Megan said. "He wouldn't hurt anyone."

"Unless he falls into you," Pilar said with a laugh.

Taylor's throat closed up, terror climbing higher and higher as she tried not to panic. She pressed her lips together in what she hoped looked like a normal smile, but from the look on the faces of the other woman, she must have looked like a serial killer.

"You're terrified, aren't you?" Kelsea asked gently. She reached for Taylor, who flinched and tripped over the dog that was still sitting on her foot and leaning against her leg.

Taylor lost her balance and started to fall. She reached out for something, but there was nothing there. Nothing to stop her from ending up face first on the ground.

Then she stopped. Her body hovering in midair, the ground still feet away. She was staring at it, her gaze locked on the hardwood floor that should have been against her cheek by now.

"Are you okay?" Dex asked, his voice sinking in through the panic.

She was lifted, righted, on her feet again. The fog of fear still hung around the edges of her vision, but she felt an overwhelming sense of peace filtering in.

"Taylor? Say something," Dex said, his voice louder than before.

She looked at him, her entire line of sight filled with his face. She drew a breath and opened her mouth to speak. "You look good with a baby."

One side of his mouth quirked up. The other side slowly followed, like one couldn't move without the other. Her head tilted to the side, rewinding her words until she figured out what she said.

"Shit."

He breathed a laugh and guided her to a seat outside on the patio. "Take a deep breath. Fresh air will be good for you."

She struggled to suck it in, the air filling her lungs in stops and starts that felt both unnatural and wonderful. She blew it out and sucked in another breath, a little smoother that time.

"Feeling better?"

She nodded, not looking at him. She never should have gone there.

"Why not?"

Shit. Did she say that out loud?

"I didn't know you were afraid of dogs," Dex said, sitting next to her on the lounge chair. "I'm sorry."

"It's fine," she said, because that was what she always said. Taylor was the big sister, the business owner. She was tough and strong and nothing got to her. She was not going to let her guard down now when there was a beautiful man protecting her and keeping her at arm's length.

"It's not fine. Will you tell me what happened?"

"There's nothing to tell. I was attacked when I was a kid. I was walking with my sister and this dog came out of nowhere. It went after her since she's smaller. She has it worse than me. The fear. But it's fine. I'm fine."

"You weren't fine a minute ago. Do you want to leave?"

"No," Taylor said quickly, and was surprised to realize she meant it. She didn't want to be there, but she also didn't want to leave. She drew a breath and held it for a minute, letting the truth sink in. "No, I don't want to go. We'll stay."

"Okay. Whatever you want," Dex said. He put his hand

on her thigh and squeezed, then he stood and walked back into the house.

Taylor looked up at the star-filled sky and decided she definitely was in an alternate universe. But she wasn't quite ready to leave it yet. And that was the scariest moment of all.

10

DEX WATCHED THE BACK DOOR UNTIL TAYLOR WALKED BACK inside. The tightness in his chest eased with the release of the breath he didn't realize he'd been holding, and he nearly collapsed from relief. Something that didn't go unnoticed by his teammates.

"She's pretty," Jack said, glancing at Taylor. "If I met her before Pilar—"

"Please," Archer said. "You only have eyes for Pilar."

Jack nudged him. "True. And I'm not sure I'm up for getting my ass kicked tonight."

Jack's pointed look at Dex drew the attention of the entire team. Dex tried to play off whatever they were seeing, but the shit-eating grins on the faces of the assholes around him said he failed.

"You and the pretty business owner?" Rocky asked, more curious than irritating like Jack.

Dex rolled his eyes and sipped his water. He was not going to answer any of their questions because there was nothing to tell. Taylor kissed him, but he kept it professional. There was nothing between them and no reason to let his team know that she was emotional and vulnerable and turned his brain to mush even worse than normal.

"Give the man a break," Mason said, stepping in and defending Dex. "Tell him what's going on with the case."

Dex gave Mason a grateful smile before focusing on Dunn and the latest updates from the case they were working on.

"All right, well, first, for Taylor, the guy who was in her house hooked an external device to her alarm system. We were in touch with the company to let them know, and they said it's how their technicians update software and check the status of an alarm. But it's also a known flaw in their system because it's an exposure, and one they've been working to update. Taylor's system was installed years ago, so they hadn't updated it yet, but it was supposedly on their list. We told them not to bother since we already installed our system. A story may or may not have been leaked to the press about this. Their customers have a right to know that they aren't as safe as they think they are. And Patrick has been notified."

Dex nodded sharply, unable to say anything in the way of thanks. His gut churned and tightened at the idea of Taylor's injuries being worse than they were. She should have been safe, but instead the company she hired to protect her was knowingly endangering customers with a crappy system they were making very little headway on updating. If Dunn hadn't leaked the story, Dex would have.

"Now, for the Parker case. The guy who took the sheriff's daughter didn't leave much of a trail. She was drunk by the time they left the bar so she couldn't tell anyone where she ended up. She gave a fairly detailed description of what he did to her, detailed enough that I'd recommend not eating for a day before you read her statement. Maybe after, too.

She's lucky to be alive from what I can tell." Dunn's face pinched with pain for the sheriff's daughter.

"Are we any closer to finding him or a warehouse or anything?" Dex asked.

"Unfortunately, no. We've come across a few options, but nothing that checked out. We tried to follow the guy's car after he took Ms. Harris, but he obviously knew how to avoid cameras and vanished. We know he's out there, and we know Parker is out there, but we don't know where they are or what they're planning next," Dunn said. His frustrated tone was repeated in quiet murmurs around the group.

Dex watched Taylor as Dunn spoke. He barely knew her, and yet the thought of someone hurting her made his stomach clench tight. He couldn't fathom how the sheriff and his wife felt after their only daughter was picked up by a man in a bar and almost didn't come home.

They needed to find these men and stop them. The things they were doing, between the drugs and the guns they were moving through the area, were bad enough, but if they'd moved on to abusing local women and asserting their control over people in that way, it was only a matter of time before things escalated to something worse.

The entire team knew how these things worked. Dennis Parker had been operating in the area for decades, but he'd gone in and out of the spotlight over time as his interests and activities ebbed and flowed. Even though Dex and the others hadn't been there for nearly as long, they knew the stories. And more importantly, they understood men like Parker. Men who thought the world was theirs for the taking, and were willing to take whatever they wanted.

The belief was that the new man, one whose name was a whisper and whose history was a ghost, was being groomed to take over for Parker. That Parker was looking to retire, if that word could be used for a man without an actual job.

"Is there a plan to try to catch the guy? Go back to the same bar?" Dex asked.

"Cops have already done that," Archer said. "They tried a lot of things to find these guys, but they don't have anything. Even the ME you two searched out was a dead end. That guy was able to avoid cameras through the hospital. He was bland enough that a database search of the sketch done of him resulted in hundreds of hits. None of them stood out to Ms. Harris."

"He's smart," Dex said.

"Too smart," Slade agreed. "So smart it's scary. It feels like he has the upper hand. Like he knows everything that's going to happen before it does."

"Does that mean we think there's an inside man?" Dex asked.

"That's one of the working theories," Slade confirmed. "It's also part of why we aren't sharing what we find with anyone."

"Not that we've found anything," Jack added.

"True, but not finding anything is showing us a direction to go. These guys are smart. They cover their tracks. They know what they're doing. All we need to do is get a little smarter." Dunn crossed his arms and leaned back. His speech made them all sit up a little straighter. They were smart, but having the upper hand was almost impossible to overcome. They had to be better.

Dex drew a breath and hated that his focus was split for this one. Even being in the room, he wasn't all there. He was watching Taylor. She laughed at something Pilar said and spoke to Kyra. She was more relaxed than he'd seen her yet.

She didn't want to go, but he was happy to see she was enjoying herself.

Howler crawled over to her, and Dex made a move to get up. All the men froze, picking up on Dex's panic.

"He wants to be friends," Kyra said, her voice low and gentle but audible in the quiet room. "He's sorry."

Kyra smiled up at Taylor, whose look of panic faded as the massive dog inched closer to her. He slid on his bottom, his head down and eyes up with a hopeful look. He was giving Taylor the power. Letting her choose if he could get closer.

Dex wanted to rush over and protect her from the teddy bear that was Howler. He knew the dog would never hurt her, but he also understood her fear. Fear was a funny thing, the kind of thing that could wrap around your throat and paralyze you or wrap around your heart and motivate you. A million times Dex would have expected Taylor to freeze and yell, like she did before, but as he watched her, her face softened and her posture changed. Her shoulders relaxed, and she leaned forward, reaching her hand out for Howler. He dragged himself a little closer and waited, letting her make the last move. He was patient.

Unlike Dex felt in that moment. Patience was the furthest thing from his mind. And when Taylor put her hand on top of Howler's head and rubbed his ears, patient was nowhere in his capabilities.

Her smile tugged at all the pieces inside him he long thought were broken, the pieces he didn't want to admit he missed having whole. But Taylor and her smile and the way she accepted Howler pulled those pieces together and something Dex thought was damaged beyond repair started to heal.

Dex noticed the conversation continued around him, his

teammates ignoring his obvious infatuation with their newest client. He was grateful for the private moment but knew it wouldn't be long before someone made a comment.

"You back with us, or you need a minute to continue your fantasy?" Jack asked with a knowing smirk.

Dex flipped him off and leaned forward. He was ready to close one case and make the people of Niagara Falls safer. The other case... He looked at Taylor again. He didn't want anything to happen to her, but he wasn't all that ready for her case to be over. The pretty business owner was definitely under his skin.

TAYLOR FELT good when they made it back to her house that night. No one asked her for anything or expected anything from her. There was some teasing about Dex, and a few requests for clothes, but those came with requests to let them pay. For the first time in a long time, Taylor didn't feel like she had to give away everything in order to have people like her.

She carried that feeling to sleep, and it lingered when she woke up the next morning to the sound of Dex downstairs making coffee.

Taylor grabbed a robe and cinched it around her waist before she pulled her hair back and made her bed. As soon as she opened her bedroom door, the scents filled her and made her hungry. The scent of coffee in the air, of a sexy man in her home, and toast... burning?

"Is something on fire?" she asked as she descended the stairs.

"Shit," he hissed, his fast footsteps moving across the kitchen. "I was trying to make breakfast for us." He paused, the scrape of a spatula the only sound as she turned the corner into the kitchen. "I think it's fine."

Taylor couldn't stop her smile as she took in the mess in her kitchen. She didn't even know she had the skillet that sat on her stove, and the ingredients in the shallow dish next to it were an even bigger shock.

"Where did all this come from?"

Dex looked up at her, his smile guilty. "I might have sent one of my teammates on an early errand. He didn't mind, though. Eggs and bacon and French toast sounded good."

"It does sound good. Wow. I don't cook much."

"I noticed." The way his eyes crinkled when he smiled made her return his grin. He was teasing her, she realized.

"I take it you do?"

He nodded as he put another slice of thick French toast on the skillet. "I enjoy cooking. It's soothing for me. It reminds me of home."

"You're not from here?"

"No. I grew up in Georgia. My grandmother raised me, and she made sure I knew how to take care of myself."

"Smart woman."

His sad smile told Taylor his grandmother was gone.

"When did you lose her?"

"Right after I went into training. She died in her sleep one night. I was able to get leave for her funeral, but not much. Saying goodbye to her was the hardest thing I've ever had to do."

"I'm sorry." The words felt empty and useless, but they were the only ones Taylor had.

"Thanks. She celebrated life with food, so I always think of her when I cook. She surrounded herself with people. She took care of everyone. If a family in town ever needed something, she would help. I remember one year when I was about seven. There was a man in town who was raising his two boys on his own. Their mom had died a few years earlier, and the dad lost his job right after Thanksgiving. My grandmother went into the closet where she'd stashed the Christmas presents she'd been buying since the previous Christmas and emptied it out. She packed up all my toys and gave them to that family."

"Really?" The laughter in his voice said he didn't mind, but she would have been mad as a seven year old to find nothing under her Christmas tree.

Dex laughed and handed her a plate with two slices of perfectly cooked French toast. "I got mad at her and told her those were my presents. She got right in my face and told me they were hers because she spent the money on them and she could do whatever she wanted with them. I cried. Oh, I was so upset. I barely spoke to her for weeks, but on Christmas morning, there were presents under our tree. And the family she gave all those other presents to came for Christmas dinner. They brought their toys, and we all played together. I don't remember what I got that year, but I remember spending the day with them." The ghost of a smile made her heart squeeze. "They were my closest friends until I joined the Navy. One of them became a doctor and the other a teacher. Both are married with kids. They told me at Meemaw's funeral they never knew where the presents came from. That they had no idea things were so bad for their family, but that once they found out, they vowed to pay it forward. They started a foundation to help underprivileged kids."

"Seriously?"

Dex nodded, a proud smile curving his lips. "They did. They do a lot of good."

"I want giving back to be a part of my company's foundation. We've set up a partnership with a local women's shelter and a few organizations that help women who were victims of violence, but something like that would be great. If you think they'd be open to it."

"I can't imagine they wouldn't be. I'll reach out to them and get you the contact info for the right person."

"Thank you." Taylor grinned, holding his gaze for a long moment. Her pulse skipped, short-circuiting her brain. It was hard not to do with a man like Dex in her kitchen, cooking her breakfast and telling her stories about his grandmother.

His gaze dipped to her mouth. Without thinking, she pulled a lip between her teeth. His eyes darkened.

Heat rushed to her cheeks, her entire body feeling warm and itchy. Impatient. She clenched her thighs together and focused on her plate. She cut into the French toast with the edge of her fork and speared a bite. Then moaned.

"Holy God, that's so good."

She closed her eyes and had a private, intimate moment with the French toast. She would marry that French toast if she could. Drop to her knees and worship it at least. And the man who made it.

She opened her eyes to thank him and praise him and found him watching her with a look that made her forget all about French toast and remember everything that made her want him on sight.

Tight tee stretched across a well-defined chest. Wide shoulders. Dark, smooth skin caressing muscles. Low slung sweatpants.

What French toast?

He swallowed, his gaze locked on hers and not wavering. The air between them thickened. So did the wetness between her thighs.

She wanted him. It had been a long time since she'd let herself indulge in a fantasy, but none of her fantasies had ever compared to Dex. Her channel clenched in anticipation of him filling her. Her heart pounded like a drum-line was in charge of the rhythm.

He took a step toward her, and Taylor sucked in a breath. He stopped, his eyes dropping to her chest as it rose and fell. The pause was long enough to deflate her confidence. Then he took another step.

And another.

And another.

Until he was right in front of her.

She looked up at him, feeling small and vulnerable with him standing so close. She watched the indecision in his eyes as he debated internally.

She wanted to grab him and pull his face down to hers, but she promised herself she wouldn't. She couldn't make a fool of herself again. She kissed him already, and while the memory of his soft, warm lips against hers was enough to melt her ice cold heart, it wasn't enough for her to risk rejection a second time in almost as many days.

"Taylor," Dex whispered, the word a pained cry as he cupped her jaw and lifted her face to meet his.

Taylor froze, her brain stalling out and abandoning her body for a long moment while her lips demanded an answer. *Kiss him back or push away? What do we do? Help!*

Kiss. Him. Back.

The definitive answer from every single active brain cell was all she needed to shift into action. Her hands slid up his firm chest, taking their time exploring the dips and hills of his body. He groaned appreciatively as she dragged her nails through his short, coarse hair.

His tongue pressed against her closed lips, demanding

an entry she hadn't consciously denied him. Again, the base parts of her brain took over, and she opened greedily for him. Her legs wrapped around his thighs and brought all of him closer.

He leaned forward, groaning as he pulled back from the kiss. He kissed her forehead and straightened, adjusting himself as he tried to move away from her. When she didn't release him, he chuckled.

"Where are you going?"

He lifted an eyebrow and looked at her with his own kiss-drunk look. "I figured you'd want to answer the door."

The pounding came again, one she recognized. "Shit."

Dex took a step away from her. "He texted me earlier. He asked if I'd met with you and if I'd taken your case. I couldn't lie to him."

"So, my brother knows you're here. And now he's here. For breakfast. On my day off." Well, that took care of her runaway train of desire.

"Pretty much. I'll make more French toast. You go let in your brother, Ms. Wright."

She scowled at him as another knock echoed through the house.

She was two feet from the door when he said, "And Taylor?"

"Yeah?" she growled, her hand on the doorknob as she turned back to look at the domestic god in her kitchen.

"We're going to continue that conversation we were just having. As soon as he's gone."

She was going to need ice water to go with her breakfast. And a cold shower.

11

WHILE TAYLOR LET HER BROTHER IN, DEX STRUGGLED TO PULL himself together. He didn't want Braden to walk in and see the way Dex was hovering over her. He would kick Dex out in a heartbeat and install himself as her protector going forward. Dex was having none of that.

He focused on the sizzle of a fresh slice of French toast while listening to the heavy footfalls of Braden's approach and Taylor's rapid steps behind him.

"Morning," Braden said, a sharp edge to his voice that made it clear how he felt finding Dex in his sister's kitchen.

"Morning," Dex said, forcing his voice to be calm and neutral. "Want some breakfast?"

Dex glanced over his shoulder and forced his gaze to stay on Braden's. He ached to meet Taylor's eyes, but he knew that would only make Braden more suspicious of him being there.

Braden took in Dex's appearance slowly, his gaze traveling from Dex's face down his body and back up. Cataloging him. Searching for a reason to kick his ass.

Dex casually turned back to the French toast and

pretended he wasn't fighting an uncomfortable squirm. He shifted his weight, listening for Braden to approach and take a cheap shot when he wasn't looking. Instead, a stool scraped the floor as Braden pulled it back and took a seat next to Taylor's now-cold plate of French toast.

"Breakfast sounds good. You cook?"

Dex kept his focus on the French toast. "I do. I've always enjoyed cooking. You?"

They weren't talking about cooking. Dex knew that. But he wasn't about to admit that he understood Braden was asking if he could take care of his sister.

"Not much," Braden said after a minute. "I can if I need to, though."

Dex shook his head and flipped the French toast. "I'm good. There's juice in the fridge. And fresh coffee. Not sure what you like to drink."

Dex turned back to the siblings in time to see Braden slide Taylor a questioning look. "Since when do you have food in your house?"

"Since Dex had someone bring food to my house."

Braden swung his gaze back to Dex and scanned him again. He knew there was more going on than he could see. Dex could feel it in the way Braden watched him. But Braden didn't press for answers. He poured himself a glass of orange juice and waved the container in Taylor's direction. "Tay-tay?"

A smile overloaded with affection and memories lifted her lips. She tilted her head to the side and nodded. A longing that surprised Dex hit him in the chest as he watched them. Braden grabbed another glass and poured Taylor juice. He carried both glasses back to their seats at the counter.

It was simple, just one person pouring orange juice for

another, but there was a story there. A story in the nickname Braden called her, a story in the way he jostled the container, and a story in the mini-glasses he used for their drinks.

Taylor nudged her brother with her shoulder and speared another bite of her French toast. Dex turned away, fighting that emotional gut-punch that had his throat tightening and his body aching for a connection like they had.

He was lonely growing up as an only child. Dex knew his parents did the best they could leaving him with his grandmother, but he missed out on the childhood he always wished he had. Seeing Taylor and Braden together, he realized he missed out on siblings. People he could count on.

He had his brothers now, but he didn't have a shared past with anyone. Not since his grandmother passed.

Dex flipped the toast off the pan and put it on a clean plate. He set the plate in front of Braden as the siblings talked about what prompted Dex to move in with Taylor. Dex grabbed another plate from the cabinet. He spent his first hour of the morning searching through her kitchen to figure out what she had and where everything was. He'd considered taking her out to breakfast, but when she wasn't up by then, Dex decided cooking at home was best.

Cooking at Taylor's home. He needed to remember that. It wasn't his home.

Dex added another piece of French toast and busied himself with making sure it was perfect. He gave that one to Taylor since he knew her other ones were cold, then set about cooking one for himself.

When the three of them finished breakfast and Dex turned off the stove, he turned and leaned against the counter, listening to Braden try to convince Taylor to stay with him.

"You have a room at my house," Braden argued.

"Yes, and you're not home half the time."

"I can take some time off."

"Why did you call Dex if you were going to go all caveman on me?"

"Because Dex owes me. I didn't know that would turn into all this. You were attacked. Someone was in your home. He could have killed you."

"I'm fine," Taylor insisted. Braden's stiff jaw and angry tilt of his head said he wasn't buying it. "Bray-bray, it's okay. You were at work the night he broke in, and Dex was here right away. He's been here. The only time we aren't together is when I'm at work and surrounded by people."

"Where you got that bird?"

"Yes, but Steven is opening my mail and nothing else has happened. You need to stop worrying."

Braden's brows pinched for a second before all the frustration in his face faded and love and admiration replaced it. "I'll always worry about you. You're my favorite person in the world. Why would I stop worrying about you?"

"Don't tell Melissa or Aaron you said that," Taylor said with a wry smile.

"They already know. You were the one who raised me. Aaron would have been happier if I'd never been born, and Melissa was always in her own world. I love them, but..."

"I know," Taylor said, accepting his thoughts as her own.

The bond between them had Dex even more in awe of her. She was a fierce businesswoman who ran her company like a compassionate drill-sergeant, and she was a kind and loyal sister who had a connection with her siblings that ran deeper than any Dex had ever known.

"Have you heard from Aaron lately?" Braden asked.

Taylor shook her head. "It's been a few weeks. I need to call him."

"Is he coming for your launch party?"

Taylor chuckled. "I've mentioned it to him, but no. I wouldn't ask him to come all that way for a party. I know he has more important things to do."

"Melissa will be there, right?"

"Yep. She said they will be." She turned to Dex and gave him an apologetic smile. "Our brother and sister. Aaron lives in Ohio, but Melissa is in Rochester."

"Do you see them often?" Dex asked, trying to piece everything he knew together. He had very little doubt her siblings could have been involved in the threats against her, but she made it clear she thought it was someone who'd known her since childhood.

"Aaron, no. He left the area when he turned eighteen and hasn't been back much. Our mom was not the best mother, and our dad was—"

"An asshole," Braden provided.

Dex looked at Braden and studied the anger rolling off him. There was more to the story, but it was a story neither sibling looked ready to share with the new guy.

"He left right after Braden was born. Braden's only met him a few times. He was in and out when we were kids, but after Braden... He wasn't father material. And our mother wasn't mother material. We fended for ourselves as soon as we could."

"What she means by that is Taylor took care of the rest of us," Braden said, admiration and love clear in his gaze. "I probably would have died of starvation if it were up to our parents to make sure I lived. Taylor raised me. I owe my life to her. I meant it when I said she's my favorite person in the world. If anything happens to her, I'll never forgive the person who does it, or anyone who lets it happen."

The threat was clear and understandable. Dex couldn't say he felt the same way, but he did. If anything else happened to Taylor, he'd lose his mind. As it was, he was spending every waking hour trying to figure out who could have let himself into her home and attacked her, and coming up with nothing was making him crazy.

So was sleeping in the room next to her, but he wasn't going to tell her brother that either.

Dex and Braden shared a silent, understanding nod before Braden turned the conversation to the rest of the day. Apparently, he was sticking around.

Dex cleaned up the kitchen while the siblings went to the couch. When he was finished, he snuck upstairs for a quick shower while he knew Taylor was safe.

Once he was dressed in clean clothes and ready to join them again, Dex opened the door to his room and stopped in his tracks. He wasn't trying to eavesdrop on their conversation, but when they weren't being quiet about it, he had no choice.

"I don't want him to take advantage of you," Braden said.

"Why do you think he is? He's here to keep me safe. Because you asked him to, baby brother."

"Yeah, but I didn't think he was going to paw at you."

She scoffed. "Oh, please. He hasn't pawed at me."

The silence between them told Dex they either knew he was listening or were having a staring contest. His money was on the latter.

"Let me stay here instead," Braden said, his voice softer, more pleading and less demanding.

"You have to work."

"I can take some time off."

"No. You're not going to tank your career because of some creep who wants to scare me. This is what Dex's company does. Why are you fighting this?"

"Because you're my sister. Because I want you safe. Because being in his bed is not the same as keeping you safe."

"He's sleeping in the guest room."

"Not for long, I'm guessing."

"Why is it an issue?" Taylor demanded. "If I did sleep with him, and I haven't, but if I did, why would it be an issue?"

Her voice faded like she moved into the kitchen. Dex wanted to lean over the railing so he didn't miss the answer, but he was afraid to move at all.

"Because if he's more worried about getting in your pants than he is about keeping you safe, then he's not doing his job."

"Trust me, he's doing his job. He's been nothing short of professional. He's a good guy."

"Tay..."

"Bray..."

They both chuckled, and Dex finally took a breath. He started to move when Braden spoke again.

"I can't lose you, Taylor. You mean too much to me. I don't think I'll recover if something happens to you. I wish you'd told me about the break-in when it happened."

"I'm still the oldest, which means it's my job to protect you. I didn't tell you because I knew you'd freak out. You helped by sending Dex to me. He's helped by being here and making sure I'm safe wherever I go. His team upgraded my security system and are monitoring the house. They're looking for whoever broke in. I'm as safe as I can be."

"And you still don't know who it could have been?"

"No. I'm guessing it's the same man who sent the bird and called me. He made it sound like it. He called me Tay-tay, so someone from our past."

"Seriously?" Braden asked.

Dex thought about moving, but he wanted to see if Taylor mentioned something to Braden that she hadn't thought to tell him.

"Yeah. I don't recognize his voice, but no one's called me that in a long time."

"Except me," Braden said.

Taylor chuckled softly, and Dex imagined the soft smile on her lips.

"Yes, but I know you aren't the one doing this."

"No, but what I mean is, we all call you that. Aaron, Melissa, and I. We've always called you Tay-tay. Could it be someone you know through us?"

Dex flipped through what he knew so far. The list of people Taylor had given the police had very few people she'd known since her childhood, which was why she said she thought it could be someone else. The things the man told her made her feel like it was someone she knew as an adult, but the nickname tricked her. Could Braden be right?

"I don't know," Taylor said slowly, carefully.

"Tell me about the man who broke in." Braden's voice said it wasn't a request. He wanted answers, and he was going to get them.

Dex turned the knob on the door to his room, letting it slip from his fingers and make a noise. He cleared his throat and made plenty of noise as he walked down the stairs. He needed in on their conversation.

When he got to the living room, he played it casual and asked what they were talking about.

"Braden thinks the man who's been threatening me

could be someone he or one of my other siblings knew, but someone I knew as an adult."

Dex rubbed his stubbled jaw. He hadn't taken the time to shave, and the rasp against his fingertips prickled. "It's a good thought. Would that person know your nickname?"

"If it's someone we were close to," Taylor said.

"You don't know your siblings' friends?" Dex asked.

"She's eleven years older than me," Braden said. "If I had a friend in high school, Taylor would have been working and starting to build a name for herself. She still lived with me and our mom because mom was never reliable enough to be around, and Taylor appointed herself as the person who was going to make sure I graduated, but I had friends over. We all did. Taylor never left home, so any of us could have brought someone over at some point..."

"Okay, but why now? What is it about right now that's driving this harassment?"

"The launch," Braden said as though that was the only thing that made sense.

It was Dex's assumption, too, but he wasn't sure if there was another reason. Both men turned to look at Taylor.

"I was on some podcasts lately. And a few TV spots. Nothing major, but enough to have my name out there a little more. Could that have garnered enough attention that someone would do this?"

Her tone said she regretted building and launching her new business. Dex wanted to pull her into his arms and tell her none of this was her fault. Because it wasn't. She did nothing wrong. Victims blamed themselves for taking on risk that shouldn't be a risk. Taylor had no reason to think some psycho would come after her because she was promoting her new business. And the psycho had no right to do it. He was the one to blame, not Taylor.

"It's not your fault," Dex said firmly.

"He's right," Braden agreed. "No one has a right to do this to you, no matter what you did."

"None of this is because of you. It's because some sick fuck thinks he has a right to any piece of you. He doesn't. So, let's figure out who this could be and start digging. We're going to find him, Taylor. We're going to figure out who this son of a bitch is and we're going to put him away for a long time," Dex promised her.

Taylor looked up at him from where she sat on the couch. The look in her eyes said she wanted him to hold her in that moment as much as he ached to. But with Braden sitting next to her, her hand in his, neither of them could move. They simply shared a too-short look and got to work figuring out who could be behind the threats.

Breakfast turned into lunch, and lunch rolled over to dinner. The three of them talked and laughed and plotted. By the time they finished their third meal of the day, Taylor was looking more like the badass Dex had come to know and less like the scared sister Braden brought out in her with his early morning arrival.

"Thank you for being here," Braden said when Taylor went upstairs for a minute. "I'm sorry I made it sound like I didn't trust you."

"Understood. I wouldn't trust me either if I had a sister."

"Are you saying there's a reason not to trust you?"

Dex returned Braden's glare steadily. "Nope. I'm just here to keep her safe, like you asked me to do. We're on the same side, Braden."

"Let's stay that way."

"Agreed."

"What are you two plotting down here?" Taylor asked as she walked back in.

"Your safety," Braden said.

She rolled her eyes like it wasn't the most important goal for all of them to have. "I'm fine. We will find whoever is responsible for all of this. We have a new list. It'll all be over soon."

Dex nodded his agreement but found himself, again, hoping the case dragged on a little longer so he had an excuse to stay under the same roof as her. He would do everything in his power to keep her safe and to find the person threatening her, but he wasn't in any hurry to race back to his empty bed in his empty home and his empty world.

Everything was better with Taylor in it.

12

———

Taylor closed the door behind her brother and fought the urge to collapse against it. She loved her brother, but he was exhausting. Especially when he had a mission, and said mission was her.

"You okay?" Dex murmured. The concern in his voice was obvious from his tone. Before her brother showed up, Taylor was hoping to spend the day playing naked tag with Dex, all over her house. But after almost twelve hours of Braden, all she wanted to do was crash.

"Yeah. Just tired."

"It was a long day," Dex said carefully. Slowly. Questioningly. He was still interested in naked games, but Taylor wanted more than a half-asleep bump and grind. Not that she was hoping for romance, but she didn't want to fall asleep mid-stride. That would be horrifying.

"I love my brother, but he is pretty relentless," Taylor said. She finally turned around and pressed her lips into an apologetic smile, hoping it said all the things she didn't want to say.

Dex's gaze never left hers. "I completely understand. Do

you want to watch a movie or something, or are you just ready for bed?"

"I think I need to take a shower and get some sleep. I'm sorry."

Dex linked his hands together. "Nothing to be sorry about. I'm here to keep you safe, Taylor. That's what matters to me. I'll double check that everything is locked and set the alarm, then be right up behind you. Unless you want me to check upstairs for you."

Taylor shook her head and forced her feet to follow each other to the stairs. "We've been in here all day. No one could have gotten past us to go upstairs. It'll be fine."

Dex nodded and waited until she passed before he went to the front door. Taylor didn't look back as she forced her exhausted body up the stairs and into the bathtub. When she got out, she dressed in boy-short panties and a tight tank top that felt good against her skin. She collapsed onto her bed with her phone and debated checking her email.

She pushed all thoughts of work away and opened her reading app, diving into a romance novel that made her sigh with all the sweetness.

Sunday was a repeat of Saturday, without Braden as an added third wheel. Dex was up and making breakfast when Taylor made it downstairs. She gratefully accepted coffee and an omelet from him before they settled into an overly polite day of dancing around each other and not discussing the way the previous morning started.

When Monday rolled around and they went back to the office, Taylor was cranky and horny and hating her brother for ruining what could have been a sinfully sexy weekend with her hot bodyguard. Damn him.

"Are you okay?" Jessica asked when Taylor barked at her

for the second time that morning. About absolutely nothing.

Taylor sighed and dropped the boss act for a minute. She glanced outside to where she could see Dex working at his desk. She licked her lips and remembered the feel of his against them. "I could have had sex this weekend."

Jessica's eyes widened, and she leaned forward. "With Dex? What happened?"

Taylor groaned and dropped her head to the desk. She closed her eyes and spewed it all to Jessica, from the kiss to Braden showing up to the uncomfortable distance between her and Dex since then.

"I was so tired Saturday night, and I think he took it as a *no* instead of *not now*. And I promised him I wouldn't kiss him after the first time I did, so…"

"The first time?" Jessica asked.

Taylor rolled her eyes at herself. "I sort of threw myself at him. He kissed me for a second, but then stopped us. I felt… not good."

"Don't you think him kissing you changes that, though? I mean, you're going to sit around forever and wait for him to make a move?"

"Is that what you're going to do?" Taylor asked.

Jessica's cheeks pinked. Taylor noticed the way her assistant looked at Braden, and the way her eyes lit up when even his name was mentioned. Taylor wasn't opposed to the idea of them together, but her brother was oblivious.

"I don't know what you're talking about," Jessica said. Her cheeks were bright red and her neck matched. She avoided Taylor's gaze and studied the tablet she had been taking notes on. "Should we finish this up?"

"Sure. Since we're both trying to avoid our love lives, work sounds like a good plan."

Jessica laughed with Taylor. "Okay, so, we have the meeting in an hour about the pre-launch, but from what I'm hearing, the response has been great. We'll get details during the meeting. After lunch, you are supposed to go to the warehouse. Have you mentioned that to Dex?"

Taylor shook her head. She forgot about it, but she didn't think it would be an issue.

Jessica made a note in the calendar, then continued. "The rest of the week is just getting prepared. You have a few radio spots, an interview on Thursday, the podcasts are tomorrow. Next week is even more booked up, but it'll be okay. I'll make sure Dex has an updated copy of your schedule in case there's anything he needs to do before you go to each of these places."

"Thank you, Jessica. I couldn't do all this without you."

She smiled like Taylor was the one doing her a favor. "I love my job, Taylor. I really do. What we're doing is going to help women feel comfortable in their own skin. It's a beautiful thing."

Taylor smiled back. She agreed, and having so many people around her who felt the same was what helped her make her dream a reality. She knew Birds of a Feather would be successful, but it wasn't a dream that she made a reality alone. And she loved her team for it.

Taylor went through her missed messages and sent replies while she waited for the meeting to start. Sharon was the one who suggested a pre-launch with a mix of potential customers, bloggers, podcasters, and influencers. It was a great idea that Taylor had never even considered. Just one more example of why she needed her team.

When it was time for the meeting, Taylor made her way to the conference room on the other side of the floor. She felt Dex's eyes on her as she walked over, but she resisted the urge to turn around. She did not resist the urge to add a little extra sassy sway to her step. *Let him say no to that.*

She fought her smile and pushed Dex from her mind as she walked into the conference room. She cleared her throat and drew the attention of the team before taking her seat at the head of the table and calling the meeting to order.

"We all know why we're here. I have nothing to say. I just want Sharon to tell us how things went."

Sharon stood and met the eyes of the entire team. All the department leaders were there. It was still a small team since the company hadn't officially launched yet, but there were strong and connected and amazing.

"The pre-launch went even better than we hoped."

A collective sigh went around the room before the relief turned to excitement and everyone let out a small cheer. Sharon beamed at the group, then continued with her results.

"Bloggers are starting to share their posts with me. Most of them are scheduled to go live next week when the website will be live. They want to coincide with the release. A few will post the end of this week, showcasing the items they received ahead of time. The podcasters are all set and ready for interviews tomorrow. Obviously, they won't have pictures for their audience, but they are all going to share links to the website."

"Will you share all of that with me?" Nora, the website manager, asked.

Sharon nodded and made a note on the pad in front of her. "Of course. I'll get you links to all the posts and podcasts and anything else I get. Some of the smaller outfits won't share, but they will post. As I find those, I'll send them along so you can include them on our site."

Nora nodded her thanks so Sharon could share the rest of the results.

"Influencers are already posting. They tend to share things before a launch, but that's good because it'll bump up our exposure and get people ready for next week. We're already running close to being sold out from the orders we've had come in for our early-bird sale, but we're working on that, right?"

"We are," the logistics manager, Harper, replied. "We've been in touch with all of our vendors and asked them to ship us more product. The team at the warehouse is running out of space to put everything until we can start shipping items out. We might need a bigger space sooner than we'd planned, but we're going to do our best to make it work."

Taylor didn't like the sound of that. She scribbled a note to talk to Harper about the warehouse and, if possible, have Harper attend the warehouse meeting that afternoon.

"What about our customers?" Maggie from accounting asked. "They're the ones who are going to keep our doors open."

Sharon's grin widened to show all her teeth and all her excitement. "I saved that for last because it's the best news of all. I haven't heard of a single negative review. Customers were asked to share their opinions of whatever they received as reviews on our website. They were also asked to share posts on social media and anywhere else they could. All of our products have reviews, and most of them are above four stars, some five star reviews."

The rest of the team clapped at the great news, but Taylor didn't get to where she was by focusing on the posi-tive. She got there by changing the negative. "I need to see any reviews that were below four stars, and especially any products with an average below four stars. We need to know if there's something that can be done about those items and then do it."

Sharon pulled out a small packet. "Already done. Printed so you can read through whenever you want to. I also sent you a copy before I walked in here in case you want to read it there."

Taylor laughed and accepted the packet. "Am I that predictable?"

Everyone around the table said, "Yes," together.

"But it works because we're all here, and this launch is going to be a huge success," Sharon said. She held Taylor's gaze for an extra minute, her smile conveying her gratitude.

Taylor looked around the room at the team she'd assembled. Most of her supposed mentors told her running a company with mostly women in charge was going to be a failure. They advised that men would do a better job at making sure things got done. Taylor resented the implication and stuck to her gut, knowing she had to do what felt right to her. As it all came together and they were on the verge of launching the business, Taylor had no doubt in her mind that the people who told her she couldn't do it were not the people she needed to go to for advice ever again.

Taylor took an idea she crafted in college, an idea that felt Pollyanna at the time, and turned it into a company that supported a staff of nearly fifty people full or part time. The loans Taylor secured when she was looking to start the company went to bringing top talent on board so she knew Birds of a Feather would not just succeed but perform beyond expectations. Seeing it happen made her proud.

They finished the meeting, and Taylor ate the quick lunch Jessica had delivered for her. After lunch, Dex drove Taylor to the warehouse to meet with the staff there. Harper was joining them, but she was leaving from there so she took her own car.

"Are these employees on the list you gave me?" Dex asked as they walked into the warehouse. His gaze swung through the wide open space and took in every inch of it.

"Of course. And there is security in the area to monitor the facility."

"Good. I'll do my best to stay out of your way while we're here."

She nodded her thanks and stepped to the front of the open space while Dex took a few steps back. She couldn't concentrate on him and run her company. Only one could win, and she long ago chose which one.

"Good afternoon, everyone. I know I'm interrupting your afternoon of training. I hope things are going well." Taylor looked at Eve, the warehouse lead.

Eve nodded in reply, not bothering to waste words and draw attention from Taylor.

"Good. I want to keep this quick. I'm going to be doing a tour, but I want to thank you all for being here. For putting your faith in me and this company. I'm really excited for us to start shipping out customer orders next week. I have a huge stack of cards in the office to sign so we can put them in with our first thousand orders."

A gentle murmur moved through the small crowd.

"I know Eve and Harper have filled you all in on the overwhelming number of orders we're expecting. I also know the shelves are already full. Unfortunately, more is coming. That's not what you want to hear, but we're looking at the possibility of sending some of these packages out ahead of time so people have orders on day one. Also to make some space. We don't want anyone at risk, so those of you driving..." Taylor looked at the group and waited until a few hands went up. "Be extra careful. Take your time. And please know you can always talk to me. I don't ever want any of you to feel you can't call me up or come to my office if there's something you need my help with."

"How about lunch?" one woman called out from the back.

"I think I owe all of you more than lunch. But that was actually part of why I'm here. All next week, I am buying lunch for everyone here."

A chorus of cheers made Taylor smile. A *thank you* from the group broadened her grin.

"You're welcome. It's the least I can do. I know Eve has already mentioned it, but the weekend after our opening is our kick off party. It's late so we can celebrate the first few days. I hope you will all be there. Bring your significant others and families."

"Seriously?" someone asked.

Taylor nodded. "Yes, seriously. I've had a lot of jobs that were just places I went for a few hours a day. I don't want to run a company like that. I want us to know each other. I want every single one of you to know you are important. Without you, this company would not succeed. I know that, and I hope you do, too."

Another soft chorus of murmurs went through the group.

"Is there anything we need to talk about right now?" Taylor asked.

They all shook their heads and exchanged questioning looks before Eve stepped forward. "It sounds like we're good. Thank you for coming to see us, Ms. Wright. We really appreciate it."

The warehouse staff clapped as Eve walked toward

Taylor and guided her toward the first of the racks of clothes.

Taylor walked through the entire warehouse with Eve and Harper, talking about where to stash the boxes coming in, what the best short-term plan was, and what was a reasonable space to need going forward.

They all agreed until they got a few months into things, they didn't want to relocate the warehouse and risk going too big, or too small.

Taylor and Dex walked out alone, Harper staying behind to talk to Eve about a few other things. It was late in the afternoon, and Taylor was feeling good. Good enough that she didn't want to go back to the office and didn't want to feel like a prisoner in her own home. She wanted to celebrate.

"Let's go out to dinner," she said when they were in Dex's large, black, intimidating SUV.

"Dinner?" he asked, like it was a foreign concept.

"Yeah, you know, where two people go to a restaurant and sit down and order food and eat and drink and talk."

"Is that what it is?" The edge of his mouth quirked up.

"Yep. I really want to celebrate. It's been a great day, and after the craziness of last week, I need a night out. Are you up for it?"

He nodded and merged onto the main road. "I'm at your service. What did you have in mind?"

She tapped her lips with her fingertip and considered her options. She hadn't gone out to eat much lately, choosing work over any indulgences. She really didn't have to think about what she wanted, though. She always went for her favorite. "Sushi?"

Dex slid her a look that said he knew she wasn't being as

casual as she wanted to pretend she was. "Is that how you always choose to celebrate?"

She shrugged like *no* was an option, but really, it wasn't. "If I say *maybe* will you believe me?"

He barked a laugh that encouraged her to join him. "You, Ms. Wright, are always surprising me. Sushi sounds good."

"Oh, yay! I wasn't sure if you were a sushi guy."

"I'm not, but I'm finding it hard to say no to anything that puts that big of a smile on your face."

"Oh," she breathed, all humor vanishing. She could think of a few other things that would put a big, fat smile on her face.

He chuckled, and she realized she said that out loud. She covered her scorching cheeks with her hands and chewed on the inside of her lip.

"I'm sorry."

He breathed a laugh. "Don't be. I was thinking the same thing."

Her gaze snapped to where he was watching her out of the corner of his eye while he drove. The side of his mouth hitched up with his sexy smile. She licked her lips slowly and pulled one between her teeth to try to stop her smile from splitting her face in two.

So much for sushi putting that smile on her face. It was all the sweet and sexy man taking her out to dinner who did that.

13

DEX COULD NOT STOP SMILING. HE TRIED TO REMEMBER THE last time he had so much fun and came up blank. Taylor was different from anyone else he knew, and it was obvious they both needed the night out.

"Another?" she asked, holding a piece of sushi in her chopsticks like she'd been using them her whole life.

He shook his head and leaned back in their booth for two. "I'll let you have that one."

She laughed at him and popped the piece in her mouth around a smirk. "No more eel for you?"

He twisted his lips in disgust. "No. I think I've had enough eel for a lifetime."

She cackled and reached for her glass. He encouraged her to have a drink with dinner. She'd confessed she never trusted anyone else enough to be her designated driver so she never had more than one drink when she went out. When the server handed over the bar menu, Dex assured her he'd get her home. Now, she was on her third mixed drink with number four already on the table and ready for her. He wasn't willing to examine the little part of him that warmed when she ordered drink after drink and showed him she trusted him.

"Did you eat a lot of sushi growing up?" Dex asked, because that was the safer question. What he really wanted to ask was if she was ready to get the hell out of there.

She shook her head while she sucked the last of the pink drink through the clear straw. He adjusted himself below the table and tried not to imagine her lips wrapped around him and sucking him dry.

He failed.

"We barely had enough money for grilled cheese or ramen noodles growing up. Sushi... I never even heard of sushi until my first job after grad school. Some of my coworkers would get together on Fridays and go out to eat. The first time I agreed to go, they were planning to go out for sushi. My friend asked if I liked it and I lied and said, of course. I'd never heard of sushi before."

"Wow. I'm not adventurous with food, so I give you a lot of credit."

She shrugged like it was no big deal, but the light in her eyes dimmed just enough that he could tell there was more to the story.

"Growing up like I did... I learned to eat whatever was there. I found a can of sardines in the cabinet once. I didn't know what they were, but I put them in a pan on the stove and cooked them. My parents were out, as usual, so I had to find things. We ate all kinds of things growing up that most people haven't eaten. Because it was cheap. My mom worked at a restaurant for a few years and would bring home leftovers. We'd eat those. Of course, she got fired because the leftovers were unfinished food from customers' plates."

Dex's eyes widened, and he pulled back. He tried to neutralize his features, but she noticed.

"Yeah. She never told us, and we were hungry, so I'm not sure it would have mattered. I think about that now and it makes me nauseous."

"Tell me about your siblings. Obviously, I know Braden, but you said you have two more?"

She nodded, a small smile teasing her lips. "Another brother and a sister. Aaron is two years younger than me, and Melissa is five years younger than him. Braden is the baby."

"You're all close."

Her nose wrinkled before she spoke. "No, unfortunately. Aaron moved away as soon as he was old enough. He lives in Cleveland. Melissa is closer to Rochester. I don't see either of them as much as I'd like. Braden and I are the only ones who stayed in Niagara Falls. I lived at home until he was old enough to leave, then I found my own place. Our mom was barely around by then. I was paying the rent and all the bills, supporting Braden. She was still his guardian and refused to sign over custody to me, so I stayed. It was just the two of us through his four years of high school. I helped him with classes and applying to college and figuring out what he wanted to do with his life. We got a small apartment close to campus when he was in college and we lived there until he was out of school and had a job and could afford his own place."

"His house is nice. Definite bachelor pad, but nice."

She laughed. "It is. I keep telling him he needs a woman to help him fix it up, but he's not ready to settle down yet."

"Does he get that from you, too?"

Her gaze lifted to his and held. The air sparked and sizzled. Dex hadn't meant for it to sound like he was asking if she was ready to settle down, but once the question was out there, he wondered about the answer.

He hadn't thought twice about settling down. Hell, not once. But spending time with Taylor had him thinking all sorts of thoughts he never had before. Like why didn't he meet her sooner and what does her skin taste like and how loud would she scream his name.

"Relationships have always taken a backseat for me. I had a boyfriend in high school and another somewhat serious one in grad school, but otherwise I've dated casually. No one has ever inspired me the same way my work has."

Dex nodded slowly, thinking how similar her words were to his thoughts. Work always came first. For him, it wasn't about the work as much as it was about the security. He didn't want to need things and not be able to have them. Not that he lived a lavish lifestyle, but his grandmother would use things like towels and dishrags until they were more holes than fabric. She hated what she called wasting. Dex would have trashed them and bought new as soon as they started to wear out, and once he had enough money to put some in the bank and not feel like he was living on the edge, he always did.

But adding a second person to his world never felt like a need. A want sometimes, sure, but never a need.

As their eyes met over the edges of their glasses, he wondered if that was changing.

"Are you ready to go?" Taylor asked. Her voice was breathy and dangerous and did things to his body that a simple question should not have the power to do.

His dick was definitely ready to go.

Dex waved the server over while Taylor finished her last drink. After he got his card back, Dex helped Taylor to her feet. She looked up at him, the moment full of all the things he wanted to say and do and have with her. If someone at the table next to them hadn't dropped a spoon that clattered to the ground and reminded Dex they were exposed and in public, he might have kissed her right then and there.

Instead, he put his hand on her lower back, feeling the warmth of her skin through her soft silky top, and guided her from the restaurant. The evening air was warm enough to not need a jacket and hot enough to send a quick pulse of desire through his body.

His fingers tensed against her back, wanting to pull her into his arms and never let go. He wasn't sure he could wait until they got back to her place to have her. But he was sure he needed to have her. They'd been dancing around their desires for days. It was time to stop dancing and start doing.

He tugged his keys from his pocket and unlocked the doors with a soft beep in the quiet night. He didn't remove his hand from her back, walking with her to the passenger door. He reached to open it, but she turned and pressed her back to the door and ran her hands up his chest. Her fingers slid around his neck and pulled him down to her.

Their mouths collided in a fire fueled moment of passion. He opened his mouth to lick her lips and found them already parted and her tongue on its way to his. He leaned against her, pressing her back to the SUV and letting her feel exactly how much he needed her.

His hands ran up her sides and around the edges of her breasts. He ached to cup them and tease them and lick them and taste them, but he wasn't willing to step back and give himself the space. She felt far too good against his erection, her leg hitched up and her warmth welcoming him in.

"Dex."

It was half-whimper-half-groan and all sexy as fuck. He

felt the same damn way and knew they'd be stupid not to stop. But fucking hell, he didn't want to stop.

"Let's go," he said, pulling back just enough to move her away from the side of the SUV. He opened her door and guided her inside with firm hands on her curvy hips. She pouted at him, but he was not going to fuck her in a parking lot. No matter how badly he wanted to.

Dex raced around the back of the SUV and had it cranked up and out on the road in less time than it took him to draw a full breath.

He reached for her hand and wound their fingers together. She was quiet, but she held on to him while he sped through the streets toward her house. His blood pumped with the quiet rumble of the engine, each mile-per-hour above the speed limit pushing them closer to her house and naked times.

He pulled into her driveway and squeezed her fingers before releasing them. He threw the SUV in park and turned off the ignition, then looked over at a snoring Taylor.

Dex allowed himself the moment of disappointment. His cock ached to fill her, but his mind knew it was wrong. He knew it was wrong before she pulled him down for the kiss, but he wanted it, wanted her, too much to stop it.

And again, he was an ass.

He got out of the SUV and went around to her door. She woke up when he opened it and gave him a sleepy, sexy smile that said she was still willing even though she really wasn't able.

She poured herself out of the seat and into his arms, then let him half-carry her into the house. He locked the door behind them and set the alarm again. He wanted to check the house, but she was his first priority. Getting her upstairs and into bed.

"I can just lay there and let you do the work," she assured him as he ushered her into her room a minute later.

"Trust me, Taylor, when this happens, I will be doing all the work, but not when you aren't a willing participant."

"I am willing," she pouted. Her eyes were glassy and her steps twisted. She collapsed onto her bed and reached up for him to follow her. "Will you kiss me some more?"

He sat next to her and leaned over her. He kissed her nose and pressed his face into her hair. He breathed in her scent and let how much he wanted her fuel his thoughts while she fell asleep without another protest.

Dex forced himself to get up a few minutes later and debated stripping her down to something more comfortable. He looked at her. One of her flats dangled off a toe, the other kicked somewhere near the door. Her dark hair wrapped around her neck and stretched wildly over her pillow. Her top was twisted tight around her waist, exposing a thin strip of her skin. He wanted to lean down and taste that strip. To press his tongue to every inch of her body and learn everything she liked.

But he knew he couldn't. Kissing her in the parking lot was a bad idea, but he didn't realize her drinks were that strong. Between the alcohol, the good news, and the stress she'd been under, he should have seen her crash coming. Instead, he was too focused on wishing he could see her coming.

Dex lifted her shoe off her toe and grabbed a blanket from the end of her bed. He set the shoe in front of her closet, then paused and opened the closet door. He had to remember why he was there.

The closet, bathroom, and upstairs were clear. Dex moved back downstairs, checking all the rooms downstairs, then reviewing the extremely boring footage of the house all day. The sun changed position, and the shadows fell as expected, telling Dex the video was not tampered with.

When he finally went upstairs to his room, he checked in once more on Taylor. She hadn't moved from her position. He stood and watched her for a long minute, then closed her bedroom door and went to his room.

He got ready for bed and laid on the sheets that smelled like the rest of her house. His cock pulsed against his boxer briefs. Not all of him was ready to go to sleep. Dex closed his eyes, but when he did, all he saw was Taylor.

Taylor with her head down at work.

Taylor with a happy smile on her face at dinner.

Taylor with her mouth spread wide around his cock.

"Fuck," Dex groaned. He wasn't getting any sleep. Not when he was so wound up.

He shoved his hand into his boxer briefs and grabbed hold of himself. One squeeze and he was already seeing stars. He hadn't been so turned on since he was in high school and didn't know how to talk to girls.

He wasn't interested in girls, plural, anymore. Just one. Her smiling face was right there behind his eyelids. Talking dirty to him and making him laugh. He stroked and squeezed himself, trying to keep his grunts quiet so he didn't wake up the object of his desire.

Dream Taylor dropped to her knees in front of him and cupped his balls. He did the same in reality, telling himself his large hand was really her small one. Dream Taylor licked him, and he jerked, his hips rising off the bed.

"Fuck," he whispered again. His balls tightened, and his throat closed up. Stars exploded behind his closed eyes. His hand pumped furiously, not slowing down as his forearm burned with the speed he needed to convince himself he wasn't alone in her guest room.

"Taylor," he croaked as his body finally took over and released everything inside and outside and all around him. The sticky come spurted out around his hand, filling his boxer briefs and settling on his body.

He laid there for a long minute, unable to move and unwilling to open his eyes and face the reality that Taylor wasn't there. When he finally did, he stripped off his boxer briefs and washed them in the sink before stepping into the shower to rinse away the mess.

He fell back into the bed naked, not wanting to have anything between him and the sheets Taylor put on the bed. His cock grew again as he thought about having nothing between him and Taylor herself, but he was going to have to wait awhile for that.

And maybe recommend a different kind of celebration next time.

TAYLOR WOKE UP WITH A START, her hand flying to her chest as it thundered and told her there was danger nearby. She strained to hear what woke her up so suddenly and jumped when she actually heard a noise.

In her kitchen.

Why was someone in her house? And why did her head hurt so damn bad?

Did she get drunk and bring someone home? She groaned to herself, then realized she was fully dressed. She groaned again as everything that had happened over the last few days came back to her in a rush. "Dex," she said out loud, a smile lifting her lips instantly.

She looked around her room again as her cheeks flamed. She kissed him and tried to get him to sleep with her. She was not lucky enough to have forgotten that for longer than a minute, and now she felt like an ass.

Taylor forced herself from her bed and went to the bathroom. She left a trail of clothes on her way and stepped right into the shower before turning it on. The icy cold spray made her yelp, but she didn't get out. She needed the cold to rinse away the last of the fogginess in her head.

She hurried through her shower while mentally reviewing her day. It was going to be busy. They were officially one week until launch, and Taylor couldn't risk anything else going wrong.

She dressed and fixed her hair and light makeup, then headed downstairs to face the day. And the man who let her celebrate then put her to bed. He was sweet. Too sweet. But Taylor knew she would be upset if he'd done anything other than exactly what he did.

"Good morning," Dex said, his voice rough and scratchy. The sound of it slithered up her spine and settled at the base of her throat, grabbing hold of her.

"Morning."

"Coffee?"

She gratefully accepted the mug he gave her. They shared a look over the top, his searching and hers embarrassed.

She lowered the mug and cleared her throat. "I apologize for last night. I put you in a difficult position. That wasn't my intention. I don't drink much, and it went to my head. I promised you I wouldn't touch you again, and then I broke that promise. I am sorry."

"I'm not," he said. He immediately rolled his lips in and sucked a sharp breath through his nose. "I... Maybe I shouldn't be saying this, but you weren't the only one that let everything go to your head last night. I wanted you,

Taylor. I still fucking do. It took everything in me to put you to bed last night and walk away. Just like it's killing me not to drag you into my arms right now and lose myself in you."

Taylor opened her mouth to say something just as her phone dinged with a notification. She dug it out of her bag and looked at it. "I have a meeting with some investors in an hour. They want an update on the upcoming launch. Really, they want to know if I was a bad gamble." She tucked the phone away and looked up at him. "Maybe we can have dinner here tonight. A quiet celebration. Without alcohol."

Dex pressed his lips together, fighting the smile sparkling in his eyes. "I think that sounds like a great idea. Until then, you have a world to takeover."

She chuckled.

The drive was quiet but not uncomfortable. Dex parked in Taylor's spot then followed her through security where Steven grunted at Dex and grinned at Taylor. Taylor almost asked Dex what that was about, but then they were in the elevator and they weren't alone.

The doors opened to Birds, and Taylor stepped off first. The motion sensing lights flickered on a moment later and Taylor's eyes widened. Her hand flew to her lips. She let out a barely there squeak as she took in the office space.

Trashed.

14

———

Dex jumped into warrior mode as Taylor stood frozen in place. Emotions pounded her, from fear to rage to worry to disappointment. All their hard work. All their ideas. All their plans. Shredded.

"No one's here," Dex said when he finally made it back to Taylor's side. She was vaguely aware of him tucking a gun into an invisible holster. "Let's go to your office."

He guided her to her office, her legs wooden and immobile. He nudged her into her chair, after he righted it. Then he picked up the phone on her desk.

She stared, her brain only catching some of the words.

Break in.

Destroyed.

Police.

Employees.

Taylor didn't know how long she sat there like that, but by the time she looked around, the floor was crawling with people. Cops, employees, security, even some of Dex's team. It was a crime scene. Everything she'd killed herself for was a crime scene. Useless.

"I want this man dead," Taylor said, the first words she'd spoken since she said good morning to Steven.

"You can't say that," Dex hissed. "If he turns up dead, you'll be a suspect."

"I will be whether I say that or not," she replied. She glared up at him. "Why is this happening?"

He held his breath for the briefest of moments, then sagged as he let it out. He shook his head and said, "I wish I knew, Tay. I really wish I knew."

"Who did this?"

Dex shook his head again. "The video was looped. They were smart. They knew what they were doing."

"What does that mean?"

"It means they recorded a portion of video of the empty office and replayed it so it looked like the office was empty. It was still running when we got here. It was set to run indefinitely. Security had no idea anything had happened, or when. All they know is there is footage of the cleaning crew being in here until ten o'clock. It shows them leaving. An hour later, the lights went out, like they're supposed to. After that, there's nothing."

"So, someone broke into my home, bypassing my security there. And now, someone broke into my office, bypassing the security here. No one should be able to get to this floor without permission."

"We're trying to figure out how they did that, too. There are cameras all over this building. We're looking to see if there's one they missed. One that can tell us when they were here and who they are."

Taylor's hands wobbled like an unsteady toddler. She squeezed them together, but the trembling didn't stop. She realized her entire body was vibrating. She looked out at the office beyond her own glass walls. Everything went blurry, fuzzy. Then a sob tore through her.

Dex kneeled in front of her, his face distorted through her tears. "Taylor."

The pain in his voice only made her cry harder. He blamed himself for what happened. She wanted to tell him it wasn't his fault, but she couldn't form words. All she could do was cry.

He lifted her from her seat and carried her to the couch. He sat with her in his lap and held her against his chest while she cried. Someone came in, but a gentle shake of his head sent them away again.

Taylor just let it all out. The pain and worry and anger and fear. The heartbreak at what was lost. The terror that she could have been there, like she was many nights. Whoever was after her wasn't done. He wanted to stop her. Stop her launch. It was personal, and it was only going to get worse.

"I hate this," Taylor finally managed to say.

"I know, sweetheart. I do, too," Dex replied. His face was pressed against her hair, his arms tight around her body. She felt safe with him. Protected. Cared for.

She couldn't remember ever feeling that way. Her whole life, she was the one who took care of people. She was the big sister and the business owner and the one people went to for advice and help. She was the one who got things done. And when her world started to crumble, Dex showed up in it. He held all the broken pieces together. He allowed her to fall apart, a little at a time, then patched her back up so she could keep moving forward.

"Thank you," she whispered.

"For what?"

"For holding me together."

He kissed the side of her head. "Always. I need to tell you something."

"What?"

"Your brother is almost here."

Taylor groaned. "He's going to lose it."

Dex nodded, his lips brushing her hair. "Yeah, he is. I think he already has. Are you going to be okay?"

"Will you stay with me? Talk to him? Tell him what happened?"

"Of course."

"Thank you."

They sat together for another long moment. Taylor forced herself off his lap and went to her bathroom. She washed her face and tried to convince herself she didn't look like she'd just gone a few rounds, but it was useless.

She heard their voices before she opened the door. Braden was not happy, but Dex was his normal unflappable self.

"You were supposed to keep her safe," Braden yelled.

"He did," Taylor answered for Dex. "I wasn't here. Because of him. And he's here because of you, little brother. I'm safe. I'm a little heartbroken." She looked around the offices at the smashed computers, tossed fabric, and shredded designs. "Maybe a lot heartbroken. But I'm fine. We can still launch. We can still make this happen. The store will probably have to be delayed. It'll take some time before we can do any new designs, and a good bit of our market research has been tampered with, but I'm here. All my employees are here. We are safe because of Dex."

Braden crossed the room and pulled her into his arms. He held her tight against him. Taylor felt him shaking and realized he was just as scared as she was.

"I'm fine, Bray-bray. I promise. It's scary, but I'm okay."

He sucked in a jagged breath and held her for a long moment. He finally released her and studied her face. "I hate this."

She breathed a laugh. "You and me both."

"I'm so happy you weren't here last night."

Taylor thought about where she was the night before, and her cheeks heated. She took a step back from her brother, moving around her desk before she answered. "Dex and I went to dinner, then home. Yesterday was a good day, and I wanted to celebrate."

"Let me guess, sushi?"

She chuckled. "You know me well."

The wry smile he gave her said he did in fact know her. Which was all the more reason she had to get him to leave. She was not interested in her brother finding out she had her tongue down his friend's throat after their celebratory dinner the night before.

"What else did you two do last night?"

Taylor's eyes widened for half a second, then landed on Dex. Her cheek heated at the sinful look in his eyes. Do? Not much. Almost do, want to do, counting the seconds until they could do? Everything.

But Taylor couldn't say any of that to her brother. Hell, she couldn't say anything at all. Her mouth refused to form words. Her hands slid against each other like a high five in a pool. And that wasn't the only place slick skin rubbed together.

Braden looked between them, his gaze deadly as he spun to Dex after Taylor's useless fish face.

"Taylor had a little too much to drink last night," Dex said smoothly. "She got great results from the pre-launch they did and sampled more than one of the fancy drinks on the menu. She poured herself into bed as soon as we got back to her place. That blank look is because she was strug- gling to remember."

Braden stared at Dex for a painfully long moment. Taylor silently begged him to believe the lies, even though it wasn't all lies. Just the last part was a lie.

Oh, God, he had to believe.

"Makes sense. I've had a few nights like that where I just crash after a long day or a few. I'm sorry you're going through all of this."

Taylor smiled weakly. "Thanks."

Braden circled her desk and pulled her into his arms. "I'm off for a few days. Do you want me to stay with you instead?"

"No," Taylor said quickly. Too quickly. Braden leaned back and examined her once more. He was taking his time looking at her, as if he could see something on her skin. Something that told him all the dirty, dirty thoughts she was having about the man he sent to protect her.

She squeezed her thighs together and forced her lips to turn up on the edges. "I just mean, I know you're tired. You never sleep well at the station. And you should get some sleep and enjoy your days off. Dex is taking good care of me."

Braden sighed heavily. "Okay. If you're sure. I just want you to know I'm always here for you. If you need anything."

"Thanks. I know. You're the best baby brother a girl could ever have."

Braden snorted. "You really know how to make a guy feel like a man."

Taylor beamed at him. "I'm your big sister. It's my job to knock you down a few pegs."

Braden hugged her once more, then turned to leave. He

nodded to Dex before he walked out, one of those nods that said *follow me.*

Dex trailed behind Braden without a glance at Taylor. She tried to watch them without being totally obvious she was watching them walk to the elevator together. When Braden got on without punching Dex, she finally released the breath she was holding.

Dex walked back into her office a moment later with a sly grin. "Your brother said he'd kick my ass if I slept with you."

"My brother doesn't get to control who I sleep with."

"He's pretty strong. I might be a little afraid of him."

She raised an eyebrow at him, daring him to say what he was implying.

The edge of his mouth jumped up, then returned to a neutral position. "Maybe this is a bad idea."

Taylor didn't protest or argue. She just nodded slowly, thoughtfully. "Your teammate, English? He's single, right? Is he available to stay with me for a few days?"

Dex growled, all humor gone from his face.

Taylor grinned cheekily at him. "I mean, since you're afraid of my brother, I'm not so sure you're the best one to keep me safe from the man with the knife who trashes my office, sends me dead birds, and breaks into my home."

Dex's scowl turned deadly, then softened as Taylor casually recounted the events that brought them to where they were. She didn't intend to sound so indifferent. Like there wasn't a very good reason for her to be terrified.

"I'm sorry you're dealing with this," Dex said, his voice quiet and rough, like the words were dragged out of him. "I wish we'd met another way."

She huffed a laugh. "Me, too."

He stayed on his side of the office and she stayed on

hers, but the connection between them stretched out and grabbed hold. Taylor felt the way his eyes slid down her body, as though his hands were the ones moving over her. She trembled at the heated look in his eyes when he met hers again.

"I'll keep you safe, Taylor."

"I know."

"I'd give my life for you."

"I hope it doesn't come to that. I kind of like having you around."

He breathed a laugh. "I kind of like being here. Even though it's really bright."

She smiled, then looked past him to the destroyed office. "I can't believe someone hates me this much."

"We'll find him, and whoever he's working with. I promise you."

She nodded. She trusted him. He would do it. There wasn't a doubt in her mind.

JONAH CAUGHT the eye of the brunette next to him, giving her his best *trust me* smile. She blushed and ducked her chin, then looked up at him through her lashes.

Got her.

He continued the game, letting it seem like any other casual hook up. The whole time, he was planning on all the ways he would make this woman pay. She was a dead ringer for Taylor, and he was going to enjoy the dead part.

When they finished their late lunch and she suggested they get out of there, Jonah let her see his canary-like grin. He nodded eagerly and let her chuckle at him. She thought she made his day. She was right.

He let her choose where they went next and followed her in his own vehicle. When she parked in front of an old apartment building and got out, he could barely contain his glee that there were no cameras in the area.

It was easy to get the woman into bed and strip her naked. It was easy to fuck her until she screamed. And it was even easier to draw a knife across her throat and watch the life drain from her eyes. Jonah smiled widely as she choked on her own blood and died by his skilled hand.

"Too bad you aren't Taylor. For today, you'll do."

He dressed and enjoyed one last view of the lifeless lookalike and promised himself that one day it would be Taylor Wright he watched die.

Soon.

TAYLOR HELD it together for the rest of the day, through the podcasts and all her meetings. She got a report from the warehouse that everything was fine there. They were getting ready to ship out early orders so the new merchandise could fit safely on the shelves. The asshole out to get her was not going to ruin her. She wouldn't let it happen.

Dex was quiet on the drive back to her house. She wondered what was going through his mind, but the watchful way he'd been taking in everything that happened that day, she wasn't entirely sure she wanted to know. He saw things she didn't, things that might terrify her if she was aware of them. She just wanted to forget for a little while.

Inside her house, Dex checked every room and closet until he was satisfied they were alone and no one had been in her place all day.

"Why don't you go upstairs and take a shower. I'll fix something for dinner," Dex said.

Taylor had just sunk into a chair at the island and dropped her head into her hands. Every time she thought she could relax for a minute, something else happened that kicked her ass. She wasn't sure she could try again.

But Dex wasn't taking no for an answer. He ushered her upstairs despite her weak protests. In truth, she was tired and a hot shower sounded good.

He turned on the shower for her and pressed a kiss to her temple before leaving her bathroom and bedroom, closing the door behind himself.

She stared at it, wishing he'd walk back through and offer to wash her body for her, but he never did. She was alone.

The shower felt good, and when she stepped out, the creepy feeling she had the week before was not there. Taylor wrapped herself in her bathrobe and took her time putting on lotion. Something that made her stomach rumble finally broke through the sweet smell of her shower and compelled her to leave the room, still in only her robe and panties.

Dex had music playing while he moved around the kitchen. He was standing in front of the sink, his hips shifting with the beat of the song, when she found him. Taylor leaned against the island and watched him dance.

He spun around and caught her watching, but instead of looking embarrassed, his face broke into a wide, seductive grin. He reached for her, tugging her into his arms wordlessly and holding her body tight to his as he moved them together in a slow, provocative dance.

"How was your shower?" he asked after a moment.

"Good. I didn't realize how stressed I was."

He nodded, not delivering false platitudes. They both knew she was stressed and scared for very good reasons.

Her stomach rumbled again, and he stopped their slow dance with a chuckle. "It sounds like I need to feed you. Where do you normally eat?"

"The couch," she admitted.

He didn't miss a beat, pointing her toward the couch while he fixed two plates and carried them over to the coffee table. He poured her a glass of wine and himself water. He joined her and started eating while she found a movie to distract her. A comedy, because she needed to laugh.

When they finished eating, they leaned back on the couch. Their shoulders brushed, but she shifted slightly away, not wanting to assume anything.

Dex adjusted his position and brought their shoulders into contact again.

Taylor tucked her feet behind her on the couch, leaning her body closer to Dex.

Dex put his arm along the back of the couch.

Taylor finally gave up the pretense and leaned against his chest. His arm fell to her side and tugged her closer. He kissed the top of her head and reached for her hand with his other one.

Taylor's eyes grew heavy as the movie played. Dex chuckled softly a few times. Taylor burrowed in deeper, wrapping her arm around his waist. He was cozy and comfortable. She didn't think he would be with all those muscles, but he was. And before she knew it, the movie and the man lost to the sleep that begged her to surrender.

15

DEX WAS PREPARED FOR TAYLOR TO CRASH THIS TIME. HE SAW it in her eyes all day. She was barely holding on, struggling to keep herself from falling apart in front of her employees. She had to be strong for them, to let them believe they were safe.

It took a lot out of her. When they got to her place, he knew a shower would help her relax because, as much as he wanted to continue the flirting they'd been doing all week, he didn't want her to do anything she wasn't completely ready for. And that meant she had to be awake.

Which she no longer was.

Dex watched the rest of the movie, then turned off the TV. He eased out from beneath her and double checked the locks and the perimeter cameras. Everything looked nice and boring, so he was ready to go to bed.

Alone.

Taylor looked peaceful on the couch, but Dex had no intention of leaving her there. He wasn't sure he could carry her up the stairs, but he didn't want to wake her up either.

He carefully scooped her up, allowing himself a healthy

inhale of her scent before he turned toward the stairs. She held on to him, no more than a gentle stirring, as he moved through her darkened home and got her into her bed. Just like the night before, he debated on helping her change, but the glimpse of skin at her neck told him she had nothing on beneath her robe. He wasn't going to see her naked without her permission. No matter how much his body demanded a peek.

She settled on her bed and tucked her hands under her chin. Dex kissed the side of her head and forced his feet to carry him out of the room.

He closed the door with a soft click, then moved to his room. He got ready for bed and settled under the covers with his phone to check a few potential leads.

He hadn't gotten all the way through the list Taylor gave Officer Shaw the day the bird arrived in her office, and he wanted to research a few more of those people.

Dex had just typed her ex's name into the database when there was a soft knock on his door.

"Yeah?" he called out quietly, just in case he was hearing things.

The door opened enough for Taylor to stick her head in. "Hi."

"Hey," he said, sitting up in bed. "I thought you were out."

"I was, but I had to use the bathroom and woke up. When I laid back down..."

"Come here," Dex said without hesitation. He pulled the covers back for her to crawl into bed with him. He put his phone away, the woman more important than anything else at the moment.

"I'm sorry."

"For what?" He turned off the lamp on the nightstand

and slid down the bed so they were face to face. She'd taken off the robe and wore a fitted tank top and a pair of pajama pants that were even more tantalizing than the robe with nothing under it.

"I fell asleep on you again. After I made it seem like—"

"You don't owe me anything, Taylor," he said, his voice like steel. He didn't want her in his bed out of some misplaced sense of obligation.

"I know. I mean, a part of me knows. Another part..."

"Another part what?"

"Sex has always been... I've only had a couple of real relationships. Most of the time, the men I've been with were very casual. People I didn't know well. It was a release, a fling. Nothing I saw going anywhere. But with you..."

"I like you, Taylor. You amaze and impress me. You are smart and creative and beautiful. If you want this, want me, I'm all for it, but if you just want to lie here and know you aren't alone tonight, I am perfectly happy to do that, too."

"You would cuddle all night?" Disbelief filled her tone.

"Absolutely. We've known each other for less than a week. And in that time, you've been attacked, your business has been threatened, and you're preparing for the biggest moment of your career. What kind of ass would I be if I said either we have sex or you go back to your own bed?"

She chuckled. "Yeah, I don't think I'd like you as much as I do if that was your answer right now."

"Then it's a good thing it's not." He rolled to his back and pulled her closer, wrapping his arm around her shoulders. She settled her head on his chest and her hand around his waist.

"Dex?" she whispered a few quiet minutes later.

"Yeah?"

"What if I want sex right now?"

"Sweetheart, that's not going to be a problem." He indicated his erection, holding the blanket up.

"Oh," she gasped, her sweet little voice wrapping around his cock and making him even harder. "I... You... Wow."

He chuckled. "Maybe we should start with a kiss and go from there."

"Yes, please," she said.

She pushed herself up, bringing her face up to his. He cupped her jaw as she slid her hand up the side of his neck. They both moaned as their lips touched and fire ignited all around them.

Dex went slow, letting her set the pace. Her tongue peeked out from between her lips in a tentative brush, then darted back into her own mouth. Dex chased her, sucking her lower lip between his teeth and biting softly. She moaned and scraped her nails into his hair. They thrust their tongues together, meeting in the middle with a satisfied groan.

Taylor leaned over Dex, her breasts against his chest. His arm drifted lower, cupping her hip. He resisted the urge to draw her on top of him. He was trying not to push too hard. He wanted her, but anything that happened between them had to be mutual or he'd never forgive himself.

Taylor pulled back after a second and drew a slow, deep breath. She kept her eyes closed, cutting herself off from him. He wanted to see her, to look at her, to know what was going on in her mind.

"I like you," she said after a painfully quiet moment. "A lot. And I don't know you, so it's weird to like you this much. I told you I haven't been in a lot of relationships, but the truth is, my work has always come first. I've let relationships fail because work mattered more. And I know..."

She cleared her throat and finally looked up at him. The

pain in her eyes made him want to kiss her until all he saw was desire and joy, but he waited. He knew whatever she was saying was important to her. And that made it important to him, too.

"I know I'm better with work than people. I've always been able to let coworkers in far enough that they feel connected without actually being connected. Most of my employees are people I've met through the hiring process. I didn't take many of them with me from old job because I wasn't actually friends with my coworkers. That's how all my relationships are. And… I don't want to hurt you or ruin this before it starts, but I felt you should know. I don't know if I can offer you more than this. More than a few stolen moments at night when I'm off the clock."

Dex cupped her jaw and let his fingertips trail over her smooth skin. He saw the way her eyes changed, the way they softened and heated with that one simple touch. He wanted more of it, even if it was just in the stolen moments between workdays.

"Your brother saved my ass. Literally. I would be dead right now if it weren't for him. There aren't a lot of people I could say that about, especially not outside the SEALs, but Braden was there for me. I took the meeting with you because he asked me to. But I came here that first night because I could hear the fear in your voice on the phone. I'm not ever the number one guy. I'm good enough, but I don't have a degree, I don't have awards, I don't have anything but me. I'm smart, but I've always thought people think I'm smart because they expect me to be dumb. I surprise them when they realize I can have an intelligent conversation. You never saw me that way. You never treated me like I was anything less than the man I am."

She sucked in a jagged breath and settled her head against his bare chest. Her fingers danced over his skin.

"I am amazed by you, Taylor, but I learned a long time ago not to count on anything. That doesn't mean I think you're not important, it means bad shit happens every day. We've seen it. It brought us together. And it sucks, but it means I'm not walking into this with a future in mind. I'm just here, enjoying the moment with a beautiful woman in my borrowed bed."

She chuckled. "I like the sound of that."

He squeezed her to his side. She lazily ran her fingertips through his chest hair and down his stomach. She danced them back up, his pulse racing in anticipation of where her sweet little hand would go next.

She spread her fingers wide on the side of his face and turned it toward her. She met his mouth with hers, the earlier hesitancy gone as quickly as his resistance to her. They clashed in a flurry of tongues and lips and fingertips.

Taylor crawled on top of him, eliciting a welcome groan from Dex when her warmth settled over his pulsing erection. She pressed her body to his and kissed him again, his tongue meeting his and making promises his dick was anxious for her to keep.

Dex's hands went to her hips where a sliver of soft flesh was exposed between her tank and her pants. He rubbed his thumbs over the impossibly smooth skin, then slid his hands up, feeling her with all his fingers.

Taylor sat up, her body positioned right on top of his, and stripped off her tank in one quick move. Dex didn't know where to look, what to touch, where to taste first. His baser instincts tried to take control and thumped hard against the part of her that still hid from him.

"Fucking hell, you're stunning," he said, his voice quiet but firm. Her company was based on plus size women not feeling good in their sportswear. They hadn't talked about her own body image, but in his eyes, she was fucking perfect. Full, heavy breasts with dusky pink nipples that begged for his lips. A soft, curvy belly he couldn't stop touching. And the rest of her... He was just as anxious to see all of her.

Taylor snorted in response to his words. She looked away from him, but he thrust up against her.

"That's not because I'm closing my eyes and imagining another woman on top of me. That's because of you, Taylor. You are the woman I jerked off thinking about last night. You are the woman I want in this bed with me right now. And if you decide to leave, you will be the woman I will jerk off thinking about again in a little while. You are stunning. You're smart and sexy and I've wanted you since the day I caught you checking me out in your office."

She blushed and ducked her head. "You weren't supposed to mention that."

"Why not? Because you're embarrassed? It was not easy for me to have a conversation with you that day because all I kept thinking about was how sexy you looked."

"You did not."

Dex nodded. "You were wearing that bright top that floated around you and black leggings, and when I first saw you, I could tell you were in charge. A force to be reckoned with. My first thought was that you didn't need protection because you could handle yourself. My second thought was, I hope you hire me, anyway. And my third thought was, dammit, I blew it and the sexy business owner doesn't want me around. Now that sexy business owner is topless in the bed I'm sleeping in, and I'm about to lose my damn mind if I don't get my lips on you again. Soon."

A sly grin lifted her lips, and she fell forward onto him, their bare torsos connecting. Dex groaned as his brain misfired. Naked breasts on his chest, a naked back beneath his hands, and full wet lips against his. He needed all of it. He needed more of it. He couldn't get enough of it. Of her.

They kissed and touched each other's bodies, their touches growing more daring with each mind-numbing moment between them. When Taylor pulled back from their kiss and dragged her lips down his throat and over to his nipple, he about lost his mind.

"Fuck, Taylor."

"I like the way you say my name," she whispered as she moved to his other nipple. "Like you can't get enough of me."

"I can't, Taylor. I want all of you."

She kissed and licked and nipped lower, rubbing her taut nipples over his skin as she let her breasts sway with her movements. She kicked the covers away as she moved down the bed until she met the edge of his boxer briefs. She looked up at him with a question in her eyes.

Dex nodded and shifted his hips, helping her strip him bare. His cock pulsed under her appreciative gaze. A drop of precum flowed out, glistening at the tip. She leaned forward and licked it, then drew him into her mouth.

"Jesus. Fuck. Taylor."

She released him with a pop and looked up at him, her lips shiny and pink and so fuckable he wasn't sure he could hold back if she did that again.

"You're dangerous," he said when she grinned seductively at him.

"And you taste good. I want more."

He tried to protest, but it turned into a strangled groan when she sucked him into her mouth and added her hand.

The two worked in tandem, pulling his shaft in opposite ways before stroking to meet in the middle. His eyes rolled back in his head and his balls pulled up tight. He was not going to survive her.

"Taylor, fucking hell, you have to stop," he growled.

She stopped immediately and looked up at him. She snatched her hand back and sat on her knees. She looked around and reached for her shirt, but he grabbed it and pulled it out of her grasp.

"It's been a while, Taylor. Since I've been with anyone. I'm not telling you no. I just can't hold back. I want to be inside you. I want to make you come. I want... Fucking hell, Taylor, I want all of this. This isn't no. Not anywhere close to no. Let me touch you, taste you. Let me take care of you."

She raised an eyebrow and smirked. "You do know I can take care of myself, right?"

"Trust me, beautiful, I know. There's not a thing in the world you can't do. But I want to take care of you. Even if it's only for tonight, I want to make you come so hard you forget everything outside the walls of this bedroom. And then I want to do it again. I want to fill you up and make you scream. I want to kiss you until our lips are bruised. I want all of it with you. And I want to do it until you're sick of me. But if I don't stop that hot, wet mouth of yours, I'll be done before we really even get started."

Her smile was slow and sinful, the kind of thing fantasies were made out of. And when she crawled back up his body and pressed those tantalizing lips to his, he felt like he won something.

Her.

She tugged him over and let him press her to the mattress. Sheets and pillows got kicked off the bed, leaving them without obstructions as Dex took his turn kissing his way down her body. She lifted her hips for him to remove her pajama pants and panties. He licked and kissed through her curls and over her thighs until she squirmed and groaned in frustration.

"Is there something you need?" he asked, meeting her gaze over the horizon of her body.

"Your mouth on me."

"My pleasure," he said, his voice a growl as he took his first taste of her.

Her hips jerked up to meet his tongue, a shared moan filling the air between them. He pressed her thighs wider and adjusted his cock against the mattress so he didn't come without her.

Taylor moaned and cupped her breast, adding her own tease to his. He watched her fingers while he kept his tongue against her slit, tasting her. He suckled her flesh into his mouth, using his tongue to probe her entrance. She moaned and pressed her hips up again.

"Yes," she whimpered.

He replaced his tongue with one finger, easing into her tight heat. She relaxed against his intrusion and sucked the digit farther inside, her body gently pulsing around him.

Dex was a big fan of both giving and receiving oral sex, but it had never felt like it did with Taylor. He'd never been with a woman who wasn't afraid to show him exactly what she wanted, or ask for it. So, when she told him to suck hard on her clit, he listened.

And he was rewarded with the most beautiful orgasm he ever witnessed.

"Dex, oh, God, Dex. Yes! Your tongue. So fucking good. Oh, God."

She shuddered through her release and he was so lost in

it himself, she was riding another wave and falling once more.

The second one left her babbling incoherently, her fingers slipping off her nipples as she lost traction to help. He added a second finger to her tight channel and toyed with her flesh while she drifted back to earth.

The blissful look in her eyes was the most satisfying thing he'd ever seen. That he could do that for her... He could die a happy man after seeing that look.

"I need you. Inside me. Please, Dex."

Dex crawled up her body, kissing her sensitive flesh on his way. He avoided her lips, unsure how she felt about tasting herself. He reached for his bag, not far from the bed, and dug out a condom. He hadn't needed one in a while, but he always kept a few with him, just in case. Especially after he met Taylor and knew he wouldn't be able to resist her.

He rolled the condom on and positioned himself between her thighs again. She watched his face with an impatient smile. He nudged against her entrance, and the tightness in her gaze went away, replaced by only desire and need.

"Dex," she begged.

He took his time pressing into her, one inch at a time, until he was seated fully inside. Sweat covered his body from holding back the desire to slam into her and lose himself. She deserved better than that.

"Please. Don't hold back," she said.

"Taylor."

"I know you think you're going to hurt me, but you feel good. So fucking good. I'm already close. And I need..." She writhed just enough for him to realize she was barely holding back herself.

And it made him snap.

He pulled back and thrust forward, his hips slapping hard against hers. She let out a squeak of pleasure, driving him forward again and again until she screamed his name.

"Dex! Fuck me. Harder! Harder! Yes!"

She squeezed him so tight he saw stars. His throat closed up as tight as his balls and he buried himself deep inside her, and let go.

"Taylor," he moaned, her name like a prayer on his lips.

She reached for him, pulling his wrung out body down onto hers. And just like everything else about her, he couldn't resist falling.

16

———

Taylor held on to Dex and tried not to cry. She hadn't had an orgasm that good in years. Maybe ever. She couldn't remember the last time she'd let go like that. It was so fucking good.

She had a friend in college who dated a guy that she didn't like much, but she said the sex made up for the fact that the guy was just okay as a person. Taylor thought her friend was crazy, but after sex with Dex, she understood.

She was not looking forward to the day everything imploded, and he stopped speaking to her. It would happen, but she was already dreading it because missing out on sex like they just had was a shame.

"Wow," he finally said. He rolled off her, shifting her with him. He kissed her forehead, then left the bed. He went to the bathroom, leaving Taylor naked and completely exposed on the now bare mattress.

She didn't have the strength to move.

He was back a minute later and chuckled. "Did I wear you out?"

"Yes," she groaned, already starting to drift. "But it was worth it."

"Agreed," he said. He kissed her quickly, the minty flavor of his breath telling her he thought enough about her to brush his teeth before he kissed her again. Her heart squeezed at the thought.

"Come on, Sleeping Beauty." Dex chuckled as he pulled the blanket onto the bed and covered her up.

She realized she was sprawled diagonally across the bed and wiggled herself until her head was in the right spot. He tossed pillows onto the bed, then slid in next to her. He lifted his arm, and she used him as her pillow, curling up against his side.

She hadn't shared a bed with a man more than a handful of times. She craved her personal space. After sharing a room and occasionally a bed growing up, she liked being able to spread out and not worry about someone else being there. She told herself she'd leave in a few minutes and let her eyes close while Dex held her close.

The next thought Taylor had was that she was warm and cozy and her bed felt better than usual. She tried to figure out why when a hand drifted down her back and cupped her butt possessively.

Her eyes opened in an instant and landed on the sexy man the hand was attached to. His eyes were still closed, his breathing slow and even.

Sunlight was starting to peek through the curtains. Taylor wasn't a morning person, but she could definitely get used to mornings like that one.

She stilled at the thought, letting it rattle around in her brain. Whenever an ex said something similar, it caused a panic for Taylor. But with Dex... He wasn't her boyfriend. He wasn't really anything. But she enjoyed spending time with him. She felt safe and protected, and the soreness between her thighs reminded her those weren't the only things she felt with him.

She wanted to taste him, something she didn't get enough of the night before. She lifted her head just enough to peek at him. He was still sound asleep. But the tent in the middle of the bed said a part of him was awake.

Taylor slowly eased her way off his chest. She wiggled under the blanket Dex covered them with the night before. Her core clenched and readied for the beautiful cock she was face-to-face with. It was long and thick and felt so good inside her she wasn't sure she'd ever be able to have sex without wishing it was with that. Maybe she could mold it and have a toy created out of it so she'd always remember how good he felt.

She'd rather have the real thing, though. And for the moment, she wanted the real thing in her mouth.

She licked the underside of him, smiling to herself when he jerked at the soft touch. She licked the glistening tip, then spread her lips wide and took him into her mouth. He thrust up, still asleep, but his body taking control.

Taylor added her hand to his shaft. She started out slow, working her hand and mouth opposite as she let him wake up. After a minute, she cupped his balls and tugged. He groaned, then reached for her.

The blanket flipped off her head as she brought her hand back to his shaft and stroked firm and fast. His hooded gaze met hers. Fire. Danger. Promised retribution. It all hung there between them with the unspoken lust that fueled her need to have him for breakfast.

He watched her, his eyes locked on her face while she stroked him. At one point, he closed his eyes, then forced them open so he could watch. She added her other hand so she could play with his balls, and he groaned and gave up on watching her.

"Taylor," he growled. His first word of the day in a strangled, husky tone that was part warning and part request.

She didn't pull back or slow down. She wanted all of him.

"Taylor," he said again, his tone higher, the warning less subtle. "Taylor, I can't..."

She tugged his testicles harder and opened her mouth to take him in deeper. A strangled growl was the only other warning she got before he swelled between her lips and exploded into her mouth.

Taylor kept stroking him until the spurts stopped and he sank against the mattress, spent and sated. She pulled back and swallowed him down, then licked the tip of him. She crawled back up beside him and collapsed against his sweaty side.

"That was a hell of a way to wake up," he said in her hair.

"I wanted to do that last night, but you wouldn't let me."

"Thank you. That was... damn."

She chuckled. "I agree. But now I need a shower. Come on. The one in my room is bigger. Big enough to share."

She got out of the bed and walked naked to her room, knowing he would follow her. She hadn't even turned the water on when his hands were sliding up and down her body, teasing her into her own morning orgasm.

When they finally made it downstairs, they were running late. Taylor hadn't been late to a job since she had her own way of getting there, but it was totally worth it for the morning she had with Dex.

They rushed through getting out the door, working seamlessly in tandem as though they'd been doing it for far longer than a few days. He started the coffee while she packed up her bags, then she fixed their coffees while he gathered his stuff. She handed a travel mug over as they both picked up their bags and rushed out to his SUV.

A few people were already in the office when they arrived, including Jessica. Her assistant gave Dex and Taylor a slow once-over, her perceptive grin widening by the second, but was blissfully silent. At least until Dex settled at his desk, after a private wink for Taylor.

"You two look cozy," Jessica said as she walked into Taylor's office.

Taylor tried not to smile, but great sex made that futile. "Yesterday was tough, and he was amazing."

Jessica raised a perfect eyebrow and gave Taylor a look that said she wasn't buying it.

"Okay, fine. The sex we had last night was amazing. And this morning."

Jessica's enthusiastic smile chased away all of Taylor's doubts about sleeping with the man who was there to protect her. It was impossible to think twice about it when someone else thought it was such a great idea.

"Well, I think you two are good together. And you deserve some happiness. You should grab hold and enjoy it."

Taylor couldn't stop her smile. "Thank you. Maybe one day my brother will pull his head out of his ass and you can grab hold of your own happiness."

Jessica's cheeks reddened, and she flapped her hands wildly like she could wipe away Taylor's words. "I don't... We're not... He's..." She rolled her lips in and shook her head sharply. "I don't know what you're talking about."

Taylor smirked at her. "Oh, sorry. I guess I misread the situation."

Jessica nodded firmly, her face and neck still beet red. "You did. Um, so your schedule for today. Are you ready to get started?"

"Yep. Only a few days left. Let's do it."

Jessica launched into their plans for the day. Taylor reminded herself this was her dream. Curling up in bed with Dex all day and all night definitely felt like a dream, but it wouldn't pay the bills. She had to focus and get through the launch and kick the ass of whoever was after her.

Maybe breakfast first, though.

DEX FINISHED the research he was working on the night before and admitted defeat. He couldn't figure out who was after Taylor. He was having just as much luck helping the team track down Dennis Parker. Nothing was going his way.

Except Taylor.

He wasn't the kind of guy who could put his personal life ahead of his professional one, though. He enjoyed his night with Taylor, but he was also there to make sure nothing happened to her. He felt like he was one misstep away from failing that job.

He checked in with Taylor before lunch and made sure she would stay in the office, then headed over to F-BOMB to see his team. He needed an update, and he needed to talk over what he wasn't finding to see what he was missing.

Everyone was in the conference room when he arrived. They gave him a warm welcome, which was strange, although appreciated.

"How are things going with Braden's sister?" Mason asked.

"Depends on the moment. Yesterday really shook her up. I can't figure out how this guy is getting in or where or anything. It's making me crazy."

"What did your woman say?" Jack asked.

"She's anxious, understandably. She's also tough and isn't backing down even though it's clear that's exactly what this asshole wants."

The room was silent, staring at Dex with a variety of surprise on their faces.

"What?" he barked.

"Nothing," Mason hurried to say. "She sounds great. Megan said she likes Taylor. What can we do to help?"

The looks around the room made Dex feel as though he missed something, but he wasn't sure what it was. He shook it off and laid out what he'd been researching, explaining to them how he needed help.

"I think you're looking in the wrong places," English said. "Your search is too big. You're looking for clues where there aren't any. Whoever broke into her home and her office knew the schedule and how to bypass the alarms. He knew just enough to get away with it without sending up any warning flags. Maybe we should be looking at employees of the alarm company. Instead of focusing on her list, we can focus on theirs." He typed in a few keys. "There, the employee list." He spun the computer toward Dex.

"This has hire dates on it," Dex said with awe in his voice.

"Yep. And it should tell you if any of these people were let go. You said we're dealing with a man so we can eliminate everyone who identifies as female or nonbinary. This is just the local office, so it's not a long list. Start searching here."

Dex scanned it. Less than thirty names. And only one he

recognized. "Steven."

"Do you know him?" Dunn asked.

"He's a guard in her building. I looked into him briefly already and nothing popped up, but I didn't dig too deep. He definitely has a thing for Taylor. I didn't like him the day I met him. She said he's friendly, but I think he's a little too friendly."

"Wouldn't want anyone moving in on your woman," Jack said.

"Yeah," Dex answered before he realized what he agreed to. "Wait. She's not my woman."

"Are you sure about that?" Archer asked.

"Of course. I'm there to protect her. That's it." Dex glared around the room.

"Jack called her your woman ten minutes ago, and you didn't notice. Maybe protecting her isn't all there is to it," Slade said.

"She's not mine. She's her own woman."

"That isn't a no," Rocky said.

"Son of a bitch," Dex muttered. "Taylor is a smart, beautiful, amazing woman. Do I like her? Yes. Is that what you want to hear? But she's made it very clear she's not interested in a relationship. Said she's not any good at them and whatever is going on between us is temporary."

Jaws dropped around the room.

"What?"

"I didn't think you'd admit it," Slade said.

"Neither did I," Jack agreed.

"Enjoy it while it lasts, but keep an open mind," Dunn added.

"Screw all of you. Help me find this guy so we can keep her safe."

They buckled down and went through all the employee

files. By the end, Dex had a shorter list of just over a dozen, including Steven, to keep digging into. He headed back to Taylor's office, feeling like he was making progress. He was going to find whoever was after her. And he was going to make sure they didn't get close to her again.

WHEN IT WAS FINALLY time to leave for the night, Taylor was more than ready to go home, sink into her tub, and forget the world for a few hours. It had been a productive day, but the closer they got to the launch, the more tension there was in the air. Adding in the threats and everyone in the office was on edge. Which meant they were snapping at each other. Not good.

Taylor had to stop more than one argument that popped up during meetings and she was more than ready for her well-deserved break.

Dex herded her into the SUV and gave her a quick kiss that left a smile on her lips. He started the vehicle without a sound, as though he understood she needed quiet time to decompress from her day.

Taylor closed her eyes and leaned back in the seat, letting peace and calm wash over her. She took a deep breath and let it out on a relaxing sigh. She was finally feeling better.

Dex jerked the wheel hard to the right, throwing Taylor toward the center console. Her eyes popped open as she looked outside at where they were. "What was that all about?"

"We're being followed."

"What?" Taylor looked back just as another vehicle took the same turn. "Who is it?"

"I don't know."

Taylor looked at the warrior in the driver's seat. His jaw was set firm, his eyes sharp and focused on the road ahead. Every so often, he'd glance at the mirror to watch for the vehicle behind them. A vehicle that wasn't deterred by Dex's sharp, last-minute turns.

"What should we do? Should I call the cops?" Taylor asked.

Dex hesitated, then nodded. "That's not a bad idea. Give them our location and tell them someone is following us. Ask for Captain Patrick, if he's on. He works with us a lot."

Taylor's fingers bounced against her screen as she struggled to dial 9-1-1. A woman answered and asked what her emergency was.

"Someone is following me. I need to speak to Captain Patrick," Taylor said.

A series of clicks said the woman was looking something up. "Can you give me your location while I get in touch with Captain Patrick?"

Taylor told the woman where they were and glanced back at the vehicle still tailing them. She felt like she was in a movie. She always told herself she'd be calm under pressure instead of stupid and reckless like so many movie characters, but sitting in the seat beside Dex, she knew she was not the calm one.

"I'm connecting Captain Patrick now. I've updated him on your situation," the woman said.

"Patrick," a brusque male voice said.

"Put it on speaker," Dex told her.

Taylor hit the speaker button, and Dex took over the conversation.

"Captain, this is Ryker Hamilton. I've been watching Ms. Wright since she received a dead bird in the mail a week ago. Officer Shaw investigated the incident. Right now, we're in one of our SUVs, but we have a dark blue sedan following us. Been on us since we left her office. No longer hiding the fact that he's tailing us."

"Can you drive here, Hamilton? Bring the guy right to the station?"

"That was my plan. I'm heading in that direction. We should be to you in about two minutes. Coming from the west."

"I'll get a team outside right now. Have you seen any weapons?"

"No, but I can't see how many people are in the vehicle or even identify who's driving. He's smart."

"You know it's a male?"

Dex looked at Taylor and raised an eyebrow. Taylor sighed and knew she had to confess. "Hi, um, this is Taylor Wright. After I received the bird, I got a phone call from someone who said they knew me in the past. A male. I didn't recognize his voice. Then a day later, he broke into my home."

"I'm not seeing any of this in the report. I'll have to speak to Officer Shaw about that." Captain Patrick's voice was laced with steel and anger.

"He doesn't know. I didn't want to tell anyone. Dex knows because he knows my brother and has been staying with me, but I wouldn't let him call the police."

"Ms. Wright—"

"Fifteen seconds, sir," Dex said firmly.

"We're ready. I see you." He paused. "I don't see anyone behind you, though."

Taylor turned back. The vehicle that was following them was gone. Vanished, like it had never been there.

"Where did it go?"

17

Dex swore and looked in his mirror. The car was behind them when he pulled onto the street. The guy must have figured out what he was doing and peeled off before he got too close to the station. Cameras surrounded it, and they would have had an easy time identifying the car and anyone in it if he drove by.

"Dammit," Dex mumbled. "We're still pulling in. You need to give Captain Patrick your statement. This is too much, Taylor."

She nodded, her face falling as she accepted the truth. Whoever was after her wasn't going to stop until he got to her.

Dex parked and waited for Captain Patrick to indicate they could get out of the SUV. The other officers walked away, leaving only Captain Patrick to speak to them.

"Well, I didn't want a call like this. I'll have one of my guys look through cameras in the area. Did he turn with you?"

"Yep. I didn't realize he was gone until you said it. Fuck."

Taylor stood next to him, her arms crossed over her

stomach. She chewed on the inside of her lip, staring out at the street as cars passed, oblivious to what almost happened right there in front of them.

"Should we go inside?" Captain Patrick asked, picking up on Taylor's anxiety.

Dex put his hand on her back, and she jumped. She looked up at him with an apologetic smile and took a step closer to him. He wrapped his arm around her waist and supported her as they made their way into the station.

The three of them went into Captain Patrick's office. He pulled up the report from Officer Shaw and asked Taylor and Dex to fill in everything that had happened since then.

"Is your team on this?" Patrick asked when Taylor was finished.

"We are, but we haven't gotten far. We're tied up with the other case also, so this has been mostly me so far. English helped a little earlier today, but I still don't have any solid leads."

"Who are you looking at?"

Dex hesitated and glanced at Taylor. She was watching him closely. He hadn't shared his latest information with her, and he was fairly sure she was going to be pissed. "Um, well, I was looking into the employees of the security company. People who could have had access to the business and home of Ms. Wright."

Captain Patrick nodded, his flattened smile saying he agreed. Taylor's face was not so happy.

"Do you still think this was Steven?"

"Who's Steven?"

"He's the security guard in my office building. He's a nice guy who likes to flirt with me. And Dex seems to have an issue with that." She pursed her lips and dared him to argue.

He couldn't.

"Is there a reason he shouldn't be a suspect?"

"Yes! He works in my building. I know him. He's a nice guy."

"They said the same thing about Ted Bundy," Dex countered.

Taylor gasped. "That's not fair."

"Maybe not, but did you happen to notice Steven at work when we left?"

"No, but I wasn't paying attention."

"Well, I was. And he wasn't there."

"It's late. He was there this morning."

"Yes, he was. And the morning after your office was trashed," Dex said pointedly. He knew he was being an ass, but he was an ass tasked with protecting her, even if that meant protecting her from her own blind spots.

"He's not... I just can't imagine that it's him."

"I've thought the same thing in the past. People suck." Dex still felt a pang when he thought about his former CO, a man who turned on them all and tried to kill them. Only after he did kill one of their teammates before they left the Navy. Brady Williams was a piece of work, and a piece of shit.

"Okay, let's keep going," Patrick said, his firm voice telling Dex their bickering wasn't getting anything done. "I think the security group is a good idea. And since we're talking about criminal behavior, including assault, I'd like to put someone on this. Did you have any issues with Officer Shaw?"

Taylor shook her head, but a twitch of her lip told Dex there was something she didn't want to admit.

"What happened?"

"Excuse me?"

"What happened? There's a reason you don't want him.

What is it?" Dex demanded. If the officer wasn't good, he didn't need to be the one who handled Taylor's case.

"Nothing. He was fine. Polite."

"But..."

She huffed a frustrated sigh and glared at him. "He was dismissive of me because of my weight. He was checking out some of the thinner, curvier employees. Which isn't a surprise, but he was there to do a job and couldn't remember my name because I wasn't hot enough or whatever."

The pink circles on her cheeks told him he embarrassed her with the questions and forcing her to answer in front of Captain Patrick. Too late, but he still felt bad.

"He's an idiot," Dex said roughly. "You're perfect, and he shouldn't have been checking anyone out. He should have been paying attention to what you said."

Taylor tried to act like it didn't bother her, but her shoulders didn't fall back down all the way. They hung up around her ears, tense and uneasy.

"I'll handle this," Captain Patrick said. "This will be my case."

"You don't have to."

He looked at the file once more. "I need to stay involved in what's going on, and this case is bigger than I'd trust Officer Shaw with, anyway. I'll dig and keep Dex posted. Or you..."

Taylor shook her head. "No, Dex is fine. He's staying with me, so I'll know when you call."

The captain's brows jumped for the briefest of seconds before he forced them back into a neutral position. He snapped the paper file closed. "I'll be in touch."

Dex kept his hand on Taylor's back while they walked

through the station and back out into the afternoon sunlight.

"Are you ready to go home?"

She shook her head and nibbled on her lip again. "I'm not sure where I want to go, but I don't feel safe there. Not right now. If you really think this could be someone from my security company, how do we know they don't still have a camera in my house or a feed or something?"

Dex drew a breath and pulled her into his arms. They were blocked from the road but visible to the cameras and anyone inside who looked out. He kept the move chaste, even as he hardened at the feel of her softness against his body.

"I want to tell you it's highly unlikely, because it is, but I can't tell you it's impossible. English and Jack are good, but they used what was there and rerouted the service to ours. If the old service wasn't turned off, or if someone had a separate link to the feed, we have no idea."

She shivered and pressed her face into his chest. "I hate this. I can't go to work, and I can't go home. Where the hell am I supposed to go?"

He knew the question was rhetorical, but he had an answer, anyway. "Why don't you come to my place? I live with English, but he's not going to be home tonight, so it would just be the two of us. Our place is not anywhere near what yours is, but it's under constant surveillance and no one has a link. We set up the system ourselves and know it's as secure as possible."

"I can't ask you to do that."

"Why not? If you'll feel safer there, then that's where we should go. We can go to a hotel if you'd rather, or a safe house, or we can stay at your place. I'll do everything in my power to keep you safe, but if you don't feel safe, you won't be able to relax."

She drew a shaky breath. "Any chance you have a big bathtub?"

He gave her a wide grin. "As a matter of fact, I do."

AFTER TAYLOR'S bath in Dex's surprisingly perfect tub, she pulled on one of his tees and a pair of panties. She looked around his simple bedroom and smiled. It suited him.

He was at the table in his kitchen when she walked out. He had a computer in front of him, but something smelled good enough to make her stomach growl.

"How was your bath?" he asked without looking up.

"Amazing. That tub is spectacular."

He closed the laptop, then turned to face her. "I agree. I use it at least once a week."

"Why didn't you join me?" she asked. He pulled her onto his lap, and she wrapped her arms around his neck. His hands held her tightly against him.

"I figured you could use a break. It's been... stressful. I didn't want to add to that."

"You're the opposite of that."

"Except when it comes to Steven." His gentle wince told her he didn't want to talk about it, but he knew they needed to.

"I don't trust people very easily. My parents were useless, and we never had anyone take any interest in us growing up. My mom's boyfriends only paid us enough attention to make her think they would give her money, then ignored us as soon as she slept with them. My dad was only around when he wanted sex from her. No one cared. Steven was the one who showed me around the office space before I moved in there. He was flirtatious, but I wasn't used to that either. I know I'm being dumb, but I just have a hard time thinking it could be him."

Dex nodded slowly. "I get it. I... I don't trust anyone. I trust my brothers, but outside our group... I don't know the last person I trusted. I am not looking into Steven because I'm jealous, even though I am, I'm looking into him because I'm worried about you. I don't want you hurt."

"I know. And I appreciate that. Almost as much as I appreciate whatever it is you cooked for dinner. Because right now, I'm starving."

Dex chuckled with her and led her to the kitchen where he pulled something out of the oven. "It should be hot enough. What can I get you to drink?"

"Water, please."

Dex handed her a glass and filled one for himself. He fixed two plates for them and carried them to the couch where they sat and watched a movie.

Taylor didn't fall asleep that time, and when the movie was over, she crawled onto his lap.

"You look a little more relaxed." His hands went to her hips and held her against him.

"I am. But I know how I could be a lot more relaxed."

"Oh, yeah? How's that?" The quirk on the side of his mouth and his wandering hands said he knew the answer to that question already.

"I think you should show me that big bed of yours and check if I cleaned every inch of myself in your tub."

He pulsed between her thighs. "I think that's a great idea. It can be really easy to miss parts when you're in the tub. Some places you can't reach as easily."

"Trust me, I can reach," she said cheekily.

"I should check anyway."

"Just in case," they said together.

They kissed as they fumbled to the bedroom. Dex's hands slid under the shirt she stole from his drawer and found her bare breasts. He groaned and yanked the shirt off her, dipping his head to capture one nipple with his mouth. Taylor moaned and leaned against the wall, holding his head in place while he drove her crazy.

"That one's clean," he said as he kissed his way around her breast. "Need to check the other one."

Taylor moaned softly as his tongue flicked her peaked nipple. He sucked it into his mouth and held it deep inside, teasing it with his tongue while she begged him to let her come.

"Can you like this?" he asked, his lips still around her nipple.

"No, but it feels so damn good."

"You feel good, Taylor." He stepped back and turned her around, pressing his body to her back and guiding her into the bedroom. One hand cupped her wet nipple, and the other cupped her wet center.

"Oh, God," she moaned as he slicked his fingers through her curls and found her clit. "Yes."

"How about like this? Can you come like this for me?"

Her legs trembled as she gave him a shaky nod. She wasn't sure her legs would hold, but she'd do her best not to collapse.

"You're wet. Were you thinking about me in your bath? I wanted to join you so bad."

"I wish you had."

"Next time." He nudged her hair off her neck and bit down on the curve leading to her shoulder.

"Yes," she moaned. The effort it took to stay on her feet

was pulling her focus from the orgasm barreling down on her. She whimpered and trembled.

"I got you, Taylor. Let me have your weight."

She leaned forward a little, testing his words, and he held her tight. Her legs quaked, her orgasm closer, and his fingers plucked at her clit. The sharp bite of it launched her over the edge and into bliss. Bliss that came with a complete loss of leg function.

But Dex held firm, the masterful man and his fantastical fingers.

"Oh, God, yes. Dex. Fuck. Me. Yes. So good. So fucking good."

She barely had time to register the end of the orgasm before he spun her and deposited her onto his bed on her back. He kneeled at the edge and gently eased her soaked panties down her thighs, the cool air of the room lifting goosebumps on the sensitive flesh between her thighs.

His hands pressed her thighs wide and lowered himself between them. She tried to fight him, knowing it made no sense, but in the bright light of his bedroom, she felt over-exposed.

"Taylor," Dex growled, not budging from his spot.

"I haven't shaved."

"I know, and I don't expect you to. You're a beautiful woman, and this is the most perfect pussy I've ever seen. I don't want some weird design or bare skin. I want a woman. A strong, sexy, stunning woman with a pretty pink pussy that's dripping for me." He eased a thick finger into her and dragged the wetness out and up to her clit. "It definitely feels like that's you, but I think I need a closer look to make sure you're very, very clean down here."

She groaned as he licked through her folds and swirled his tongue around her clit. His finger made another sweep inside her, sending her already spiraling thoughts into the stratosphere. The only thing that mattered was Dex and her and the moment in front of them.

Dex took his time, licking all over her with long, slow licks that felt like heaven, then quick, short licks that were definitely on the road to heaven. She couldn't decide which she liked more and decided it didn't matter as long as he never, ever stopped.

He added a second finger and the quick, short licks became the preferred option as her body demanded another orgasm. She was along for the ride as Dex licked and sucked and fucked her until lights flashed behind her closed lids and everything she thought she knew about life righted itself in the man in front of her, the man who self-lessly protected her, thought of her, and made her boneless and quivering all at the same time.

Dex kissed his way up her body, taking his time to follow the trail of flushed skin. He sheathed himself, then lined up with her entrance and thrust inside her in one fast, thick stroke.

Taylor erupted around him instantly, the orgasm pulsing through her at the sudden, intense feel of him buried deep inside her.

"Are you okay?" he asked, holding deep but frozen.

"More," she begged, her voice rough from screaming. "So good."

Dex didn't hesitate to repeat the punishing move, holding her knees wide as he pounded into her over and over again. Her body spun up and up and up until she fell over, coming with a shout that convulsed her body and made her wonder, again, where sex like that had been all her life.

"It's you," she said quietly, the words slipping out without a thought.

"You, Taylor. Us. So fucking good," Dex grunted. He buried himself deep on the next stroke. Veins on his neck pulsed in time with the swell and eruption inside her. He groaned with the effort it took to stay upright, his arms shaking as he twitched inside her.

Taylor wrapped her arms around him and pulled him onto her. Their legs were off the bed, but her back was on it and she could hold him. She could give him something. After everything he'd given her, she could give him this.

His breath escaped him in rough pants while she held him. Hers did the same, but she knew it wasn't just the amazing sex that had her struggling to breathe. For her, it was the knowledge that the man she kissed when she was drunk, and slept with when she was scared, and let into her body, hadn't stopped there. He was buried deep in her heart, too.

And she was pretty sure he wasn't going to get out of there anytime soon. Because love was like that.

18

DEX WOKE SLOWLY TO THE WARM, COZY FEEL OF A WOMAN IN his bed. He couldn't resist the pull of her body, teasing and toying with her until she was wet and ready for him. Which made them late. Again.

Taylor was googly eyed as they walked into her office, so Dex figured he didn't upset her with their sleepy morning sex. He was beginning to wonder how he was going to go back to sleeping alone, and it had only been two nights that he'd held her. He was in trouble.

They made it through the morning without another incident. Dex was starting to breathe a little easier. He did his research into the employees from the security company and had to admit that Steven wasn't a legitimate suspect. He still didn't like the guy, but his whereabouts were easily accounted for on multiple occasions that left Dex with the knowledge that the man harassing Taylor was not Steven.

Eliminating Steven and a few others also narrowed his list down to three. One was a long-time employee with a shady past, which made Dex wonder how he got a job at a security company. One was new to the area and new to working security, and had very little information available online. And the third was not new to security, but was new to the company and started less than a month before Taylor's attacks began. Like the second one, the last one had little information available publicly, and what was there gave Dex an odd feeling. It felt like his profile was faked.

He wanted to ask Taylor if she recognized any of the men, but she was in a meeting. Dex walked over to Jessica's desk to get on Taylor's calendar. And to steal a piece of her candy.

"Hey," he said. He pointed to the visitor's chair next to Jessica's desk. She nodded for him to sit.

"What's up?" she asked, typing furiously while he sat.

"Does she have any free time today? I want her to look at a few pictures."

Jessica clicked a few things, then studied the screen in front of her. "It looks like she just added a meeting at the warehouse in a few minutes. I'm assuming you'll go with her. Do you need more time than the drive over there?"

"No, probably not. The warehouse meeting wasn't on her calendar before?"

"No. I would have remembered that. She doesn't go over there often. We review her schedule every morning and didn't talk about that."

"Does that mean there's an issue?"

Jessica shrugged. "I don't know. She should be off her call in a minute."

Dex looked through the glass walls to Taylor. She was laughing at whoever was on the other end, and his lips lifted in response.

"She's a force, isn't she?" Jessica asked.

Dex nodded. "She sure is. She's impressive."

"It's nice to see her happy, too."

Dex snapped his focus back to Jessica, who was looking at him with an all-knowing gleam in her eyes. He didn't know how much Jessica really knew, but he wasn't about to share any secrets with one of Taylor's employees.

"Anyway, I'm glad you're here. Do you want me to look at the pictures? Is it something I can help with?"

Dex held up a finger and went back to his desk. He grabbed the laptop he had all his research on and carried it back to Jessica. "Have you seen any of these men? They work for the security company, so you might have seen them in the building, but if you've seen them at all, it could help."

Jessica took her time studying each photo and dismissed each one. "No, I don't recognize any of them. Do you think it's someone from the security company who's doing this? Someone's watching us?"

At the panicked rise in her voice, Dex snapped the computer shut and kicked himself for worrying her. "It's just a theory. We don't really know. We're looking into every possibility. Taylor's list after the bird arrived didn't point us in any directions so we expanded the options. Looking at the security company was a good next step, but if we rule out all of those people, then we'll keep digging. We'll find whoever is behind this."

Jessica hugged her arms to herself and shivered. Her shoulders pulled up and her lip slid between her teeth.

"My team is looking into everything and we have a copy of everything happening. We're not relying on a company we aren't sure we can trust. You're safe here."

Jessica nodded again, a quick, jerky movement that told Dex she didn't believe him.

"Hey, I have to go to the warehouse. Do you want to go with me?" Taylor paused. "Jessica... Are you okay?"

Jessica forced a smile for Taylor and loosened her grip

on herself. She met Taylor's gaze and lied more easily than Dex thought she'd be able to. "Of course. Just got a little cold. How long are you going to be at the warehouse?"

"Not long. Eve said there's a delivery for me there. It came in this morning sometime. Something from one of our suppliers, I guess. I'm going to go over there and pick it up."

"Are you sure that's a good idea?" Dex asked. He hated being on edge and untrusting all the time, but it was his job.

"It'll be fine. If there was anything to worry about, they would have told me." She gave him a look like he was being crazy, but Dex didn't feel crazy. He felt like they were getting closer to whoever was after her, and that usually made people more dangerous.

Dex took in Taylor's irritated look and said, "I'll come with you."

"Good. Jessica, do you want us to pick up lunch while we're out? Then you don't have to worry about it?"

Jessica shook her head. "It's fine. I already put an order in. I'll head down with you now if you're ready and go get it. I ordered for Sharon and Emily, too."

"Thank you. I know I don't say it enough, but I really appreciate all you do. I couldn't keep my head above water if it weren't for you."

Jessica smiled what looked like a real smile. She grabbed her purse and her jacket, then turned and followed Taylor to the elevator. Dex hung back, carrying his laptop so he could ask Taylor about the men while he drove, and giving the women a chance to talk without the reminder of why he was there.

Jessica was back to her normal self by the time they made it to the garage. Dex waited until she was in her vehicle and pulling out before he backed out and left the garage behind her. Jessica turned right, and they went left, so he lost her quickly, but he told himself there was no reason to worry about her. She hadn't been a target yet. It wasn't likely to change. Especially not in broad daylight.

"Open that up and look at the pictures." Dex pointed to the laptop he slid against the center console.

Taylor did as he asked and asked, "Who are they?"

"Suspects. They all work for the security company. Do you recognize any of them?"

Taylor shook her head, then stopped. "Wait. I know this guy. He looks different from the last time I saw him, but I know him. He was friends with my brother. We went to grad school together."

"What?"

"Yeah, his name is Jonah Hampton, right?"

Dex glanced at the photo of the man he knew as Matt Warner. "That's not the name he used when he got hired."

"What? Why would he change his name?"

"Maybe because Jonah Hampton has a record. Or maybe because he doesn't want a trail. Or maybe—"

"There's a perfectly legitimate and legal reason?" Taylor asked.

"Yeah, sure, maybe. But maybe not. We're in the middle of a fight for your life, Taylor. And you just picked a man out of a photo who probably knows your childhood nickname. How well did you know him in college?"

"Not well. We had classes together in grad school. We actually applied for the same job after grad school. I got it... over him."

"And there's motive." Dex gripped the steering wheel so tight his knuckles ached. He clenched his jaw and resisted the urge to tear into her. "Why wasn't he on your list?"

"Because it's been years. I finished grad school forever ago. I've moved on from that job and forgotten about those days. Do you honestly think he's still carrying a grudge from almost two decades ago?"

"I honestly think he should have been on your short list of enemies. And yes, I think it's very possible he's carrying a grudge from that long ago. People are fucking crazy."

Taylor sulked in her seat while Dex drove the rest of the way to the warehouse. He had a name, and a lead, and he'd managed to piss her off. He was having a great fucking day.

When they made it to the warehouse, Taylor slammed the door shut while Dex grabbed his laptop. He wasn't taking any chances that someone got a hold of it while he was inside. He called Dunn as he followed Taylor, needing help to find Jonah Hampton.

"Dunn," the other man answered, even though Dex knew his name showed up on his phone.

"I think I have a suspect. I need some help finding him. He works for the security company, but he's using a fake name."

Dunn listened as Dex detailed everything he knew about the man supposedly named Matt Warner and asked Dunn to find everything they could about Jonah Hampton.

"We're on it. I'll be in touch soon."

"Thanks." Dex hung up and went over to where Taylor was speaking to Eve and touching the petals of an oversized bouquet.

"Very sweet," the other woman was saying.

"It is. I didn't even know he knew what I was doing. We haven't had much of a relationship. I didn't realize he was in the area," Taylor said.

"Who?" Dex asked.

"My father." Taylor gave him a pointed look that said not to ask any other questions.

Dex let it go. It was more than a little odd that her father sent flowers to the warehouse instead of to her office, and that he sent anything when they hadn't been in touch for years. But he wasn't about to question her about any of that with another employee standing nearby. Not after the disaster he made of things with Jessica.

"So, how are things going with the early shipments? Everything okay?"

"Yeah, absolutely. It's made a huge difference around here. Safer. Much better."

"Excellent. I'm happy to hear that." Taylor glanced around the space. "Do you mind if we walk around a little?"

"Of course not. Just wear your hardhats so you're easier to see. We don't want anyone getting hurt."

"Absolutely."

Taylor looked way too cute in her neon orange hardhat. Dex chuckled when she puckered up for him. They walked silently for a few minutes before Taylor started talking.

"I don't know what to think about my dad sending me flowers."

"When's the last time you heard from him?"

Taylor stared at the floor and thought about it. "I can't even remember. A long time."

"Years or decades?"

"Maybe a decade. He wasn't around when we were growing up. Not much. Every so often he'd show up, but he never stayed. He never provided for us. He's not really a father to me."

"Why does it upset you?"

Her shoulders were tense and her movements unsteady. "I told you I don't trust people. He's why. He would come back for long enough to sleep with my mom and take whatever money she had. He'd leave her broke and pregnant and not care. And now..."

"You think he wants your money," Dex finished for her.

Taylor nodded slowly. "It's hard to imagine there's anything else he's after. He's never been interested in anything else."

"What does your dad do?"

She shrugged. "I have no idea. He never talked about a job. He would say he had things going on, but he never shared details, and he never brought home money for us. I always assumed he really didn't work."

"Or he was involved in something illegal."

Her brows lifted quickly in consideration, then settled once more. "Yeah, that's possible. I wouldn't put it past him, I guess. But this... I don't like it."

"You're entitled to that feeling. You don't have to roll over and do everything your parents say."

She considered his words carefully. "I always wanted him to be around. Thirty years ago, I needed him. I needed someone. But now... why is he trying to be a dad now?"

"It might be like you said. You've been getting a lot of publicity lately. Maybe he saw some of it and decided you were a good way to repay his debts or make a quick buck or any number of things."

"I wish I could ask him. He wasn't the kind of person who would lie. For all his faults, he never promised to stay or to be there or to help. He told us the truth."

"I'm not sure that makes him trustworthy, but—"

"Not a liar and trustworthy are definitely two different things. If I knew what he wanted, I'd give it to him so he would go away."

"You'd give it to him? If he wanted money, you'd hand it over?"

She nodded without hesitation. "I have enough. And if it

meant he was out of my life, and my siblings' lives, yeah. I absolutely would."

"Wow. You're better than me. I'd tell him where he can shove his request."

She chuckled. "I don't know if that makes me better. I think it makes you smarter."

Dex pulled her into his arms, resting his cheek against the top of her head. They embraced for a long moment before Taylor pulled back and announced they should get back to the office.

Dex carried the flowers to the SUV and put them on the floorboard in the back. Taylor glanced back at them every so often, but she was quiet.

He turned onto the street that led to her building and stopped dead. Police cars and an ambulance surrounded the building. It was a busy area, but the sinking feeling in his gut told him it wasn't a coincidence.

Taylor gasped, then her phone rang in her bag. She dug through it, her attention half on the flashing lights and half on finding the phone.

"It's Jessica," she said before she answered. "Hey. We're in front of the building. What's going on?"

"Ms. Wright?" a man's voice said.

Dex heard the tone through the phone and met Taylor's gaze. Speaker, he mouthed.

She pulled the phone back and tapped the speaker button. "Yes, this is Taylor Wright."

"My name is Officer Shaw. We met last week."

"Yes, I remember you."

"I'm at your office again. One of your employees has been attacked. Jessica German. She's hurt badly and asked me to call you before she's transported to the hospital."

Dex watched as a stretcher was wheeled to the back of

the ambulance. He couldn't see details of who it was, but the dark hair against the white sheet, combined with Officer Shaw's confirmation, told him exactly who it was.

"Is Jessica okay?"

"She will be, Ms. Wright. If you'd like to meet her at Saint Nicholas's Hospital, she'll be there soon. I'll be handling the investigation into what happened."

"Call Captain Patrick," Dex said loudly.

"Who is this?"

"My name is Ryker Hamilton. I work for F-BOMB. Ms. Wright and I spoke with Captain Patrick yesterday. He has more information on this case. Please call him."

"Yes, sir," the officer said in a tone that told them exactly how he felt about the request. "I'm going to give Ms. German her phone back. I'll be in touch when I have something to share."

"Thank you," Taylor said. Her phone nearly slid from her hands. She swung a watery gaze toward Dex and clamped down on her shaky lower lip. "Jessica is on her way to the hospital. Because of me."

Dex knew she wasn't to blame and tried to reassure her as the ambulance pulled away. "This is not on you. Jessica will be fine. I'll call Lily. She works at the hospital and will make sure Jessica is taken care of. I promise."

Taylor nodded as tears rolled down her cheeks. Dex wanted to comfort her, but until they knew how badly Jessica was hurt, he couldn't make her any promises.

He hit a button on the dashboard and told the SUV to call Lily. She picked up on the first ring.

"Well, this isn't the usual number I get calls from. What's going on?"

"Hey, Lil. I'm with Taylor. One of her employees was attacked. She's on her way to your hospital right now. EMTs are bringing her in. We don't know any details, but wondered if you could make anything happen."

"Of course." Lily's voice was calm and soothing, and Dex hoped it helped Taylor. "Can Taylor hear me?"

"Yeah."

"Taylor, we'll do everything we can to help her. I'm heading down there right now to make sure everyone knows she's a VIP and to be catered to. Are you guys on your way?"

"Yes," Taylor said weakly.

"Okay. I'll meet you there."

"Thanks, Lily."

"Any time."

19

———

Taylor sat at Jessica's bedside and held her hand. Her friend had only opened her eyes for long enough to say Taylor's name, then passed out again. The doctors warned her that might be the case for a few hours, but it still scared the hell out of Taylor.

She'd spent many nights holding hands in the hospital, but usually it was out of an abundance of caution because they were kids and her parents weren't there. This was different. This was Taylor's fault.

"You should get something to eat," Dex urged. He put his hands on her shoulders, and Taylor ached to lean against him and let him help her feel better, but she couldn't. She was the reason Jessica was lying in a hospital bed instead of at work or home or anywhere else.

"I don't want to leave her."

"I can go get something for you," Lily offered. "I know the best spots in the hospital to get food. What are you in the mood for? There are great sandwiches and pizza and salads and even full dinners like turkey with mashed potatoes and gravy or roast beef. What sounds good?"

Taylor forced a smile for Lily. She liked her and appreciated all she'd done, but Taylor didn't deserve to be catered to. "I'm not really hungry."

Lily's smile faltered at Taylor's dismissal, then resumed its normal position as she swung it to Dex. "How about you?"

Dex rubbed his temples. "I could definitely go for some food. Something easy. Whatever you recommend."

Lily nodded. "I'll take care of it. Do you need anything for your headache?"

Dex glanced back at Taylor. "I'm fine."

Lily gave him a pointed look that clearly said she didn't believe him.

"I don't have anything with me."

"I think we can find something here."

"I'm not a patient." His tone was gruff, but the wince that immediately followed hurt more. He locked eyes with Taylor, and she felt tears spill over the edges of her eyelids again.

Dex closed his eyes and drew a slow breath. "Sure, Lil. Thank you."

Lily left them alone and went in search of food and meds and whatever else she was going to find. Taylor was learning quickly that Lily was a very resourceful woman, one who could make anything happen.

She managed to get Jessica prioritized and moved up to a room instead of requiring a long wait in the emergency department. Her head injury was minor compared to what it could have been, but the doctors, by way of Lily, insisted she stay the night and have a private room. Taylor was fairly sure the doctors would have required that anyway since Jessica lives alone, but Lily didn't give them a choice, all while making it seem like it was their idea.

Taylor could use someone like her to negotiate contracts. Assuming she still had a company after all this.

Dex was strong and silent while Taylor sat in the plastic chair that was painfully uncomfortable. She wanted to sit somewhere else, but the other option was a recliner that was jammed against the wall. Taylor wanted to be able to hold Jessica's hand, to know she was okay.

She racked her brain as she searched for answers to the whole mess she'd gotten her people into. Until Jessica, the attacks and threats had been focused on Taylor. Obviously, that was no longer the case.

Taylor promised herself when the bird arrived in the mail that she would not let whoever was behind the whole thing scare her into shutting down her company. She still bristled at the thought, but she couldn't risk her people. She cared too much about them to take a chance that anything would happen to them again.

She never should have taken a chance in the first place. She should have kept her head down and not brought attention to herself by starting a company.

There were plenty of people who wanted to see her fail. Dex said he'd dismissed most of the threats she first identified, but Jonah was one she never considered. She wondered if he was responsible for all of this, for hurting Jessica.

And why?

"Are you okay?" Dex asked, interrupting her inner thoughts.

Taylor shook her head. "Not really, no. One of my friends is hurt because of me."

"This is not your fault. The only person to blame is the one who actually hurt her. Why would you blame yourself?"

"Because I should have stopped this last week ago. I should have shut down the company."

"Why? Because some asshole thinks you should? Because he's jealous of your success? How is that helping women? Or anyone? You're telling the bad guy that you'll do whatever he wants you to do. That's no way to live your life."

"Is this?" she shouted, pointing to Jessica. "Is this better? Having my friend and employee lying in a hospital bed with a head injury all because I wanted to start my own company."

"This is not your fault," Jessica groaned from the bed.

"Jessica! Are you okay?"

She waved her hand, but still didn't open her eyes. "My head is killing me. He hit me pretty hard. But that's not on you. That's on the asshole who hit me."

"He hit you because he knew I'd back off if he attacked you."

"You better not," Jessica growled. Her voice was rough and scratchy, but the steel in it could not be mistaken.

"Jessica—"

"Do you know why I came to work for you?" Jessica asked.

"Because I bugged you until you did."

She chuckled. "No. I mean, yes, you did, but that's not why I followed you. I jumped to Birds of a Feather because you had a vision. Because you wanted to help people. This isn't a company for you. It's not a place you go to work. It's a calling, a life, a place where you're building a better world for the people around you. Birds isn't just selling clothes." She turned to Dex and opened her eyes just enough to see him standing there. "She refuses to make it public, but fifty percent of the profit from every sale is going to help women. She's funding shelters and providing clothes and bedding and toiletries to women. All the models she used for the website and marketing materials are women who were forgotten by society. She's a hero. And you don't even know it."

Taylor couldn't breathe past the lump in her throat. She mentioned charity to Dex, but she never told anyone about the other things she did because she wasn't doing them for the publicity. She believed it was the right thing to give back and to help others. Apparently, her staff agreed.

"I... I... Thank you. I don't really know what else to say."

"There's nothing you need to say. Taylor, you're the best boss I've ever had. I love working for you. It's hard work, but I know it's for a reason. And this isn't going to stop me. I don't think it'll stop any of us. We know you're doing the right things for the right reasons."

"I never wanted anyone to get hurt. I never thought he'd go after someone other than me."

"I'm not surprised he did," Dex speculated. "You weren't available for him to attack again. He knew the only way to get your attention again was to push the limits. Harder. Farther."

"What I don't get is why. I haven't seen him in years. Why now? What changed?"

"You know who's behind this?" Jessica asked, her voice stunned.

"We figured it out. Well, mostly Dex. He was a friend of my brother's, of Aaron's. We went to grad school together. We applied for the same job leaving school. He really wanted the job, but I ended up getting it. I took it because it was a job. He stopped speaking to me and Aaron. It created some problems with my brother and me. But it's been forever. I almost forgot about it. He wasn't even on my list."

"Then how did you figure out who it was?" Jessica asked.

"Dex went through the employees of the security firm. I recognized him. He looks different, but it's him," Taylor said.

"Do you have a picture of him?" Jessica asked, sitting up in her bed.

Dex stepped forward with his phone held out. "This is him."

"That's the man who attacked me," Jessica said. "He started chatting with me, then grabbed me. He tried to drag me to his vehicle, and I fought back. But that's definitely him."

"Excuse me," a furious voice said from the door.

Taylor turned with Jessica and Dex to see who was there. Officer Shaw. She turned away and rolled her eyes. Dex caught the move and stepped between the cop and the women.

"Can I help you?" Dex asked, his voice equally harsh.

"I'm here to question the witness, but it seems you've already tampered with her memory. Are you impeding this investigation?"

Dex scoffed. "Are you kidding me?"

Taylor turned enough to see the two men toe-to-toe. She couldn't lie about enjoying the show, but pissing off a cop was not a good idea. Even that one.

"She's the one and only witness. No one else saw anything. People heard her screaming and found her on the ground. No one saw another person or a car leaving the garage around the same time. And now, you're telling her what she saw."

"Actually, I'm not. I'm doing your damn job for you since you couldn't be bothered to do what needed to be done."

"Is that so?"

"Yep."

"And what is it I didn't do?"

"You didn't investigate this situation the first time there was something to look into. You let a threatening package become an anecdote. You left these women unprotected and at risk."

Shaw snorted. "I was under the impression you were a mythical hero who could do everything for everyone at once. Are you telling me that's not true?"

Dex's fingers coiled into fists. He rocked back on his heels, then forward again. Every muscle in his body was tense, ready to strike.

"Officer Shaw," Taylor said, hoping to diffuse the situation. "Jessica is my friend and employee. I have been the target of repeated attacks. Mr. Hamilton has been helping me figure out who is behind them. *I* mentioned the man to Jessica. This has nothing to do with Mr. Hamilton."

"You should be more careful about the company you keep, Ms. Wright. Mr. Hamilton and his team aren't always on the right side of the law. Not everyone is willing to see the line. His team never should have been given the freedoms they've been given, but my captain doesn't see the whole picture."

"And you do?" Dex blurted.

Taylor shot him a glare, but he didn't notice. Dex and Shaw glared at each other. Taylor wanted to trust the officer, but Captain Patrick didn't seem all that confident in his skills. It made her wonder if he could have been involved in the whole thing from the start.

"I do. I've been going through the list you gave me last week. I haven't found anyone of any concern. I'm not sure who your supposed suspect is, but you have no authority to do anything. This is an open police investigation. Not a case your ragtag team is responsible for."

"Actually, that's not true. Ms. Wright is my responsibility. Her safety is my responsibility. And our suspect isn't on your list. It's one I found on my own because my team is skilled at finding people who don't want to be found."

"Is that why the other case you're involved with is still open?" Officer Shaw asked with a cocky smirk.

"Gentlemen. I think we've gotten off track. How about we share information? Work together. Solve this so no more of my employees get hurt," Taylor said in her best I'm-in-charge voice.

Both men looked at her and nodded reluctantly. They shot glares back at each other, and Taylor was sure she heard them growl.

Fucking men.

DEX HAD zero interest in sharing anything he knew with Officer Shaw. He'd only had the displeasure of working with him on a few cases, but he'd always been a pain in the ass. He made it clear he wasn't interested in working with their team or willing to hear what they had to say. Working with him on Taylor's case would not be easy.

"What have you found?" Dex asked, pretending to be the bigger man.

"I think you should go first. Since you think you have a suspect."

Dex wanted to punch the smug grin off the son of a bitch's face, but Taylor cleared her throat in a way that warned him to play nice.

"Fine. We looked into the security company that monitors the office building and Ms. Wright's home. We found employees with shady pasts, and one of them was familiar to Ms. Wright. He's using a different name, but she's sure it's a man she knew decades ago."

"Decades?" Shaw asked, giving Taylor a once-over that was not at all appreciated.

Dex growled and took a step toward Shaw. Taylor put her hand on his arm, holding him back from beating the other man into the ground, and Shaw flashed him another look that said exactly how whipped he thought Dex was.

If it were anyone else, the idea wouldn't rankle him, but because it came from Shaw, it bugged the shit out of him.

"Yes, decades," Taylor said with a syrupy sweet smile. "Because I'm not a child."

Jessica snorted from the bed. She tried to cover it with a cough, but everyone in the room knew Taylor put Shaw in his place.

"What's this man's name?" Officer Shaw asked.

"Jonah Hampton, but his employee record says his name is Matt Warner. I know it's the same man, though," Taylor said.

If Dex hadn't been watching closely, he might have missed the way the officer's mouth tightened or the way he gripped his pen just a little tighter.

"Do you recognize the name?" Dex asked.

Shaw looked up at him, his face carefully blank. "Never heard of him."

Dex didn't argue, letting Taylor lead the conversation again.

"He wasn't on my original list because it's been so long since I've spoken to him. He was friends with my brother and we went to grad school together. We had a falling out over a job and he hasn't spoken to my brother or me since."

"And you didn't think to mention him before?"

Taylor shook her head. "No. I couldn't imagine someone holding a grudge for that long. It's still hard to believe, but Jessica confirmed he was the man who attacked her."

"Well, I'm not so sure that's really what happened, Ms. Wright. You told her about the person you assume is attacking you based simply on the fact that a man who works for your security company looks like someone you knew twenty or so years ago. They have different names and you asked yourself, why would he be holding a grudge for so long? Ms. German could easily believe the picture you showed her is the person who attacked her, especially if they share any similar features. These incidents could be completely unrelated. There's no way of knowing until a full *police* investigation is complete."

Dex swore his jaw popped from how hard he clenched his teeth. It took everything in him not to blast the arrogant asshole for his dismissive attitude toward all of them. Dex had found more suspects than the other man had ever heard of, but he couldn't tell him about the people he brought in. So he had to stand there and take it from the shithead who thought he knew what he was doing.

"Regardless of who completes the investigation, I think Matt Warner and Jonah Hampton need to go on your list as people of interest," Dex said. He was proud of himself for saying it without a sneer. Until he caught sight of the self-righteous smirk the asshole flashed at him.

"I'll take it under consideration. But for now, I'd like to speak to Ms. German alone for a few minutes." He turned a friendly grin toward Jessica and took a step forward.

Dex didn't like the idea of leaving her alone with the man, but he wasn't going to go far. He'd be outside the door. With his guns.

Dex met Jessica's gaze and waited until she nodded. "I'm fine. You guys don't need to stay here all night."

"We're staying," Dex and Taylor said at the same time. "But we'll be right outside the door for now," Dex added.

He reached for Taylor and guided her out of the room. He closed the door so Officer Shaw didn't accuse him of obstruction or another trumped up charge that made it sound like he was trying to slow or stop the investigation instead of being the only one doing anything about it.

"I can't stand him," Taylor whispered.

"I don't trust him."

"Really? I think he's a dick, but do you think he's going to hurt her?"

Dex shook his head. "No. He wouldn't dare. But I think he knows our suspect."

"Jonah?"

Dex nodded. "He didn't like when you mentioned him. He pretended it was nothing, but he tensed when he heard the name."

"How would he know him?"

Dex shrugged. "Could be anything from acquaintances to partners in crime. There's no telling. All I know is he's not going to look into him."

"Who's not going to look into who?" Archer asked from behind Dex.

Dex jerked his head toward Jessica's room. "Shaw's here."

Archer rolled his eyes and groaned. "Fucking really? I just can't with him."

"Yeah. What are you doing here?"

"Lily told me you guys were here. Dunn sent me over. We need to talk."

The four words that sent fear through the heart of every man. If Archer was saying those four words to Dex, it was bad.

"What's going on?" Dex asked. He resisted the urge to run. He wanted to, but he wasn't going to.

Archer glanced at Taylor and pressed his lips into what was supposed to be a casual smile. "Lily should be back in a few minutes with dinner for everyone. We can talk while they eat. Assuming Officer Shithead is gone by then."

Taylor snorted.

Dex drew a breath and nodded. If it was something that could wait, it wasn't that bad. On the other hand, if it was something he needed privacy for, that wasn't good.

Taylor leaned against him, finally letting him give her some of his strength. He took the first good breath since they heard Jessica was hurt and took some of her strength back. He closed his eyes for half a second before the door to Jessica's room opened.

Officer Shaw's eyes widened, and he drew back in shock at finding Dex and Archer right outside the door. "Gentlemen," he said roughly, the disdain loud and clear.

"Let us know if we can help in any way, Officer," Archer said, his voice kind and welcoming to anyone who didn't know Archer well enough to hear the threat beneath.

Shaw nodded sharply, then walked away quickly.

Taylor was already inside and at Jessica's bedside, holding her hand and asking if she was okay.

Jessica rolled her eyes. "I'm fine. He tried to convince me I was wrong because I hit my head, but he's an ass. I know what I saw. I could have described him to you before I saw the photo. It's the same guy. And if you think he's the guy you knew years ago, I believe that, too. That cop is an ass."

"You ID'd the guy?" Archer asked.

Dex nodded just as Lily walked into the room. "Yeah, we think so. Nothing concrete but it tracks. I was going to do some digging but—"

"Hello, husband. Are you hungry?"

"Yeah, but Dex and I need to talk for a minute first. Are you ladies okay for now? We'll be right outside the door."

Lily kissed Archer and walked past him to Jessica and Taylor, where she introduced herself to Jessica and dove in like they'd known each other forever.

Dex followed Archer into the hallway and closed the door. "What happened?"

"Our guy. He didn't stop at a beating this time. He killed one. And I think you need to see it."

20

DEX TOOK THE PHONE FROM ARCHER AND WAS GRATEFUL HE hadn't eaten yet. His first glance at the photo had his stomach flipping over and threatening a revolt.

"Fucking hell," he breathed. Past the blood and the light bruising on her face, she could have been a double for Taylor. "She looks just like Taylor."

"That's what we thought, too," Archer admitted. "That's why I'm here. We don't think these two cases are really two cases. We think they might be one case that's linked somehow."

"What?"

Archer pushed his phone back into his pocket and leveled Dex with a worried look. "The sheriff's daughter had some resemblance to Taylor, not as much, but some. If we step back and look objectively at this, it seems like this guy is going after women who look like her. Which means it could be the same guy. You said you have a suspect?"

Dex nodded and focused on the task at hand instead of letting the photo get into his head. He wouldn't be able to look at Taylor, and he definitely wouldn't be able to let go of her. He peeked through the door to see her as he dug his phone out to show Archer their suspect. She had a cheerful smile on her face. She glanced over and winked when she saw him looking.

His heart felt too full. He smiled back and got lost in her for a second. He never thought he could feel the way he did about her.

"It's hard, isn't it?" Archer asked quietly.

"What is?" Dex pulled up the photo instead of meeting his friend's gaze.

"To keep yourself from falling in love. I tried with Lily, but spending so much time together when there's chemistry makes it easy to fall into bed. Falling into bed and sharing another part of yourself makes falling for her that much easier. We've all been there."

"I'm not in love with her."

Archer chuckled and took the phone. "I said that, too. Love might be a four letter word, but it's a pretty fucking great one." Archer gave him a look that said he was going to keep pushing, then focused on the phone. "Send this to us. English can try to run facial rec on the guy. Do you have a name?"

"Two. Taylor knows him as Jonah Hampton, but his employee records list him as Matt Warner. We're assuming he's hiding his identity, but Officer Shaw thinks they're two different people and that Taylor's memory sucks."

"What do you think?"

"I'd never doubt her. If she says that's who he is, that's who he is."

"Then we'll find him. All of this can't be a coincidence."

Dex shook his head. "We don't believe in coincidences. They're convenient excuses for not doing the job."

"Yeah. We need to look into this guy. We need to know who he is. Do you have notes on the case?"

"I do, but I haven't been on the network so they're stored on my laptop."

"Is your laptop in the room?"

"Yeah."

"I'll take it with me to upload everything. I'm not sure you and Taylor should be exposed tonight. I'm thinking you two need to be in a safe house."

Dex knew that was even less likely than when Dunn suggested it the first night he spent at Taylor's. "She won't leave Jessica. I have a feeling we'll be here all night. And she's still working. It wouldn't help."

Archer glanced around the hospital hallway. Dex saw the same risks and threats as his teammate. No security, nowhere to hide, and multiple entrances and exits. It was a nightmare to hide in plain sight.

"I'll get the team here. Have you spoken to Patrick?"

Dex shook his head. "I was hoping to follow the chain of command, but Shaw wasn't really willing to listen to anything I had to say. I don't even know if Patrick knows what's going on."

"Go back in there and eat something. I'll get in touch with Dunn and the others and make a plan. We'll reach out to Patrick and figure something out. We're not going to leave you here alone."

"You have a newborn. You don't need to be here."

Archer shrugged. "I also have a responsibility to my brothers. We will figure out the best way to make this work. If Patrick has officers he can trust, we might have them here, but I think we'll both feel better with some of our team here. Just in case."

"I will, yes. I hate to admit that, but after the way Shaw

acted today, I'm not sure who we can trust besides Patrick. I get the feeling Shaw knows more than he's willing to share. I don't like it."

Archer drew a breath and nodded slowly. "We'll dig into that, too. Especially since Patrick wasn't too big on Shaw keeping this case. Go eat. I'll be there in a minute."

Dex let himself into the room while Archer made his calls. Dex was used to being the one who did that, who followed up and checked in with Dunn and made sure everything was on the right path. It was a role he was comfortable in, but it wasn't his role for this assignment. His role was more important. His role was making sure the beautiful woman who was looking at him with a tempting smile was safe from whatever harm might come her way.

He'd never had a role more important than that one.

"Sit and eat. I need to stand for a little while," Lily said, offering her chair.

"You don't have to," Dex argued.

Lily waved him off. "I'm sitting all day. The baby weight is coming off, but I need to get up and move more during the day. Sitting here isn't going to help."

"Baby weight?" Jessica asked.

Lily nodded, but Taylor answered for her. "Lily had a little girl a month ago. She's adorable. Do you have pictures you can show Jessica?"

Lily pulled her phone from her purse and gazed at it lovingly before she handed it over to Jessica. She and Taylor cooed at the baby, and Dex hated himself for getting hard watching Taylor talk about babies.

The woman was messing with his head. The entire case was messing with his head. He'd always been able to put things into boxes, to separate work and personal. But with Taylor, it all blended together. From the first time he saw her, he couldn't figure out what box to put her in. He went back and forth, but the truth was, she deserved her own box. A Taylor box. One that held only her and everything about her. The way her eyes crinkled on the edges when she smiled freely. The way her cheeks turned pink when he caught her doing something she thought no one noticed. The way her body responded to his when they were alone together.

Everything about her overflowed any box he tried to put her in. He sat back and watched her talk to Lily and Jessica and realized it was because you couldn't contain Taylor Wright. She was a force to be reckoned with. And she'd swept into his world and knocked him on his ass.

Archer was right. He was in love with her.

Archer walked in the door at that moment and grinned at the women. He crossed his arms and stood close enough to Dex that they could speak without being overheard.

"Dunn is sending backup. We're going to have three men here. You'll stay in the room with Jessica and Taylor. The nurses are going to bring in a bed for Taylor to sleep in. You'll have the chair. One of them said something about bringing you meds?" His brows went up in silent question. He wanted to know about the meds.

Dex knew it was time to come clean. "My TBI still gives me trouble. Lack of sleep can cause me some problems. When we got here, Lily asked me if I needed anything for my headache. I'm not sure how she knew, but—"

"She's very observant."

Dex nodded. "She is. I shouldn't have hid it from everyone for so long, but I had trouble admitting it. I haven't gotten a lot of sleep during this assignment and it's been giving me more trouble than usual. I take ibuprofen during the day as needed and a muscle relaxant at night, but that one knocks me out. I don't take it often."

"There's nothing wrong with that. And you know I'll happily have you on my six any time, right?"

"Thanks."

Archer nodded and held out his knuckles to tap.

"You said three guys are coming, or am I number three?"

"Three coming. Jack, English, and Slade. They should be here soon. Lily and I will stay until they arrive, and I'll give them the rundown. They'll do their best to blend in, but you know that's unlikely. Slade is bringing food for all the nurses and getting food delivered for night shift to make sure they're okay with you guys staying here."

Dex nodded. "Thanks for handling all this."

Archer nudged him with his shoulder, understanding the deeper meaning behind his words. Without his brothers, Dex would be in a very different place. A place he didn't want to be. The team had given him a purpose after the Navy, and being second in command was good enough. But it kept him in his place. It kept him from stepping up when he could have. He was comfortable being a little held back.

Until this mission. Where the woman he loved was in danger. Now he needed to be in charge. Focused. Ready.

TAYLOR TRIED to pay attention to Dex and Archer, but they were too far away and too quiet for her to eavesdrop. She gave up after a little while and focused on Lily and Jessica and baby pictures.

She'd never wanted kids. After raising her own siblings, kids weren't a part of Taylor's plan. Her goals in life included building something no one could take away from her and making sure her siblings were okay. After that, she didn't think twice about it.

But then she saw the baby pictures of Lily's daughter and she wasn't so sure she made the right decision.

After so much turmoil growing up, Taylor wasn't willing to bring other people into the world she lived in. She needed to know she'd never end up back in a shitty apartment with too many people and too many threats. She lived there far longer than she should have, but she never wanted to return to a place like that. She wanted security. Freedom. Knowledge that she had enough in savings that if something ever happened, she wouldn't have to worry.

And she'd done all that. She had a loan for Birds, but she wasn't worried about being able to pay it back. As long as she didn't close the company.

Birds was supposed to be her baby. It was her baby. But maybe she wanted a real live baby, too. With brown skin and dark brown eyes and his daddy's ability to turn her to mush.

She looked up at Dex and tried not to picture him with a baby in his arms. A blue blanket wrapped around the tiny little thing they created together. Or pink. She didn't care. She just wanted more of Dex. More of their time together. More people to share their love.

She yanked her gaze from him. Her love. It was one-sided. She loved him, but he hadn't given her any indication he felt the same. She couldn't start imagining a future with him when she didn't think he wanted the same thing.

Taylor was quiet while Jessica and Lily talked about families and babies and futures. Lily wanted more kids, but she wasn't sure when they would consider another one. Jessica said she always wanted kids, but needed a man first. Taylor kept her mouth shut, not wanting to risk spewing all her feelings out and telling Dex she was in love with him.

Archer and Dex walked out into the hall a few minutes later. Taylor followed him with her eyes and wondered what was going on. She didn't get to wonder long when a nurse opened the door and wheeled in a second bed.

"Hello, everyone. I've been asked to deliver a second bed so you can sleep here tonight. Your husband said he didn't think you'd leave your sister. He's going to take the chair."

"Oh, she's not—"

Lily put her hand on Taylor's. "She knows. Shh."

The nurse winked, then locked the bed. "We wouldn't normally let family stay the night, but since your husband worried your sister might be in danger, we wanted to keep you both safe. His friends are getting set up out there now. Make sure we're all safe."

"He is? They are?" Taylor looked between the nurse and Lily, who just shrugged.

"This is what they do. Let them do it."

The nurse spoke to them a few more minutes before telling Jessica she'd be back to check on her before she finished her shift in an hour. She promised the night nurse would be up to speed on everything and wouldn't give them any trouble.

When she left, Taylor turned to Lily. "What's going on?"

Lily shook her head. "I honestly don't know, but if they're bringing more people here, they think there's a reason to worry."

Jessica gasped. "Do they think that Jonah guy is going to come back?"

"I don't know who Jonah is, but I'd trust any of these men with my life. They won't let anything happen to you. And whoever Jonah is probably isn't stupid enough to come here. There are cameras everywhere and too many people to avoid being seen."

"I'm not sure if that makes me feel better or not," Jessica admitted.

"I'm so sorry this happened. You shouldn't have to be afraid. This is my fault," Taylor said.

Jessica grabbed her hand and squeezed. "It's not. I've already said that. It's not your fault. It's Jonah's fault. He's a deranged psycho."

Taylor laughed lightly. "He definitely is."

"Deranged psycho. My favorite kind," Lily deadpanned.

Taylor and Jessica laughed. It felt good to laugh. Weird after the day they'd had, but good. Taylor only hoped they were feeling the same way in the morning.

Jonah was fed up with being summoned. He was going to be in charge one day, and being ordered around made him seem like he wasn't worthy of the title he intended to claim very soon.

He growled at the door and dragged his feet, but he went inside. He knew it would only get worse for him if he didn't do as he was told. The old man wouldn't think twice about killing him. But Jonah wasn't going to let that happen.

The men at the door stepped aside to let Jonah into the office. He glared at them, letting them know he was the one in charge. They barely acknowledged him.

Two more on his list of men to kill when he took over.

Jonah stepped into the office and closed the door behind himself. The old man didn't look up, which pissed Jonah off. He insisted Jonah come right over, which he had, then ignored his presence for a long minute while Jonah stood there.

"What the hell is wrong with you?" the quiet, steely

voice said. It echoed lightly against the marble floors and bounced around, sounding like he was all around Jonah.

"I'm not sure what you mean."

"I mean you've been identified."

"That's not possible."

"Really? Well, I just got off the phone with Officer Shaw, who has your name and photo, plus Matt Warner's name, and this fucking team of SEALs are the ones who told him, so they know who you are."

"And you believe him?"

Dennis slammed his hands onto the desk and stood, leaning forward with each snarled word. "Yes, I fucking believe him. Why would he lie to me?"

"Because he knows you're considering getting out. If he makes me look bad, he's in. Aren't you supposed to be the smart one?"

That was definitely the wrong thing to say. Dennis was around his desk and in Jonah's face before he could take another breath. The older man was slowing down, but he could still pack a hell of a punch, one he was quick to showcase.

"I am the smart one, you fucking idiot. That's why I'm telling you what you're going to do now. You're going to stop sticking your dick where it doesn't belong. You're going to stop going off on your own. And you're going to stop putting all of us at risk by exposing yourself. Taylor told Shaw she grew up with you. How long do you think you can go without getting caught? You know I'll never let that happen."

The threat hung between them, a cloud Jonah felt settling over him. Dennis wasn't willing to let any of them get questioned. That was why Shaw was on the team. If any of them got picked up, Shaw was the one who questioned them, if he couldn't eliminate them first. Elimination was always Plan A.

Jonah wasn't going to give up his goal. And he wasn't going to be Plan A'd. He was going to run the organization. He just had to get rid of the heir.

"I will eliminate the threat," Jonah said firmly.

Dennis scoffed. "Do you really think she's going to leave herself exposed? That she'll just give herself to you so you can get rid of her? She's not as dumb as the ones you get from the bar."

"Then I'll dangle some bait in front of her."

"What bait?"

"The thing she's always wanted the most in her life."

That got Dennis's attention. He tilted his head to the side, silently asking the question. Jonah smirked.

"Her father."

21

———

TAYLOR CONVINCED JESSICA TO TAKE THE WEEKEND OFF WORK to recover and rest. Jessica didn't like it with the launch so close, but Taylor insisted.

Dex tried to talk her into the same, but she refused. She had a company to run and employees to reassure. Assuming they were all still willing to stand beside her and fight.

After missing half of the previous day, Taylor was busy all day. She was in meetings and talking to suppliers and employees and making sure everything was set. They were only four days from the launch. Nothing else could happen. She trusted that her people were handling work and that Dex's people were handling Jonah.

He was on the phone and busy whenever she saw him through the day, which meant she didn't get an update at all from him until they were back at his place for the night. With English as their guest protector.

"What have you guys figured out today?" Taylor asked as she settled onto the couch.

English slid Dex a glance, silently asking how much they

were willing to share. Dex nodded, giving English permission to speak freely. At least, that's what Taylor hoped.

"We ran background checks on Jonah Hampton and Matt Warner. It's impossible to prove they're the same person, but the absence of proof is sometimes proof," English said with a satisfied smirk.

Taylor raised her brows at him, waiting for him to explain.

"What he's saying is that we can't prove they're the same person, but there's enough that we believe they are. Matt Warner didn't exist more than a few years ago. He could be in witness protection, but more likely, it's a faked identity."

"So, I was right?" Taylor asked.

"Yes," Dex said. "We also spoke to Captain Patrick. He said Officer Shaw didn't include any of what we told him last night in his report. He was going to ask him about it, but Shaw didn't answer his phone today. He wasn't on duty, which could explain it, but that's not what I think happened."

"He's involved?"

"We believe so," English said. "We can't get into his files or find any direct connection, but there are a lot of indirect ones between Shaw, Hampton, and Parker."

"Parker?" Taylor asked, the back of her neck tingling.

"Dennis Parker. The case we've been working on was focused on him. We've known about him, but he's a ghost. He controls a lot of guns and drugs in the area and has connections to bring anything he wants across the border, both ways. One of his men, we believe Jonah, attacked the sheriff's daughter a few weeks ago. Got a lot of attention. We were called in to help with the case after that."

"Dennis Parker is a kingpin?" Taylor asked, her throat

dry. Her voice felt hollow and strained to her ears. She was sure Dex heard it, too.

"Yes. Do you know the name?"

She nodded. "That's my father's name."

"What?" Dex barked. "How... What... Explain. Now."

Taylor nibbled the inside of her cheek and pulled her knees up to her chest. She wrapped her arms around them and rested her chin on one knee. "He was absent most of my childhood. He came back to my mom when he needed something. Usually sex or he paid her in sex, as far as I can tell, because she had four kids and no money. She was faithful to him, although I never understood why."

"Your name?" Dex asked.

She shook her head, understanding his ill-formed question. "We all have our mother's name. Wright. She was pissed off at him by the time each of us was born and put her own last name on the birth certificates. That's what she told me. For Melissa and Braden, she didn't even consider my father's name so all of us had the same last name."

"How the fuck did we not know this?" English asked, furiously typing as Taylor spoke.

"Your father is Dennis Parker?" Dex confirmed.

Taylor nodded. "He is. It's what he always went by. Technically, his last name is Andrews, but he never used that name. I've never heard anyone call him anything other than Dennis Parker."

"So, it might not be the same man?" English asked.

Taylor shrugged, feeling small and ashamed. As a child, she hid the truth about her family. Her classmates had two parents who were married and lived together. They had cute homes and picket fences and perfection. Taylor learned quickly that her family was different. She was the only one in her class who wore hand-me-downs and had lunch provided by the school for free. She never participated in clubs or after-school activities because she had to take care of her siblings. And as soon as she could, she started working.

Now Dex was telling her that her father wasn't just a deadbeat dad, but he was a rich criminal deadbeat dad. He had money, and a network, and did things she didn't even want to think about.

If it was the same man. She couldn't imagine there were two men by the same name, but maybe...

"Do you have a picture of him?" she asked. If she saw him... Maybe she was wrong.

English clicked a few keys, then spun the computer toward her. The photo was grainy and unclear. It looked like it could be him, but it also could be just about any older white man.

She wrinkled her nose and tilted her head. "I'm not positive that's him. It looks like him, but it's not clear. And I haven't seen him in years."

English spun the computer back toward himself and clicked something else. When he turned it to her, her hope shattered around her.

"That's him," she breathed. "That's my father."

"Fucking hell," English said. He stood and walked into the other room, on the phone before he was out of earshot.

Taylor couldn't look at Dex. She felt like she let him down. Like she lied to him. Like she was no better than her evil father.

But she didn't know.

"Taylor," he implored as the first tear slid down her cheek.

She wiped it away and stared past him to the blank wall on the other side of the room.

"Look at me, sweetheart."

"I didn't know," she stated. She bit hard on her lip, knowing how weak and useless the excuse was. She had no idea who her father was. He was her father, and he was—

"Wait. Why would he attack me?"

"That's what we need to figure out. When was the last time you spoke to him?"

Taylor tried to remember. "Years. Like I mentioned at the warehouse. Every so often he'll send a card or flowers or something, but he doesn't show up. I didn't even know he was in the area."

"The last time you saw him, did something happen?"

"No. Braden had just graduated from the fire training academy. I had a party for Braden at my house, and Dad showed up to say congratulations. It was a surprise to all of us."

"Did you two have a falling out? Argue? Anything?"

"No," Taylor rasped. "Why is he doing this? If Jonah works for him, which is what you think, right?"

"Yes, it is."

"Then why would he do this? Why is my father trying to ruin my company and hurt me?"

"Maybe he's not. Maybe Jonah is acting alone. But we can no longer even consider the option that the cases aren't linked."

"Dunn is getting the siblings," English said as he walked back into the room. "They'll be safe."

"My siblings? Why do you think they wouldn't be?" Taylor asked.

"We don't know what this is about, Taylor. If it's a power grab by Jonah, he could be using you to threaten your dad. Or using any of you. We need to make sure your siblings are safe."

The tears Taylor thought were at bay broke free and raced down her face. She'd never been so scared in her life. The first time someone came to her apartment as a kid and asked where her dad was, she wasn't playing dumb when she said she hadn't seen him. By the third time, she understood the men who had the nerve to show up weren't leaving without something. She would answer the door with a knife and the promise that she knew how to use it. It wasn't long before men stopped coming by to find her father.

But even during all those times, Taylor never felt as scared as she felt in that moment. Her father was the one behind all her trouble. Her father and Jonah.

"Jonah's grandfather worked with my dad when I was in middle school," Taylor said suddenly, the memory bursting forward in her mind. "Jonah's parents didn't want him and dumped him with his grandfather. We first met him when he came to our apartment one of the times my dad was living with us. My dad bought a new video game system for Aaron, and Jonah sat and played with him while his grandfather and my dad talked. After my dad moved out again, Jonah and Aaron stayed friends."

"Do you know his grandfather's name?"

Taylor tried to think back, but her mind was blank. "I don't remember. I used to go to the bedroom when they were there. They smoked a lot, and I couldn't stand the smell."

"We'll find it," English said.

"Do you have a way to contact your father?" Dex asked.

Taylor handed over her phone. "I have a number, but I'm not sure if it's still good."

"Do you remember anything else?" She hated the

gentleness in his voice that said she was fragile. She wasn't fragile. Not usually.

"Not that I can think of. I'm sorry. I should have told you all this before. Or put it together. I'm sorry."

"Taylor, you have nothing to be sorry for. You aren't to blame for any of this. You didn't know who your father was. You didn't know what he did. And you had no idea Jonah was behind all this until yesterday. It's been busy since then."

Taylor still felt like she should have seen it all coming. She wanted to believe that Dex wasn't upset with her, but why wouldn't he be? Why wouldn't he hate her? She hated herself.

DEX LEFT the details and research to English and talked Taylor into going to bed. She hadn't looked at him since she admitted the man he'd been chasing for weeks was her father. It was a blow to Dex, but it was obvious Taylor didn't know what her father was capable of before he told her.

He hated seeing the look in her eyes when she figured it out, but she was strong. She was determined to take her father down. She wasn't going to let him or Jonah get away with whatever it was they were planning. She was helping to stop them.

Taylor used the bathroom to get ready for bed, then wrapped her arms around herself and moved toward the door. "Where do you want me to sleep?" she asked, her voice small and timid.

"In my arms."

"But—"

"Taylor, look at me," Dex growled. He was done with her blaming herself.

She closed her eyes and drew a breath before blinking her eyes open and looking at him. The fear and pain and worry in her gaze tore a hole through him.

"The last mission I was a part of before I left the Navy was supposed to be an easy snatch and grab of a high value target. We had intel we thought was good, and we were going to pick up someone that had power. The capture would have been a huge move for us. What we didn't know going in was it was an ambush. Our own commanding officer was bitter and resentful and hated the Navy. He set us up, using our informant to arrange the whole thing. The informant was secretly seeing Dunn, who felt betrayed. During the ambush, Williams killed one of our own, but he made it look like Archer did it. He nearly destroyed our whole team."

"Oh, my God."

Dex sucked in a deep breath. "I was near one of the buildings during the fight. Shit was going wrong, and I still believed I could secure the target. I went against all protocols and went toward the building alone. I knew I shouldn't, but I did it anyway. I wanted to claim a victory. I hadn't re-upped and knew it would be my last chance to be a hero, to prove that I wasn't second best like I'd always been, and I made a stupid choice."

"What happened?"

"The building blew as I was about to walk inside. I was thrown twenty feet to the sand. I thought I was dead. But my team grabbed me and dragged my stupid ass back to safety. The blast rocked my brain and damaged my hearing, but more than either of those, it rattled me. I never thought I'd be whole again. I saw myself as half a man because I couldn't trust myself to make smart decisions. My nickname became a burden. I wasn't the man I used to be. My brain wasn't working the same as it used to. Nothing was."

"I'm so sorry, De—Ryker?"

He appreciated her consideration but shook his head at her question. "It's taken me a few years, but I almost feel like myself again. I'm more cautious than I was that day, which is good, but I still felt like a part of me was missing. A part of me was... broken. Until I met you."

"What?"

"I know you're scared right now. And I know you're blaming yourself for all this. I wish I could take that away from you. For me, meeting you and knowing you and loving you has changed everything about me. You've been that piece I was missing. I didn't know it, but I'm not going to let you sit here and blame yourself for the actions of others. I love you too much to let you go through that."

"You love me?" she squeaked.

"Hell, yes, I do," he told her honestly. Vehemently. He needed her to believe his words because he believed in her. He wasn't searching or hoping she'd say the words back to him. He only needed her to know how amazing she was.

"I love you, too," she confessed.

"Oh, yeah?" He couldn't contain his smile, and didn't want to.

She nodded and finally moved toward him. They met at the foot of his bed. Her eyes were bright and happy for the first time since before Jessica was hurt. She was Taylor again, his fierce, smart, kick-ass woman.

"I've never imagined sharing my life with someone, Dex. Or Ryker. What do you want me to call you?"

"I'm Dex again. All the way. With you."

"I'm not sure how good I'll be at sharing my life."

"I'm not sure either. But we'll figure it out together. We don't need to worry about that right now."

"Yeah? What do we need to worry about?"

"All I'm worried about tonight is making you feel good, Taylor. I want to show you how much I love you."

She gave him a happy, lazy, blissful grin and wrapped her arms around his neck. "Sounds good to me."

Dex kissed her, taking his time with her lips. He was nervous, not because he wasn't sure about her, but because he wanted her to feel his love. To know he wasn't just saying the words. He needed her to know that if things ever ended with them, she was loved fully and completely for being exactly the woman she was.

Taylor slid her hands up Dex's torso and bared his chest. He reached back and tugged his shirt off, then reached for her tank top and helped her pull it off. She wrapped her arms around him again and brought their upper bodies into contact, making them both groan as their lips connected with passion.

Dex guided her to the bed and followed her onto the mattress. She pulled his weight on top of her. Her hands roamed his back as he stroked against her center.

"I need you, Dex."

He understood all the words behind the simple request. He needed her, too. He needed the connection they had, the love they shared. He needed to feel her come apart while he was buried deep inside her, to know the soft moans and quiet demands were for him alone.

Dex crawled off the bed and shoved his shorts and boxer briefs to the floor. He grabbed a condom and rolled it on while Taylor shimmied out of her shorts and panties. When he settled between her thighs again, nothing stopped him from thrusting into her.

She cried out at the intrusion, reaching for him as her body stretched to make room for his. He held himself still inside her, counting to ten until he could move again. She was perfect. Every damn thing about her was perfect.

"Dex," she whispered.

"Yeah?"

"I love you."

He leaned down and kissed her. "I love you, too."

She smiled up at him, a happy, love-drunk smile. He started to move, and her smile widened to allow her to moan. "You feel so good."

"So do you, Taylor. So do you."

Dex withdrew and slowly slid back in, his strokes short and even at first. Her body pulsed around him, letting him know she was just as affected by their lovemaking as he was. She never stopped touching him, her hands spread wide on his chest, then her nails scraping down his back and her fingertips dancing over his face. Every change tightened his balls and pushed him closer to letting go.

"Dex," she whimpered.

He knew her enough already that he was pushing back and reaching between them before she spoke. When his fingertips found her swollen clit, he didn't go slow. He tugged and rubbed and plucked at it. He pumped his hips faster, harder. And when she came apart, her moans restrained with English home, Dex followed her over the edge.

His dick pulsed hard as he collapsed onto her, the aftershocks making them both shiver. Dex rolled to the side, their bodies staying linked as she rolled with him, one leg thrown over his hip.

"I can't get enough of you," he admitted.

"The feeling is mutual," she said with a soft laugh.

"I love you, Taylor. I never thought that would happen, but I do. So much."

"That's good because I love you, too."

It wasn't long before she drifted off to sleep, her face peaceful and happy. Dex took care of the condom, then curled himself around her and followed her into sleep.

22

___

TAYLOR WOKE SOMETIME DURING THE NIGHT. THE ROOM WAS dark, and outside was no different. Then there was a light. Her phone.

She leaned over and grabbed it off the nightstand. A text. From her father.

Dad: Did you get my flowers?

Taylor glanced at Dex and wondered what she should do. He was her father. Did she really think he could hurt her? Or that he would? What if all of it was really Jonah and her father was innocent? Or what if the picture they had of her father was mistaken identity? She didn't think to ask Dex or English why they had that picture.

Taylor: I did. They were beautiful. I was hoping to thank you.

Dad: I'd love that. Can we meet? I can pick you up from home.

Taylor looked at Dex again. She could find out. Just ask her dad. Or warn him. Make sure he was safe. Or make sure he was the man Dex thought he was. She'd been afraid of plenty of his associates over the years, but never of her father.

Taylor: I'm at a friend's.

Dad: Send me the address. I'll be there soon. We can get breakfast at that all-night diner we used to go to when you were little. Do you remember?

Taylor smiled at the faded memory. It was the only thing she shared with her dad. He would breeze in and out of their lives, but every time he was in, he would take her to the diner. She'd forgotten about it, but now she thought back on all the times they went there.

Taylor: That sounds good. I miss you.

Dad: I miss you, too, Tay-tay. I'll see you soon.

Taylor clicked the phone off silently and eased out of bed. She wasn't crazy, even though she'd felt it when they told her he was the man they were looking for. He was her dad. She would talk to him and prove to Dex and the others that her dad wasn't the man they thought he was. He wouldn't have left them so poor growing up if he had money. He was a shitty father, but she couldn't believe he was that shitty.

Taylor grabbed her discarded clothes from the floor and dressed quickly. She tiptoed out of Dex's room, past English's room, and out the front door without saying anything to either of the men.

The night air was cool and refreshing. She took a deep breath and realized she was alone for the first time since the night Jonah broke in and attacked her. Fear tried to slither up her spine, but she shook her head and refused to be afraid. She was meeting her father. She would be safe.

A car drove up a few minutes later. He flipped on the interior lights so she could see him.

"Hi, Dad."

"Hi, Tay-tay. You look good. Being a business woman suits you."

She chuckled. "Thanks, Dad."

She got in the car and buckled her seatbelt as he quietly pulled away from the house.

"So, how's business? Are you ready for your launch?"

Taylor nodded. "We are. Things have been a little crazy lately."

"Oh, yeah? How so?"

"Do you remember Jonah Hampton? I think his grandfather used to work with you?"

"Of course I remember Jonah. Why?"

"I think he's trying to destroy my company. He broke into my house. He attacked one of my employees. He also trashed my office space. I don't know why he hates me so much."

"You were always taking things personally," her father said. His voice was harsher, rougher. Angry. "Not everything is about you."

"Do you know what it's about? Are you still working with his grandfather? Or Jonah?"

Her father was silent for a minute. Taylor catalogued him. His hair was more gray than brown now. His skin was wrinkled and worn. He had a scar across his right eyebrow. His clothes looked expensive, a direct contrast to the crappy car they were in. Taylor wanted answers, but she knew forcing them wouldn't help her. He would get mad and tell her she was being unreasonable and childish.

So many memories of her childhood were coming back.

She realized after another long minute that they were heading out of the city instead of toward the diner. "Where are we going?"

Her father grunted but didn't respond.

"Dad?" The fear she pushed away earlier wasn't listening anymore. She was in a car with a man she didn't really know. A man she suspected was working with the one who was trying to ruin her business and hurt her. She left the warm bed of the man she loved to question a man she thought loved her, but she realized all of a sudden she was wrong.

She looked at her father and saw the ruthless kingpin she feared he was when she saw the photo. All hope that he would help her was gone in an instant as Taylor accepted the fact that she wasn't going to survive to see daylight again.

Her father was going to kill her.

DEX WOKE up to a dark room and an empty bed. He sat up quickly, his head spinning as he did. He was exhausted from their night in the hospital with Jessica and hadn't heard Taylor get up, but she couldn't have gone far.

Dex sat for a minute with his head in his hands and waited for the dizziness to pass before he went in search of Taylor.

The bathroom was empty.

He dragged on the shorts he was wearing the day before and left the bedroom. *Maybe she couldn't sleep and is watching TV.* Even as the thought went through his head, he knew she wasn't there. What he couldn't figure out was why she would leave.

He went back to his bedroom and realized her clothes were gone. So was her phone.

He rapped on the door to English's room. "Taylor's gone."

"What?" he called back, his voice scratchy and rough. "What do you mean, gone?"

English's hair was sticking up on one side of his head and flat on the other. His eyes were glassy and dazed, unfocused as he struggled to force the sleep away.

"She's gone. Her clothes and phone aren't here. The bed's cold."

"You didn't sleep in there with her?"

"I did, but I crashed hard after... Anyway, she's gone. You need to track her phone."

"Yeah, okay."

English went back into his room and came back with his computer and a shirt on. Dex grabbed a shirt then met English in the dining room. Dex started the coffee while English did his magic on the computer.

"She got a text from her dad two hours ago. He wanted to go to a diner. She agreed."

"Cameras?"

English spun the computer around to show Dex the footage from the front door. "She waited outside and got in the car. You can't see him, but I got a partial on the plate. It's stolen."

"He's smart," Dex said.

"He didn't survive as long as he has without being smart," English said.

It wasn't a reminder Dex wanted. Taylor's father was dangerous. He was the kind of man most people cowered from. And she'd willingly gone to him. She'd put herself in danger, risking her life even though she knew who he was.

"Why did she go with him?"

"I'm guessing she wanted to believe he wasn't the piece of shit we told her he is," English said dryly.

Dex glared at his friend and tried to stay calm. Taylor left on her own. She wasn't taken. Which meant she might come back.

"Where is she now?"

"Her phone's off. I have no way of knowing."

"Fuck!" Dex paced and wiped a hand down his face. He needed to find her. He couldn't lose her. He had to figure out where she was and save her from her father.

And Jonah.

"Do we have anything about where they are? What about Jonah? The backgrounds you ran on them?"

English clicked through and stared at the screen for a long moment. "There isn't much useful. We have a lot more than we had before, but I'm not sure how much it'll help us. Although…"

Dex waited for him to continue. When he didn't, Dex said, "What?"

"Sorry. I was reading. Jonah's grandfather is Vincent Hampton. Darcy Harris talked about a few cases that were from a long time ago. Vincent Hampton was one of the suspects in a few of those cases, but nothing ever stuck."

"Okay?"

"We have his address. A current one."

"What? We need to get over there. Now."

"Hold on," English said, halting Dex as he moved toward the door.

He paused and turned back to his former friend. He wasn't waiting to get Taylor. He needed her back in his arms.

"I know you want to go break down his door and

demand he tell you something. I think this will go a lot better if we have a plan. Let's call the team."

"I need to get her back."

"We will. And if you could think clearly, you would know this is the best way." He glanced down at his phone. "Dunn is up and on his way here. He's letting everyone else know."

"I can't lose her," Dex said, his voice low and painful. The admission was hard. Not because he wasn't willing to admit how he felt about her, but because he knew losing her was a very real possibility.

"I know."

Dex paced while they waited for the rest of the team to show up. They all walked in with somber looks, each one tightening the invisible band around Dex's chest. He wasn't sure how much longer he was going to be able to breathe.

"Tell us what happened," Dunn said when everyone finally arrived.

English looked at Dex and stepped forward when Dex couldn't open his mouth to say anything. English told them everything they discovered the night before about Taylor's father and the background checks, everything right up until Taylor disappeared out Dex's front door into the hands of the man he was supposed to protect her from.

"Do we know she's in danger?" Archer asked.

"How could she not be?"

"I'm not saying we sit on our hands and do nothing, but if we're wrong about this, it'll get ugly. I'm ready to smash and grab whenever I'm needed. Just point me in the right direction," Archer said.

"That's part of the problem," English said. "We don't know where they went. We have Vincent Hampton's address, and we can go lean on him, but we don't know where Taylor and Parker are."

"So, what do we do?" Mason asked.

"We fucking find her," Dex growled.

"How?" Rocky asked.

Dex pinched the bridge of his nose and tipped his head back. He was about to lose it. He knew they were trying to help, but all he wanted was for one of them to say something useful.

"I've tried following them on cameras, but they avoided too many, and I lost them. He said something about a diner, but they never mentioned which one. Her phone is off, so I can't find her."

"Where did it last ping?" Dunn asked.

"North of the city. Not far. But there's nothing near where it was so it's likely they were on their way somewhere, not at their destination."

"Where is the grandfather's house?" Dunn asked.

"Downtown."

"Call Patrick. Have him bring the grandfather in. Get something. We're going north," Dunn said.

"Blind?" Archer asked.

"What would you do if it were Lily?" Dunn replied.

Archer glanced at Dex and nodded. "Let's go."

Dex nodded back at his brothers. They would get him through whatever they were about to face. Together.

TAYLOR STRUGGLED against the zip ties binding her wrists together and glared up at the man in front of her. Jonah Hampton was a dick when they were kids, and as an adult, he was only worse.

"I told Jonah I was going to turn everything over to you, Tay-tay. I don't think he liked that, but he's put me at risk, so I knew I had to do something," her father said.

"So, you brought me here so he could kill me and end the argument? No worries. I don't want your organization. I'm good with the one I have." Taylor's tone was sharp and biting, but inside she was terrified. She didn't know where they were, and her father had not only taken her phone, but he'd handed her over to the man who wanted her dead.

"You don't get to choose about things like this, Taylor. If I say you're in charge, then you're in charge. If you refuse, I'll have you killed because you know too much." Her father's voice was calm, like he didn't care about killing his oldest child.

He probably didn't. If he was half as bad as Dex and English told her he was, she was just one more dead body. His hands were stained with blood.

"I didn't ask for this. I never wanted to be a part of this life."

"You're my child. You were born into this life."

"I don't want it." She hated that her voice wobbled.

"Shut up," Jonah growled. "Just shut the fuck up."

"Why should I shut up? You're an evil son of a bitch. Why the hell did you attack Jessica? She had nothing to do with this!"

"She was pretty. Her hair's a little too dark for me, but those curves of hers were nice. I'm more of a junk in the trunk kind of man. Brown hair and eyes. Nice rack. Thick thighs and ass that I can hold on to. Leave my mark on you." His gaze stripped her bare as he spoke, leaving her feeling dirty, exposed, and sure death wouldn't come fast enough. Death was better than whatever Jonah had planned.

A tear rolled down her cheek. She squeezed her eyes

shut and brought Dex's face to mind. She wished she'd told him when she first fell for him. He needed to know he was a good man. That he did his best. He was going to blame himself for her walking away. She hated that.

The crack of a slap had Taylor's eyes popping open. Her father was standing over Jonah. Jonah held his cheek, blood seeping between his fingers.

"Don't you dare talk about my daughter like that. Don't you fucking dare."

Jonah looked up at Dennis. He took his time standing to his full height and wiping the blood from his cheek before he spat, "Are you serious, old man? You brought her here. You delivered her to me. You tied her up and called me. Why? We both know she's not making it out of this room alive. For years, I've put up with your shit. Your endless talking about how great your kids are. How perfect they are. How I should be more like them. How Taylor got that job over me because I'm worthless. She's my trophy. She's what I've worked all these years to overcome. And you think I'm not going to take every fucking ounce of flesh I want from her sweet ass?"

Dennis moved to hit him again, but Jonah pulled out a gun and pointed it at him.

"You wouldn't dare," Dennis growled. His voice was low and deadly and said exactly what would happen if Jonah hesitated.

"Didn't you pay attention to the women I always picked up? The sheriff's daughter and all the others? You never even realized they looked like Taylor. All those women were preparing me for her. For taking everything I wanted from her. She's mine. And you're both going to die knowing she's mine."

"No," Taylor breathed. She looked at her father, hoping,

praying he would do something. He was a monster. A deadly, vicious, evil monster. But he was still her father. That had to count for something. Even if it was self-preservation.

"She's not yours. She was never yours. She'll never be yours."

Jonah's laugh made Taylor shiver. It was cold and dark and promised pain. Pain Taylor couldn't fathom. He was going to make her pay.

"What makes you think you're going to get out of here alive?" Dennis asked.

"Because your men are now my men," Jonah said simply.

Dennis's eyes narrowed. Confusion was never a good look on a man staring down the barrel of a gun.

"They all knew you were getting out. I told them you were losing it. That you were looking to bring in an outsider just because she shared your blood. The minute you brought her here, they all pledged their loyalty to me."

"You're lying."

Jonah shook his head and shrugged. "You're welcome to ask them, but they're under orders to shoot whoever opens that door if it isn't me."

Dennis looked at the door, his gaze staying there for far too long. He believed Jonah.

All hope was definitely lost.

"What do you want?" Dennis asked.

"What do I want? What do I want? Wow. I never thought you'd ask me that question. Hmm." He tapped the gun against his lower lip and smiled the kind of smile that sent shivers through the strongest of people. "I want you to leave. Now. Walk out the door and never come back. Disappear. You can have your freedom, if you leave now."

Dennis looked at Taylor, his eyes sad for the first time.

"You have to leave her behind," Jonah said firmly. "She will be mine. And if you leave, I'll wait until you're gone. Or I can shoot you right now and let you watch while you die."

"I'll go," Dennis submitted. "I'll go."

"Excellent choice."

23

TAYLOR'S HEART SANK. TEARS POURED DOWN HER FACE. SHE wanted to yell at him, to beg him to save her, to fight, but it was pointless. He wasn't going to protect her. He was never there to do it before, and she had no reason to think he would be in her death. She was going to suffer and die at the hands of a man who thought she should belong to him. A man who'd been plotting revenge on her partly because of her father.

She stared at him as the door opened and closed behind him.

"Alone at last," Jonah said with a smile that made her skin crawl. "I've been wondering what your skin would taste like since the day we met. Do you remember that day?"

"No."

"It was the best day of my life. My grandfather brought me to your apartment. You were so pretty with your pigtails and skinned knees. I dreamed of you that night, of scraping those knees up some more while you sucked me off."

"I was barely a teenager," Taylor gasped.

"Old enough. Over the years, I tried to get close to you,

but you weren't ever interested. I stayed friends with Aaron so I could watch you. When he told me you were going to grad school, I made sure I got into the same program. I thought you'd give me a chance then, but you were never interested."

"I don't like slimy, creepy, disgusting men."

He slapped her again, making her ears ring. "Shut the fuck up, you worthless cunt. You don't get to talk. Your mouth is only good for one thing."

He started to unbuckle his pants.

"I told you before, I'll bite it off if you put that thing in my face."

"Not if it's so far down your throat that you can't breathe. This one woman, she fought it, but after a few minutes, she relaxed and let it happen. She was a good one. She was one I thought about going back to, but she wasn't you, Tay-tay. None of them were you."

"You're sick."

He laughed. It started slowly, then became hysterical and manic. Like a lunatic who couldn't stop.

"What is wrong with you?"

"You! Fucking hell, Taylor, you are what's wrong with me. First, my grandfather told me I should be more like your brother, then your father told me I should be more like you. He tried to give all this to you instead of me. But he's gone now. And everything here is mine. Including you."

He grabbed the zip ties holding her hands together and yanked her roughly to her feet. The hard plastic cut into her skin, but that was nothing compared to the feel of his tongue on her cheek. He licked her tears, then plunged his tongue into her mouth.

She bit down hard, and he pulled back and slapped her. He shoved her into the chair and mumbled while he undid his pants. He shoved them to the ground and wrenched her head back. Tears stung her eyes, and bile rose in her throat.

"You fucking whore. You're going to learn how to behave before I kill you."

Everything in her revolted at the idea of any part of him touching her. She thought about Dex and how gently he caressed her. How loving he was. She wished he was there, protecting her, saving her.

Jonah moved closer. The smell of his body infiltrated her nose. She gagged, and he slapped her again. The metallic taste of blood flowed over her tongue. She tried to breathe through her mouth so she didn't choke on his stench.

He seized a chunk of her hair tight enough to make her wince. She cried out and tried to pull away, but he held firm. He fisted his cock and pushed her head toward it. She squeezed her lips shut, letting his half-hard dick bump against them.

"Open your fucking mouth," he shouted, yanking harder on her hair.

She winced and shook her head. Tears ran down her cheeks. Fear had taken over her body. She wasn't ready to accept that she was going to die, but her hope that she might not be raped was fading quickly.

"Open your fucking mouth or I'll—"

He broke off, staring at the door. Something in the hallway drew his attention. Taylor didn't know what it was, but she was grateful for the moment of relief. He was silent, and she heard the rapid pop of gunfire.

"Dex," she whispered. Hope flooded her. He was there. Help was there. She was going to be okay.

She tried to get up and go to him, but Jonah tightened his fist in her hair. He dragged her to her feet and positioned her in front of him. He pressed his naked lower half against her, his cock hardening against her ass. She tried to fight him, to free herself, until she felt the cold steel of a knife against her throat.

DEX FOLLOWED his team through the maze of hallways that led them deeper and deeper into the building. Their drive north of the city felt futile until Patrick called and said they had Jonah's grandfather. The old man wasn't overly cooperative until Patrick told him they were after his grandson. Then the son-of-a-bitch sang like a canary and told them everything.

Including the location Dennis Parker used for his base of operations. And that Officer Shaw was on the payroll.

Parker was on his way out of the massive building when Dex and the others arrived. He had sunglasses on and looked like he was out for a casual stroll, but as soon as he saw them, he took off. It was easy for Dex to catch up to and tackle the older man.

And he was less than gentle with his interrogation. He had a woman to save, and Parker was standing between Dex and Taylor.

The firefight escalated the deeper they went into the building until they were face-to-face with the door Parker assured them was where Jonah was holding Taylor. Where Jonah intended to rape and kill Taylor.

"She's in there," Dex told Dunn, barely holding himself back. "That's the door."

"We need a way to get in there. His men seem to be multiplying," Archer said. He wrapped a bandage around his bicep where a bullet grazed his arm. He winced, but Dex couldn't pay attention to Archer or the others in that moment. He had to get to Taylor.

"He's going to kill her. He knows we're here," Dex said, his impatience winning.

"Jack?" Dunn said into his earpiece.

"I don't have a shot."

"Can you see them?" Dex barked.

"I can see two people inside. I don't have confirmation of who they are. All I know is it's two bodies," Jack said into Dex's ear.

Jack set up across the street on top of a building. As their sniper, they were hanging a lot on Jack being able to take Jonah out without harming Taylor in the process. If she wasn't already hurt.

Dex's heart pounded with every second she was alone with that man.

"Slade?" Dunn asked.

"It's not like I have something set up. I can toss a flash at them, but it might not do enough," Slade said.

Dunn looked at Dex. "Do it. We need an option. Guns up gentlemen. Shoot anyone who moves."

Dex squeezed his eyes shut and said a prayer that Taylor was still alive when he got to her. The bang echoed in the small space, tossing Dex's brain and making him dizzy. He leaned against the wall for half a second, but he wasn't willing to stay put and risk Taylor's life. He moved in with his team, ignoring his own pain. The flash did its job and the men guarding the door Taylor was behind were blinded long enough for F-BOMB to put them down.

Dex made it to the door first and froze. He didn't know what he was going to find inside. The pictures of the other woman were enough to make him sick. This would be

Taylor. His Taylor. He'd never get it out of his head if he saw her the same way.

"Let me," English said, moving ahead of Dex. He opened the door and Archer moved in first.

"Not who I was expecting," a voice said from inside the room.

"Yeah, well, we come in teams," Archer replied, his voice steely and pissed.

"I think the rest of your team should stay outside. One is enough."

"And why the hell would we listen to you."

"Because if you don't, this knife will do more than scratch her pretty little neck."

Dex lurched, his body moving into the room without conscious thought. Taylor was alive. With a knife to her throat.

"Dex," she whimpered when she saw him.

"Taylor." Her face was bruised where he'd clearly hit her multiple times. Blood dripped down her neck as she strained to get away from the knife he held against her skin. His other hand had a gun trained on Archer.

"You're the one I expected. Why don't you tell your buddies to get the hell out of here?" Jonah gestured toward the door with his gun.

"Why don't you let Taylor go?"

Jonah chuckled, his laugh vacant and deadly, like he had nothing to lose and everything to gain. "How stupid do you think I am?"

Dex shrugged. "Stupid enough to be trapped in a room with no way out."

"There are more ways out of this place than you know about. I've been coming and going from here for half of my life. I'll be gone before her body hits the floor."

"Yeah, well, that's not going to happen." Dex squeezed the trigger of his gun, searching for a way to shoot the son of a bitch without hitting Taylor.

"Why is that?" Jonah asked, his voice taunting.

"Because she's not going to die."

Jonah shook his head. "Someone else told me that earlier, but see, he was wrong, too. She knows too much. And the deal was either she takes over or dies. Except that was kind of a trick because if she decided to take over, I would have killed her, anyway."

"Get your fucking hands off her," Dex growled.

"Tay-tay is mine. She doesn't belong to you. And before you came in here, we were having some fun, weren't we?"

He nudged against her back, and she moved forward to get away from him. Her movement pressed the knife to her throat, and she cried out.

"Dex."

"Do you remember what I told you last night?"

She nodded.

"Never forget that, okay?"

She nodded again, a single tear rolling down her cheek.

"Never forget," Jonah mocked. "You know what I'm never going to forget? The way you look when you die. I'm getting hard just thinking about it. Do you feel me, Taylor? Maybe I'll fuck you after you're dead, too. I'm familiar with the morgue. I know how to get in and out without being seen."

"Fucking hell," Dunn said. "He's the ME we were looking for. He's been everywhere."

Dex's stomach flipped at the realization. Jonah was behind everything. He was the one who did all of this, from the love letter in the autopsy to the woman who looked like Taylor and the sheriff's daughter. It was all Jonah. And all because he had some sick fascination with Taylor.

"I don't have a shot. Not without risking Taylor," Jack said through the comms.

"We're not shooting the hostage," Slade said.

"We need another option," Dunn said.

"If he moved to his right, I might be able to get him," Jack said.

Dex took a step forward, hoping to make Jonah move.

"What the hell are you doing?"

"Making sure the woman I love is okay."

"You don't love her. She's not yours. She's mine."

"You have a knife to her throat. You hit her. You're talking about killing her. Why would she be yours?"

"She's always been mine. Since long before you met her."

"That doesn't mean she's yours." Dex kept walking around the office, forcing Jonah to turn. "She's repulsed by you. Disgusted. You're some sick fuck who gets off on hurting women. Why would anyone want you? Your own grandfather is the reason we're here. He gave you up in a heartbeat. Happy to surrender himself if it meant taking you down."

"That's a lie! Shut up!"

Dex chuckled, knowing it would piss Jonah off and keep his focus on Dex instead of thinking about what Dex was doing. "It's not a lie. He's in custody right now. All the cases you told Darcy about were cases your grandfather was involved in. He knew you were the one running your mouth. He wanted to kill you himself, but he was happy to let us come down here and find you. He's hoping to share a cell."

Jonah finally turned far enough, stepping between Dex and the window.

"Got a shot. It's risky, but—"

"Take it. Now!"

The next sound Dex heard was the glass behind Jonah shattering and the sharp whistle of a bullet speeding into the room. Jonah's face twisted in pain before he fell to the ground.

The gun and knife fell from his hands, his body lying half-naked on the ground. He wailed and coughed and spat up blood as a dark pool of death formed around him almost instantly.

"Dex," Taylor whispered, drawing his attention.

He looked at her and saw a matching blood red darkening her collar.

"Taylor!"

He raced to her and caught her as she fell. Her hands were still bound, preventing her from catching herself as she collapsed to the ground.

"Taylor, where are you hit? Did you get shot?"

"The knife," she gasped.

"Rocky!" Dex yelled. "Taylor's been cut."

Rocky was pushing Dex out of the way a second later, taking control of Taylor's injury. He pressed a bandage to her wound and held it tightly against her neck.

"She needs a hospital. Now. Pick her up. I'll hold pressure. We need to move fast."

Dex's hands were shaking as he reached for her. The bandage was already turning red beneath Rocky's hand. The color drained from Taylor's face.

"Stay with me, Taylor. I love you. You can't die on me. I won't let you."

"Never thought I'd see you again," she stammered. "Love you so much. Never forget me."

"I won't. Because you're going to be with me, Taylor. Stay with me, Taylor."

Dex cradled her on his lap in the back of the SUV while

Rocky held pressure on her neck. He had no idea how they got to the hospital, but they made it in record time with a full staff waiting for them.

Dex and Rocky got Taylor out of the SUV and onto the gurney. Dex refused to let go of her hand and hurried inside with her. Her bandage was soaked through, her neck and shirt coated.

Rocky detailed what happened to the staff, using language that sounded foreign to Dex. He wasn't sure if it was the flash bomb that was still making him dizzy or if it was seeing Taylor slowly slip away that had him unable to make sense of their words.

The nurses and doctors shoved him out of the way as they started to work on Taylor right there in the hallway. He was jostled to the side, his view of Taylor cut off. People moved, giving him glimpses of her, pale and lifeless against the stark white sheets.

"We'll take her from here, sir," the doctor told Dex, getting his attention.

Dex looked at her and begged, "Save her. Please."

"We'll do everything we can. She's in good hands."

Dex watched the doctor and the rest of the staff run down the hall with Taylor on the gurney. Then he collapsed to his knees and did the only thing he could.

Said another prayer she wouldn't die on him.

24

THE FIRST THING TAYLOR SAW WHEN SHE OPENED HER EYES
was a brightly colored bird. Her eyes slipped closed again as
her brain tried to figure out what was going on. She heard
beeps of machines and smelled the pungent telltale scent of
antibacterial cleansers. She slowly tested that her fingers
and toes were moving, feeling the rasp of the sheets against
her body.

She opened her eyes again, and the bird was still there.
She stared at it, holding on to the vision and wondering if
seeing it meant she had a brain injury.

She tried to move, but her body felt heavy, like she was
being held down. She couldn't move her neck at all, which
she realized was because of a brace holding it still.

She cleared her throat and movement to her right told
her someone was in the room with her.

"Taylor," Dex breathed before he came into view. "You're
awake. How do you feel?"

"Sore. Tired. What happened?"

"You don't remember Jonah?"

She nodded as much as she could as the memory

returned. Her hands went to her throat, stopped by the brace.

"You had surgery," Dex explained. "You're not out of the woods, but so far, they're telling me everything looks great."

"Is Jonah...?"

"Dead."

"And my father?"

"In custody. We caught him leaving the building. He told us where you were."

"After he left me there to be raped and killed."

Dex's eyes blazed with anger. "I know. I'm so sorry you went through all that."

"It's my fault. I should have stayed with you. Or told you my father reached out to me. He..."

"You wanted to believe he wasn't who he was."

She tried to nod as tears welled in her eyes. She hated that she hoped there was something good inside him, and that a part of her still hoped, but she did.

"I'm sorry things didn't work out that way."

Taylor gave him a sad smile. "Me, too. I want to believe there might be good in him, but... I guess he did the best he could, and staying away from us was his best. I just wish he'd kept that up a little longer."

Dex chuckled at her wry tone.

"I have a question."

"Anything."

"Do I see a bird?"

Dex laughed and turned the bird so she could look at it. "You do. I asked Lily to find it. It's stuffed so you can put it on your desk or something, and so if it fell it wouldn't hurt you. I figured you would want something familiar to look at when you woke up."

She reached up and put her hand on the side of his face. He nuzzled against her. "Thank you."

The heat in his eyes warmed her as much as the thoughtful gift.

"I'm surprised my brother isn't in here. Or my sister. How did you manage to stay?"

"Braden and Melissa were both here. Lily told the nurses I was your protection and that I needed to be with you at all times. We're gathering up everyone involved in your father's organization, but we aren't sure if anyone else will come after you."

"Do you think...?" Fear pulsed through her. She glanced at the door and wondered if someone was lurking outside.

"We don't have any reason to believe anyone else would come for you. Your father kept meticulous files on everyone involved in his organization. They were in his office, and we now have them. We know everyone who was or is involved, and we're bringing them all in. All this is a precaution, and a good excuse for me to be here."

"Are you sure?"

"I am. I wouldn't lie to you. I'm just happy to see your eyes again."

She smiled sleepily. "I'm happy to see you."

"Good. Your meds are kicking back in, and you're fading. But I want you to know I love you."

"I love you," Taylor said as she fell asleep again with a peaceful smile on her face.

TAYLOR WAS DISCHARGED from the hospital on launch day. Dex wanted to take her home and have her rest, but she wanted to be at her office with her team.

When they walked in, everyone gave her a standing ovation. She blushed and smiled and accepted hugs from all of them. When she finally made it to her office, Dex could see the exhaustion on her face.

"What do you need?" he asked.

"I think I just need to sit for a minute. I haven't been up this much in days. I'm tired and weak."

"You will be for a week or so. I'll get you something to eat while you sit down."

"Thank you," she said, giving him a weak smile that revealed just how worn out she really was.

Dex left her office and closed the door behind himself. "Jessica, keep an eye on her, will you?"

Jessica was already walking toward him. "Of course. If you aren't in there, I will be."

"Thank you. How are you feeling?"

"I'm better. Just worried about Taylor." She looked into the office as if seeing Taylor was enough to confirm she was okay. Dex understood the feeling.

He hadn't been alone with Taylor since she was hurt. He ached to hold her and kiss her and tell her how much he loved her. Something had changed between them, though. Something he couldn't put his finger on. Something that worried him.

He told himself things would get better when they could be alone again. He glanced back at her once more and trusted Taylor was in good hands while he went to the kitchen. He grabbed a banana and a muffin, knowing the sugar and the carbs would help give her energy. If he could talk her into it, by the time they wore off, she'd be tucked into bed and taking the rest of the day off.

Taylor ate, then started working. She kept working and working and working until most of the staff had gone for the day. Dex barely left her side all day, hovering over her in case she needed anything.

"Are you ready to go?" he asked for the twentieth time.

"Almost," she said, avoiding his gaze. "You can go if you need to."

"I'm not leaving until you do."

"Why? Jonah is dead. My father is in jail. His organization is gone. You don't need to be here."

"What's going on?" he asked her, the earlier anxiety he felt about the distance between them flaring up.

"What do you mean?"

"Taylor, look at me."

She sighed and looked up at him.

"What's wrong?"

She drew a deep breath and let it out slowly. Her gaze was distant, but not cold. Disguised. Like she didn't want him to see the truth. "I don't know if this is going to work between us. If we can be together."

"What? Why?"

She threw her hands up, frustrated. "Because of what happened. I lied to you and was almost killed. I can't close my eyes without seeing Jonah, thinking about what he did, or tried to do. I see the look on your face and know you're trying, but you can't get past this. You're angry. And you're probably hurt. And it's my fault. We just need to end this now before we let it drag on and we both get hurt more than we already are."

He moved closer to her and kneeled on the floor next to her chair. "Taylor, I love you. None of what happened is your fault. Your father tricked you, Jonah attacked you. You didn't do anything wrong."

"But—"

"No, sweetheart. No buts. You were hurt. You were

attacked. I don't know what happened in that room, but if you ever want to tell me, I'm here to listen. If you want to talk to someone else—"

She opened her mouth to protest, and he held up his hand.

"I know. The therapist at the hospital tried to talk to you. I also know trauma can come in waves. Maybe you were mostly okay then, but now you aren't. Or maybe in a month you aren't. Whatever the case, nothing that happened since we met is your fault. As for me being angry, hell yes, I'm angry. I'm angry at myself for not protecting you. For letting you sneak away from me. For not having someone else with us on the couch or something to make sure no one came in or out. And I'm hurt because I hate seeing you in pain."

He took her hands in his and held them together. Her eyes softened at the touch.

"If you don't want me here, I will have someone else stay with you until you feel safe, but I am not giving up on us, and I am not walking away from you. I will be here, fighting for us. Because I know we should be together, Taylor. I love you."

"I love you, too," she whispered, the words pained like she didn't want to admit it.

"But?"

She shook her head. "But nothing. Maybe I'm selfish, but I want you. I want you in my life. I know you deserve better because I'm broken. I'm not sure when I'll be able to let you in again, but I want you."

"We're all a little broken, Taylor. That doesn't mean we should be alone."

"I just... I don't want you to get frustrated with me if I'm not willing to have sex or anything."

"Taylor... I'm sorry, sweetheart. I would never. Yes, I want you, but part of that is you wanting me, too. You have to be sure. Always."

She nodded. "Okay."

"Good. Now, can we get out of here? You've looked like you were about to fall asleep since we arrived."

She breathed a laugh. "I am."

Taylor was asleep before they made it to her house. Dex carried her to the couch so he could watch over her while he fixed dinner. She was awake long enough to eat, then went to bed.

The next few days were similar. She would wake up in a panic after a nightmare. Dex didn't share her bed in case his presence scared her more, but he slept in her room on a chair. His neck was killing him by the weekend, but it was worth it to make sure Taylor felt safe.

Saturday was the day of her launch party. She'd reserved a private room at the casino for her entire company to get together. All day, Taylor was anxious. She changed her outfit three times before settling on a simple black skirt and a Birds tank that hugged her breasts and made Dex's mouth water and his dick ache.

Not that he was going to tell her.

Taylor hadn't touched him once since the night they talked in her office. He was frustrated by the situation, but not by her. He loved her and hated that she was scared. He hoped she would feel better one day, but if she never did, he would still be there, waiting. Hoping.

"Will you help me?" she asked as she walked downstairs. Her heels clacked on the tile floor as she crossed the room to where he was standing near the door. She held up a dainty necklace.

Dex struggled to clear his throat and settled for a nod.

He took the jewelry from her, their fingers brushing. She didn't pull back, which he took as a win. Baby steps.

She turned and waited for him to loop the necklace around her front, then lifted her hair out of the way so he could secure the clasp. His hands quivered, but he managed to hook the sides together. He set the chain against her neck and breathed her in. She dropped her hair and turned to face him, closer than she'd been in over a week.

"Thank you," she whispered, her voice soft and breathy and sexy. His dick rose at the sound, hoping it meant something good was coming.

"You're welcome," Dex said, his own voice rough and scratchy, desire clawing at him. He wouldn't touch her, though. He promised himself he was not going to push, and he wouldn't.

She stared at him, the air between them charged. Dex squeezed his fists tight and waited for her to say or do something.

"Um, should we go?" she finally said.

"Yep."

Dex watched her all night. She radiated with joy and excitement as all her employees celebrated their launch. To his surprise, she'd also invited the entire F-BOMB team and all three of her siblings, all of whom showed up.

"Thank you," Aaron said to Dex when Braden introduced them. "I can't believe what she went through. Braden tells me you're the only reason she's alive."

Dex shook his head. "Your sister deserves a lot of that credit. She's an amazing woman."

Aaron beamed. "Yes, she is. She even got my husband and I here and to repair my relationship with my other siblings, in the middle of everything she was dealing with. She's unbelievable."

Dex looked at the woman he loved. The woman he'd do anything for. "She really is."

"Listen, I wasn't totally fair to you," Braden said.

Dex forced his attention back to Braden. "About what?"

"You and Taylor. I'm protective of her. She's tough, but she's special. She's vulnerable. She doesn't show it, but when she lets someone in, it's hard for her to not get hurt."

"That's why she doesn't let people in," Aaron added.

"I love your sister," Dex told them, meeting their eyes. "She's already tried to push me away, but I'm not going anywhere. I want her in my life forever. And I plan to tell her that every day."

Braden and Aaron shared a look, then turned matching smiles toward Dex. "Good answer," Braden said.

Dex chuckled. He spoke with them a little longer before they went to mingle with others. Dex smiled when he caught Braden watching Jessica, and again when he saw Braden approach her and them talk for a while.

"How are things going?" English asked, walking over to Dex.

Dex forced a neutral look. "Seems to all be good."

"You know the party is not what I'm asking about."

"Yep, but that's the only thing I can judge right now."

"No improvement with Taylor?"

"She's working through it. She asked me to put her necklace on tonight, so I'm hoping that's a good sign."

"It is," Slade said, coming up on Dex's other side. "There will be days, but eventually, you'll have her back. She knows she's safe with you."

"I hope so. I'm not giving up on her."

"That's love, man. It's fucking amazing."

Dex smiled. It hurt, but it was still amazing. Slade was right.

TAYLOR LOOKED for Dex every other minute. She thought he'd have given up on her, but he was still there. And he showed no signs of leaving. She wasn't testing him, but having him stick around and not waver was one more reminder that he was unlike anyone else she'd ever known.

And that suit he wore... She was pretty sure the flutter in her belly and the wetness between her thighs were saying the same thing.

She needed him back in her bed.

The party was better than Taylor hoped it would be. Jessica, Sharon, and a few other staff members gave speeches. Taylor thanked everyone for all their hard work. She was happy to tell them they'd exceeded their first month's projections in the first week, which was an impressive start. And the better news was that the threats that plagued them were over. Taylor, her siblings, and her employees were all safe.

At the end of the night, Dex was by her side, ready to take her home. Taylor was exhausted, but the good kind of exhausted. The kind that said it was a good day, not a draining one.

Dex followed her inside and lingered in the living room. It had become their routine to watch TV and for Taylor to fall asleep on the couch. The only time Dex would touch her was when he'd wake her up to go to bed.

Taylor stopped at the bottom of the stairs and said, "I was thinking I might go to bed now."

"Oh. Um, okay. I'll turn off all the lights and meet you up there."

She turned away so he wouldn't see her smile. He was

disappointed, which was perfect. It meant he missed her as much as she missed him.

Taylor tried not to race up the stairs, but as soon as she was, she hurried through her actions, getting ready for Dex to arrive. She was practically vibrating by the time she heard his footsteps approaching.

When he knocked softly on her door, she drew a shaky breath and said, "Come in."

He pushed the door open and froze.

Taylor had stripped down to her panties and matching bra and was sitting on her bed, waiting for him.

"I'm sorry," he mumbled, his eyes locked on her body. "I thought you said to come in."

"I did." Taylor got off the bed and walked to him.

His eyes grew wider as she walked closer. When she stopped in front of him, his gaze flickered across her skin.

"I was wondering if you could help me again." She turned her back to him and lifted her hair once more, showing him the clasp on her necklace.

"Sure," he said. His voice was rough as his breath fanned over her shoulders.

She could feel the heat from his body as he removed her necklace. Once it was free, she dropped her hair and spun to face him. "Thank you."

He nodded, just like when he put it on her.

"Do you think you could help me with something else?"

"Of course."

"My bra and panties."

"Taylor," he groaned.

"I love you, Dex. And I need you. I want to kiss you and touch you and love you. I want to feel you on top of me and have you hold me all night."

"Are you sure?"

She nodded slowly, deciding right then and there she would no longer live in fear. She was going to embrace every minute of life with Dex.

"I'm barely holding it together right now because I want you so much, Dex. Please."

"Thank God," he breathed as he stepped into her. "I love you, Taylor."

He finally, finally kissed her. And he didn't stop all night long.

LAST MAN STANDING. English never thought he'd be the only single one in the group. As he watched his brothers fall in love one by one, he couldn't help but wonder if he'd ever find someone who turned him upside down and inside out like they were.

English had never been close. He was the nerd in high school, the kid voted most likely to succeed because he was smart. Salutatorian with a full ride to just about anywhere he wanted to go. He thought about it, too. Harvard was appealing, but he knew a place like Harvard, or Yale or Columbia, wouldn't give him the kind of life he wanted. So, he declined all of them and took a scholarship offer at a small college in California. One that offered an ROTC program run by one of the top SEAL recruiters in the country.

His life was set from the time he was seven. He knew what he wanted to do. The only time he ever considered giving that up was when he started working with computers. That was his first love. Not a woman, a computer.

He was still a nerd.

His home was empty without Dex around. He hadn't

officially moved out, but English knew it was only a matter of time before Dex left.

English didn't bother sitting around the quiet house. Instead, he went into work to do some digging on a new case. They always had new cases. People who needed help. People in danger.

The office was deserted so early, but English was used to it. The hum of the computers was all he needed. That and coffee.

As the computer ran a search on the latest missing person case, English fixed his coffee and looked for a gift for his parents. Their fortieth anniversary was coming up quickly, and he wanted to get them something nice to make up for all the anniversaries and parties and events he'd missed.

The program he was running finished, and English groaned. He had no idea what his parents wanted or needed. Maybe Lily would have some ideas for him.

He scanned through the search. The woman was missing for almost a week. Her friend was the one who reported it, and since there'd been no word from her, the local PD turned it over to the feds as a kidnapping case. Since it was likely to be a dead-end, they turned it over to F-BOMB.

English was almost to the end and about to give up when he read the woman's bio. Jeanine Waterford lived in his hometown. She moved there after college. English read back through the information he found out about her.

He wondered why his parents hadn't mentioned her disappearance. There wasn't much to go on, but English couldn't help but feel like he had to look into it.

After all, his parents' anniversary was coming up. Maybe he could show up instead of sending them something. And he could figure out where the missing woman was in the process.

THANK **you** for reading Dex and Taylor's story! They were a lot of fun to bring to life. I loved Taylor's fire and how strong she was, and Dex is that perfect strong and silent type of man who makes you swoon. I loved them, and hope you did, too!

The last book in the series is English and Caitlyn's book. Caitlyn was one of the popular people in high school, the kind of person who was friends with everyone. English kept to himself and knew he'd leave their tiny hometown as soon as he could. When he goes back for a visit, they run into each other, and before he knows it, English is helping her unravel a deadly mystery. Read Finally today!

ARE YOU READY FOR MORE? Newsletter subscribers get *exclusive* bonuses like short stories, bonus scenes, and a first look at everything new. Sign up for my newsletter today so you never miss a thing!

ON AN IMPULSE, flight attendant Allison takes home a passenger who is so drunk he can barely walk. She's trying to be nice, but the first thing he does the next morning is try to pay her off like she gave him more than just a place to sleep for a night. Insulted, she throws him out, and hopes she never sees him again. She does not get that wish. Start reading Wish For It now!

ABOUT THE AUTHOR

USA TODAY Bestselling Author Mary E. Thompson spent most of her childhood wishing she had a few less curves. She hid between the pages of books because her favorite characters never cared what size her clothes were. Now, neither does Mary, and she writes stories about women like her. Real women who have curves, chase dreams, and find love, because we should all be happy, no matter what size we are.

When Mary's not reading or crafting stories, she's playing with her two kids or living out her own real life romance with her amazing, curve-loving hubby. She has a weakness for chocolate and will fight you for the last peanut butter cup. Unless you trade her for a glass of wine. Then everyone can be friends.

Visit https://MaryEThompson.com/subscribe/ to sign up for Mary's newsletter, **Romancing the Curves**. You'll get free ebooks and other fun stuff, like exclusive, members only content and giveaways, plus be the first to know about new releases and sales!

For even more great stuff, find me at:
MaryEThompson.com